DAUGHTER OF CAREFUL-ISH

WHAT HAVE WE LEARNED? NOTHING.

HONEY PARKER

SLOW BURN MARKETING LLC

This book is dedicated to anyone who, during COVID, lost someone dear, struggled with work and bills, or was isolated from family and friends for too long... a moment to hope, laugh, and remember who we are.

PROLOGUE

From over Jerome Perkins' shoulder, Karen Perkins watches her husband as he watches their son on TV. She can feel the pride Jerome is taking in this young man with whom he has such a challenging relationship. This is good.

Suddenly, the TV cuts away from the story of their son's achievement to breaking news: the white police officers connected to the death of a black man in Minneapolis are being charged with murder. Once again, the world changes...

WAKE UP!

SHAD & BENJI'S APARTMENT

"What the hell? What the hell?"

In a voice that's more moan than actual speech, Benji slowly mumbles the same three words over and over. "What the hell?" All six-foot-four inches of this gangly, white guy are draped over an armchair. His mop of black hair is going in five different directions. It makes him look like he could be Harry Potter's overgrown brother with no glasses and a hangover.

A stream of New York daylight is slicing into the apartment and inching its way over to Shad, a fit-looking black man, lying on his back on the floor. There's nothing about his face that would make him easy to spot at a party. He's almost handsome. His shorts and t-shirt are stained with... Better not to know. He feels his head. "What the hell?"

Benji moans, "I know. Right?"

Shad lies there with his eyes now open. "Did that actually happen?"

Benji's too focused on the cotton in his mouth to answer.

"Must. Have. Coffee." Shad calls out, "Alexa, make me coffee!"

"We don't have an Alexa."

"Alexa, buy yourself and make me coffee!"

Benji looks at the whistle he has hanging around his neck. "At least you did it. You crossed the finish line."

"Not that anyone saw."

"But you did it."

"Thank you, Wingman." Shad is still staring straight up but focusing on nothing. "Didn't you think that after college we'd know better than to drink that much? I mean, I thought I had the capacity to learn from my mistakes."

Benji tries to move, but thinks better of it. "I wonder how much money we raised."

"Less than we would have."

"Yeah. Bummer."

Shad covers his eye with a forearm. "Seems insensitive to call a major civil rights tragedy a bummer." He lies there and allows himself to picture the moment of glory that might have been. Him crossing the finish line of the lockdown charity marathon he helped create. Being interviewed for the cameras. Getting praised for all the money they'd raised for restaurant workers. His father witnessing his fifteen minutes of fame. But now? If only the timing had been better. Suddenly, Shad feels like a complete jerk for thinking that. Major civil rights tragedy. Out loud he says, "How self-absorbed am I?"

"You want me to answer that?"

They both lie still for a long moment. Douglas, Shad's dog, a small boxer-mix gets up from his spot in the sun, walks between Shad's legs, spins for a moment and makes himself comfortable. Was that a bit of dog wind?

Benji thinks back to the video call after yesterday's race. God, they were hammered. He tries to remember what everyone was laughing at. It seemed so funny last night. He comes up empty. All he can picture is a montage of grinning teeth. He considers that his friends all practiced excellent dental hygiene. That's good. No. Wait.

Who was that girl? There was a girl. She was dark and mysterious and he now can't get her out of his head. He mumbles, "Who was that girl?"

"What girl?"

"Last night, on the call."

Shad sees a can of beer near him on the floor. Hair of the dog? He grabs the can, tilts it to his lips and takes a sip. Warm hair of the dog. Blech. "Girl? There was Kimi, The Joy and Steph. Those are *the* girls."

Benji now sits up. "No. There was someone else. Who was that?"

"If you're getting up, I'll take coffee. And a beer."

Benji gets up, steps over Shad and heads to the kitchen of their one-bedroom apartment. The kitchen is in the corner, under the loft he uses as his bedroom. Benji mumbles "Who's that girl? Who's that girl? Who's that girl?"

"Is this a new spiral?" Spirals are Benji's life. He fixates, particularly when he's stressed, then can't break out of it until it releases him. It's something Benji's lived with for as long as he can remember. Yet one more thing that sets him apart from everyone else.

Benji ignores Shad and goes about making coffee as quietly as possible. "Who's that girl?"

Shad muses, "I wonder if everyone else is as wrecked as we are."

THE JOY'S APARTMENT

A cluttered, one-bedroom brownstone apartment. It is floor-through and packed with weird clutter. Color is everywhere. The space feels alive. From the eclectic mix of furnishings, pillows and throws to the exotic tchotchkes that cover all the available surfaces, it's an exercise in visual overstimulation. So much to take in. The curtains on the tall windows are pulled tight. Something in the kitchen area falls over and crashes into the sink.

A pile of colors on the sofa moves. A head appears. From beneath mats of blond hair, The Joy moans, "Oh, that cat."

At the other end of the sofa, from beneath another pile, a hand emerges. It moves aside a blanket, uncovering another face. This one is Asian and looks pained. Kimi mumbles, "You don't have a cat."

"Oooooh. That's right. But if I did." The Joy shakes her fist and then sits up. She's Rubenesque with lots of white-blond hair. Down the side of her face is a streak of mascara. "Well, that was fun."

Kimi pulls the blanket back over her face. "Was it?"

The Joy spots a plate on the coffee table and reaches for it. "Hey, toast!"

Quietly, Kimi warns, "You don't know where that's been."

The Joy immediately drops the toast back onto the plate. "Yes, I do."

Kimi rubs her face. "The outside world certainly kicked us square in the clam yesterday."

The Joy leans down and looks under the sofa. Maybe there's something under there to eat. Bag of chips? Empty. Bag of pretzels? Empty. Box of Cheez-Its? Who is she fooling? Ugh. This is going to require getting up. As The Joy carefully rises from her cocoon, she brings her ocelot-print blanket with her. Once up, she looks down and does inventory. Hmm. Seems she has no pants. Just a tutu.

"Hey, there's a surprise."

"Not really."

In the kitchen area, The Joy starts putting random food items into bowls. Savory, sweet, it doesn't seem to matter. When she's done building the breakfast treats, she looks around the counter. It's covered in the aftermath of last night. She spots two cocktail monkeys and puts one on the rim of each bowl, then returns to the safety of the sofa. The Joy hands Kimi her bowl.

"What is this?"

"Does it matter?"

"Fair point." Kimi takes a bite. "The cocktail monkey makes it."

"I thought so."

They sit and eat in silence, except for when one of them hits something crunchy. It seems like they're both in the same trance. Finally, The Joy perks up. "Hey, we have a video call with the gang tonight."

Kimi shakes her head slowly, trying not to disturb the contents of her skull. "Too soon."

"We can't break a long-standing tradition. It's bad luck."

"We saw them last night. That counts. And I think I hate them."

"Wrong."

"Wrong? You're not the boss of me."

"I'm your landlady. That makes me your boss."

"I don't pay rent, so technically, you're not my landlady."

The Joy is flustered. She loves their weekly video calls. How can Kimi consider interrupting their standing date? The Joy cannot allow a shutdown of the potential for fun. She stands and takes on a parental air.

"Fine, then I'm your guardian. And if you're not going to listen... just...go to your corner."

The Joy points to a corner of the apartment. Kimi's corner. A visual departure from the rest of the space. It's like its own little world with its own little force field. In it is a La-Z-Boy, a bureau, a box fridge with a computer sitting on it, flowers in a vase and a few other personal items arranged in a purposeful way. In front of the space, there's a curved shower curtain rod with a white curtain hanging open to one side. This has been Kimi's home since the beginning of COVID lockdown and the end of her paychecks. The flower shop she worked in closed and her life as part of this very odd, odd couple began.

Kimi looks up at her. "Seriously, Joy?"

"You forgot the *The*."

"Oh, I didn't forget."

They stare at each other for a moment. With a huff, Kimi pulls an afghan around herself, gets to her feet and takes her bowl over to her corner. In thick socks, she stands about five feet tall. It's striking how physically opposite they are. Once inside her space, Kimi pulls the shower curtain closed, separating her tiny sanctuary from Land of the Joy.

The Joy grabs something off the floor and follows her. "You lost your monkey."

Kimi's hand comes out from behind the curtain, palm up.

The Joy places the cocktail monkey in her hand.

From behind the curtain Kimi says flatly, "Thank you."

JACKSON'S APARTMENT/BALCONY

On the large balcony of his Park Avenue apartment, Jackson is still sleeping it off. He's stretched out on two plush, cushioned chairs that have been turned to face each other. He's wearing nothing but handsome. Even in this state, he is searingly good looking. His dark, Middle Eastern features are matched in attractiveness by his toned frame. Offering him a bit of modesty is a popcorn bucket sitting upside down over his manhood. He sleeps completely peacefully, like few people ever do, wearing the bucket and a smile.

Behind him, in the dim light of the massive apartment, a dark figure passes. She stops, raises a camera, takes his picture, then continues on her way.

STEPH'S APARTMENT

Steph's apartment is your standard New York box. But it's clean, has a real bedroom, an updated kitchen and features big windows that look out onto the city. There are just a few knickknacks about. These personal touches relate either to Steph's job in broadcast news or to her family. Her artwork, like the Lichtenstein Wonder Woman hanging on the wall, would be staggeringly valuable if original. Someday.

Stephanie Weiss is young and attractive with Semitic good looks. She's at her laptop, which is set up on the dining table. Behind it are two monitors. She works in the Land of the Screens. She's sitting up tall on a video conference with work. Lots of little heads in lots of little boxes. Everyone is paying attention to Bill, trim, sharply dressed and pushing 60. He's wrapping up the meeting. "So, you are all on call. We don't know what direction this thing is going to go, but it's about to take off. The police are gearing up. We're hoping the protests will be peaceful, but who knows? Stay safe, wear your masks, carry hand sanitizer, and know that you could get a call at any time. Oh, and this comes directly from Mason. Now more than ever, nothing political. I don't want to hear about any of you posting your opinions on social. You got that? You want to share a dog picture, fine. An apple pie recipe, great. But don't be careless. At work you report. Online you have no opinions. You are not the story. Got that? Repeat after me. I am not the story." Everyone on the call looks around uncomfortably, but does as told. They all chant, "I am not the story."

Bill continues, "Good. Smart. Now, Jim is going to be our face on this. We're all going to give him our complete support. You have your assignments." Then his tone changes a bit. "Oh, and Steph, sorry about your story getting pre-empted. It was good work." Almost to himself he says, "Who here thought that something would knock the pandemic from above the fold? Crazy." He looks back at his team. "Stay safe, people."

With that, Bill's screen goes black. Everyone else signs off.

Steph's alone. She thinks about how much nicer it is to work for Bill than her last boss, Janis. No drama. No berating. Just the facts, ma'am. She pushes her chair back from the table. Her professional decorum vanishes. She slumps with hangover. She's all business up top, but from the waist down, it's a pajama party. She collects herself for a moment, then removes her tailored blouse. Hey, pajama party up top, too. She gets up and heads to the kitchen area. On the way, she catches herself reflected in the glass of one of her art prints. She looks mostly like her young, fit, attractive self. Her rich, brown hair is organized. What's off? Something. "Shit." She leans closer at her reflection. She's only got fake lashes on one eye. Did anyone notice? Of course they did. They're news people. She thinks, I'm an idiot. Correction. A hungover idiot.

What kind of smoothie is going to help? Steph puts some protein powder and frozen blueberries in a metal cup, then adds almond milk and counts out eight almonds. After mixing it all with a handheld blender, she tastes her concoction. It's good. She drains the drink then absently grabs an unfrosted Pop-Tart.

Her phone vibrates on the kitchen counter. It's a text from The Joy. *Weekly video call tonight.*

Steph texts back, *Fuck you.*

GETTING BACK TO IT

SHAD & BENJI'S APARTMENT/SHAD'S BEDROOM

Shad's dressed for work, head to toe. He checks himself in a full-length mirror that's hanging on his closet door. No sign of last night's debauchery. Good. Just to be sure, he slaps himself in the face twice. That was bracing. Ready. He takes a seat at his computer. There's not much room between chair and bed. He logs onto his work account and looks at numbers. Looking good. Again, Wall Street is living by its own rules. He checks his watch. Almost time. Shad pops two strong mints, knowing that no one can smell his breath, but it makes him feel fresh and ready. He clicks onto the office video meeting and waits.

How is he the first one here? After five minutes of waiting and trying to hold a "man of action" pose, he looks back at his watch. Son of a bitch. He's an hour early.

SHAD & BENJI'S APARTMENT

Shad walks through the living room, loosening his tie. He sees Benji in the kitchen. Something smells good. "Something smells good."

"I'm making yaka mein."

"Yaka-who?"

"Yaka mein. It's a New Orleans Creole beef soup with wheat noodles, green peppers, black pepper and a hard-boiled egg. They also call it Old Sober. The origins are in question. Some say it was adapted by Cajuns from a dish brought to Louisiana by 19th-century Chinese railroad workers—"

Shad cuts him off. He's not in a headspace for one of Benji's long, geeky food explanations. "Is it hot?"

"Yes."

"Hand it over."

Benji ladles soup into a bowl, sprinkles some chopped green onion on top and hands it to Shad. He watches in anticipation as Shad tastes it.

"Damn, that's so damn good."

"You said damn twice."

"This is seriously double-damn good. You spoil me." As Shad goes back to eating he thinks that living with Benji has had its downsides, but the food more than makes up for it. Benji's a savant in the kitchen. Or maybe he's just a savant.

Benji takes a bowl for himself. They eat in silence. One after the other, they each get a text from The Joy. Shad looks up. "Is she serious?"

"She's The Joy."

"Ask her if she's serious."

Benji shoves more soup in his face and shakes his head. Through a mouthful of noodles he says, "No, you."

THE JOY'S APARTMENT

The Joy is on her sofa looking at her phone. She's still wearing her tutu, but has added a flowing, floor-length skirt. She looks over her shoulder and calls out. "Everyone is really excited about the call tonight!"

From behind the curtain Kimi calls back, "No, they're not."

JACKSON'S APARTMENT

Jackson, now wearing more than a popcorn bucket, is putting in some miles on his Peloton bike. He knows he'll feel better if he can get in a good workout. And beating Steph's Peloton time is always rewarding, but she hasn't logged on today. He smiles to himself thinking about what kind of pain she's probably in. Last night was rough, but they all needed it. Well perhaps not Kimi and The Joy, but they at least deserved it.

His mind drifts. Now that the Marathon In Place is over, what's his next move? Should he try to leverage their efforts and expand that charity for restaurant workers to include restaurant owners? Should he focus on getting a running start for law school? He remembers why he'd stopped caring about serious things and started calling himself an out-of-work actor. So much easier. Maybe he'll spend the day building another obstacle for his in-home Ninja Warrior training. He needs a set of rings. He imagines himself swinging across the living room and smiles.

Jackson smells something and calls out, "Ruby, are you smoking?"

SHAD & BENJI'S APARTMENT/SHAD'S BEDROOM

Shad's back at his computer. He checks his watch. Yes, it's time. The right time. He clicks onto the video call to find his teammates Collin and Sandra already on the line. Both white. Both dressed for work. Both slightly uncomfortable.

Shad greets them: "Hey all."

A bit overly motherly for a thirty-something, Sandra says, "Hey, Shad. Great job on the race. Really sorry you got cut off."

Shad tries to be cool about his disappointment, "Yeah, well. Life."

Collin: "You were robbed."

Shad: "I'm trying to not be negative. We did raise money."

Sandra: "Good for you."

Just then, two more video screens join the call. It's their team leader Max, full name Maxabillion. Max had his name legally changed from Maximillian when he was still in high school. This guy came out of the womb as a flaming A-type. Max is healthy by anyone's measure, but for a fifty-year old, he's well above the curve. From what can be seen of his home office, it says, "You'll never be as ready to crush it as I am." He's mid laugh with someone off screen. Over his shoulder Max says, "I'll do the test drive, but I'm not buying the red one. My dick is way too big for a red sports car." He then turns his attention back to his team. To the new person whose screen has joined the call. "So, new team member. Everybody, meet Sandra."

Sandra, a very attractive black gal with almond-shaped eyes looks to be in her late twenties. The first thing you notice about her is her posture. Damn she sits straight.

The team's other Sandra says: "Hey, my name is Sandra, too."

Max: "No. You'll now be known as Old Sandra. And this is New Sandra. That way there's no confusion."

Old Sandra looks like she was just slapped in the face. Which, of course, she was.

New Sandra jumps in. "Why don't you call me Sandra D. The D is for Davenport. Perhaps Sandra can be Sandra O. For Original Sandra."

Shad's impressed with this new person. Attractive and a diplomat. He wonders what else she's got going... and if she's available.

Max approves. "Brilliant. Love it. Done. Team, this is Sandra D. She comes to our team by way of Stanford Brothers. In your face, Stanford Brothers! She's a U of P grad and she's smarter than any of you all. There. Now. We are up, up, up people! Supply chain, strong. Building, strong. All of our go-tos are on the rise and we are so not done. Will we go down? Sure, but I think we have a little more time. This new unrest will eventually hit the market, which of course, means opportunity. Up is good. Down is good. I need you to impress upon our people that there are always ways to win. And what do we do on Team Maxabillion?" No one answers. "Oh, my God, you people kill me. Come on. What do we do?"

Slowly, the three original team members say, "We win."

Max: "Thank God almighty. Finally. That's right. We win! So, next, we're making calls, we're letting people know that the market has no emotion, we respond only to facts, and the facts point to an up, a down, and an up. Good. Done. New Sandra..."

Sandra politely interrupts, "Sandra D."

"Yes, Sandra D. is taking over Christopher's people and she's also doing analytics. So, Shad, talk to her. A lot. I think you can learn a few things."

Shad, sensing, or maybe just hopeful for an opportunity beyond work, snaps to, "Got it." He smiles at Sandra D. No response on her end.

Max notices nothing. "Oh, Shad, nice work on the Marathon. Sucks that you got cut off. Life. That's it people. Go. Please pick up a damn phone. Collin, stay on. I want to talk to you about Bambridge."

Collin: "Um..."

With that, Shad clicks off from the call as quickly as he can push the exit button. If you linger, you could get sucked into a trap. Max is like a vampire. Never look him in the eye. Shad sits back, puts his hands behind his head and thinks for a moment. He then leans forward and Googles "University of Pennsylvania Alumni. Sandra Davenport."

THE JOY'S APARTMENT/KIMI'S CORNER

The curtain is closed to the rest of the apartment and Kimi is in her La-Z-Boy with her feet up. She's under a bundle of blankets with a red bucket hat down low on her head. It's like a pile of laundry with a face. Her computer is open on her lap and she's staring at a text message from Carmen, the woman she's technically engaged to. The text reads, *Are we ready to try again?*

Unsurprisingly, Kimi's hangover is doing nothing to help her ability to deal with her relationship. It's been on-again/off-again more times than Kimi can remember. What she can remember is that it's been mostly her own fault. God, she sucks at commitment. Finally she texts, *Let's try quietly. Totally hungover.*

You [cocktail emoji] too much.

I know.

Long pause. Kimi fills the lag time by looking at her online sales. She created an original line of face masks that are all graphic scrolling designs with sarcastic sayings. She likes to describe them as "floral/smartass." Not that she has many people to describe them to. But if she ever gets interviewed by *Entrepreneur Magazine*, that's what she'll say. It's good to be prepared. She thinks back on how her mother used to make her prepare for winning the Publishers Clearing House prize. They'd open the front door, standing next to each other, pretending they were looking at the giant novelty check. They'd both do a gasp, turn and look at each other with wide-eyed surprise faces, then look back at the check with their heads leaning together. That would make for the best picture. Kimi shakes her head. Her mother. So complicated. She sees that she had an okay week of sales. And while she's not setting the world on fire, business is decent and getting better. It just might give her enough money to start paying her way again. She thinks about how she hates feeling needy. Needy sucks. Needy is pathetic.

Then, from Carmen, *Tell me how you feel.*

Ahh! There it is. How do I feel. How do I *feeeeeel?* Trapped. Stupid. Indecisive. Backed into a corner. Kimi looks around her and notes that she's literally backed into a corner. She takes a deep breath and texts, *Good.*

Bullshit.

Harsh.

True.

Fine. Harsh and true.

You know this is all your fault.

What?

You make me needy.

I don't see that.

Of course you don't. But you don't say shit. So you force me to pull everything out of you.

Kimi thinks about this. Is that really a thing? Can you make someone needy? It actually makes some sense. She knows that her style is to reveal nothing. She decides to switch it up. *Tell me a joke.*

???

Tell me a joke. Make me laugh.

There's a very long pause of dead text air. Kimi sits and looks around her space then back at her computer. She really likes the masks that she's designed for her new business, OnYourFaceMasks.com. They balance her love of flowers with her true strength, sarcasm. Which is her favorite mask? Hmm. Just as she is basking in the glow of herself, she gets Carmen's next text.

A piece of string goes into a bar, jumps up on a stool and says, 'Bartender, give me a beer.' The bartender looks at it and says, 'We don't serve string in here. Get out.' The string jumps off the stool, goes outside and into the alley, ties itself in a knot, and frays the end. The string comes back into the bar, jumps up on a stool and says, 'Bartender, give me a beer.' The bartender says, 'Aren't you that piece of string that was just in here?' The string says, 'Oh no, I'm a frayed knot.

Kimi laughs to herself, letting just a bit of her laugh hit the air.

She smiles and texts, *You [beer emoji] too much. [wink emoji, heart emoji].* She thinks, That's right. I texted a heart. Kimi feels she's making real emotional strides.

SHAD & BENJI'S APARTMENT

Benji's stretched out on the sofa, head over one end, feet over the other, elbows over the sides. He's a lot of man for any sofa to deal with. He's watching an anime cooking competition on TV. He could trance out on it for hours and often does. It's not like he has anything else to do since the pandemic closed all of the restaurants in New York. What's a sous chef to do? As a new episode starts, Benji sings along to the theme song in Japanese. He's not bad. In fact, he's good.

Douglas wanders up and tries to find a space for himself on the sofa. Good luck. He finally settles for a spot on the floor right below Benji whose hand drifts down and pets him on the head. Benji does everything in a zombie-like state when he watches TV. He reaches into his t-shirt pocket, pulls out a Q-tip and starts working it in his ear. He knows they say you're not supposed to do that, but it feels sooo good. And really, it's what they're for, right? He keeps digging.

THE JOY'S APARTMENT

The living room is empty. There has been very little picked up from the night before. Perhaps a dish got washed. Perhaps not. Kimi's curtain is closed. It's a good bet that she's back there. A deep male voice comes from The Joy's bedroom. He's laughing, but not in a "that was funny" way. More like a "can I put my finger there" way. Now The Joy is laughing with him.

THE JOY'S APARTMENT/BEDROOM

The Joy's bedroom is part hippie lounge, part hair salon. Her bed seems to be giving birth to colorful pillows of all shapes and sizes. In her styling chair is Dennis, a large, rough-looking, well-tattooed man. Her tutu from the night before hangs on the upper right corner of the full-length mirror in front of them. The Joy removes the smock from over Dennis revealing a good amount of leather. They're both laughing. She gets down behind him and they look at themselves in the mirror. "See, everyone's beautiful when they laugh."

Dennis sounds offended, "Are you saying I'm not beautiful?"

The Joy gets up and folds his smock. "Oh Dennis, you're so ugly."

He laughs, "I know. Right."

"But you're sexy ugly."

Dennis considers this. "Sexy ugly. That could be a tattoo. You in?"

She laughs. "No."

He gets up. He's even larger than he looked sitting down. The Joy holds out her hands. Dennis fishes a wad of cash from his vest pocket and places it in her welcoming mitts. "That enough of a" —he makes air quotes—"gift?"

Ever since The Joy got her license pulled for operating a salon during the pandemic, she's had to call all of her clients "friends" and all of their payments, "gifts."

"That'll do it."

"I love comin' to see you. You always plus my sexy."

"That's me job!"

"And a big job it is."

They both laugh again. "Oh Dennis, at least *you* get me."

The Joy sees her Powerpuff Girls clock and snaps into action. "Oh, look at Bubbles, you have to go."

"Bubbles?"

"Bubbles. The Powerpuff Girl." He has no understanding of

what she's telling him. "The clock. The time. My video cocktail hour is in an hour and the place is—"

He finishes for her. "A shithole."

STEPH'S APARTMENT

Steph is sitting on her Peloton bike. Done. She can't believe she made herself work out. Yes, she can. She thinks, I'm an animal. She looks at Jackson's workout stats on the bike's video screen. He crushed her today. That's OK. He can have this one. God, he was sexy last night on the call. She could stare at him for hours. Then, the bigger question. What is she doing with him? Besides what she's "doing" with him. Can this really be going somewhere? She lets herself muse about the best version of what life with Jackson would be like. She'd be a news celebrity and not even need the money. She'd keep the money, of course. The pandemic would be over and they'd travel the world in style. And they'd have two beautiful children. How could they not? She thinks about a scene from *Funny Girl*. She assumes all Jewish girls have seen the movie multiple times. She certainly has. In the scene, Barbra Streisand coos over the baby, then hands her baby off to the nurse for care. With the infant gone, she falls into Omar Sharif's arms. How lovely. Yes, she and Jackson would have a baby nurse. A new thought hits her. Barbra and Omar. A Polish Jew from New York and an Egyptian. They made it work. Well, onscreen. What religion was Omar? Don't know. But she's positive that she and Jackson can make it work.

The spell of this beautiful new life is broken when Steph's phone rings. It's her mother, who may not be thrilled at Steph's new fantasy Middle Eastern family. She steadies herself and answers. "My mother."

"Hello, New York." This is the standard greeting from her mother since Steph moved to the city. Her mother's Philly accent, mixed with her tendency to overenunciate, makes for a distinctive speech pattern. And it only emphasizes to Steph that introducing change to Ida in the form of Jackson would be a challenging proposition.

Ida starts in. "Have a minute? I would like your sage advice."

"Seriously?"

"Yes."

"Shoot."

"OK. You know that some of my neighbors have a rock band." Steph knows nothing about a band, but why interrupt? "And, my friend Barbara Beach is in it. You don't know her. Barbara asked me to sing back up. How 'bout that? Your mother in a band. But then Cora O'Shea, the lead singer who I never trusted, said that I could only sing in the band if my mic is turned off."

"A, that's crazy. And B, how can you have a band during lockdown?"

"So, I shouldn't tell her where she can shove her mic?"

THE JOY'S APARTMENT

The Joy is doing her best to clean up the kitchen without actually touching anything. Yick. The smell of whatever that was in the sink is brutal. She washes all her cocktail swag by letting them swim in a bowl of super-hot water, kissing each plastic animal as she towel-dries them and sets them on the counter to await their next assignment.

Looking for a break from the little work she's accomplished, she checks her social media streams on her phone. Lots of hair pictures. She tries to scroll past all the political posts. Isn't life hard enough? There's so much about protesting police and supporting minorities. She's about to close her phone when she sees it. A post from her mother in Florida. Without even realizing she's audible, The Joy lets out, "Holy pancakes!" She starts messaging Betty as fast as she can.

SHAD & BENJI'S APARTMENT

Benji's got a clean anime t-shirt on for the weekly video call. Since the start of lockdown, the call has been his only social time. Not that he was a social animal before. He wasn't. And not a babe magnet either. So, he wants to look extra nice in case that girl is there. He can't really picture her clearly, but there was something dark and mysterious about her. In his mind, she's like one of his anime girls. That's a good thing. He goes to the bathroom and checks his look. He gels his hair so it's purposefully sloppy. Then he checks his temperature with an infrared digital thermometer gun. Benji's been checking his temperature every day since the beginning of lockdown. Even though he hasn't had much outside interaction, just a few trips to the bodega and the handoffs with the pizza delivery guy. Yet, he's paranoid about getting sick. 98 degrees. Dodged another bullet. He looks at himself again and is pleased with the level of brooding his look has achieved. He's ready.

ZOOM! WE MEET AGAIN

THE JOY'S APARTMENT

The Joy is at the counter, preparing cocktails. Big cocktails. She always preps the drinks for their weekly video meetings, but these are exceptional. Kimi's curtain opens and she shuffles over to the kitchen, where the action is. She remarks, "Big cocktails."

"The better to see you with."

"What are they?"

"Long Island Iced Teas."

Kimi looks concerned. "I know you. Long Island Iced Tea means something's wrong. Spill it."

Is she that easy to read? The Joy pulls up her mother's social media post on her phone and shows it to Kimi. Kimi's mouth is agape for a good ten-count. "Holy shit!"

"I know."

"But I mean, holy shit!"

"I know! I haven't gotten her to take it down yet. There goes my good name."

"You don't have a good name."

"Well if I did, it would be all gone now."

Kimi thinks how glad she is that it wasn't her mother and her good name. That she doesn't have either. She shakes her head. "Damn. That's one crazy bitch."

The Joy takes a long swig of her cocktail and steadies herself. Kimi grabs hers and raises it in support of her friend/land-lord/guardian. They drink. Wow, that's potent. Yet, is it what's needed, in a hair-of-the-dog kind of way? Kimi lifts open The Joy's laptop which is also on the counter. "You ready for this?"

Warily, The Joy answers, "*Je suis pret.*"

"You speak French?"

"*Je ne sais pas.* I guess that's a *oui.*"

Kimi wonders how many more layers of this large blond onion The Joy can reveal. She's a bottomless pit of surprises. Scary thought.

They poise themselves on their stools, assuming their positions for the call. The Joy logs in and watches the screens of their friends pop up. Shad, Benji and Douglas are on their sofa with beers and a bowl of something. Jackson is wearing a smoking jacket and holding a yard glass, which looks like a trumpet with a bulb at the bottom. Steph is finishing shaking out her hair. The Joy tries to sound positive, "Hey you!"

Shad: "Which 'you' do you mean?"

The Joy: "You know. The collective, you all. Hey, you all!" She forces a smile.

Steph: "Someone is trying too hard. What's wrong?"

Kimi: "Her mom shit the social media bed."

The Joy: "She didn't shit it. She maybe peed it."

Steph: "Details please."

Everyone looks at The Joy waiting for her to spill it. Finally, "Stop the inquisition! Fine. You cracked me. She posted a picture of an Aunt Jemima bottle on Facebook and said how sad it was she's becoming a victim of political correctness. There are positive things for the black community to learn from the Aunt Jemima story."

Steph: "She! Did! Not!"

Kimi: "But wait. There's more."

Jackson leans forward. "Do tell."

The Joy: "Fine. I texted her to take it down, like, immediately. And she argued with me that she was encouraging black people to be proud of their history. And that I'm being insensitive, as usual."

Shad: "Wow. Just, wow. I thought I'd heard it all."

Kimi: "Right?"

Steph: "Did she take it down?"

The Joy: "Like a minute ago. After a bunch of hate messages."

Benji: "Man. I thought I was bad at social."

Kimi: "You are. Said with love. Nice hair, by the way."

Benji: "Thanks."

Jackson: "That is epic."

Steph: "It's OK. Your mom's just... I'm sure she just... No. It's bad."

The Joy: "Augh. Can we talk about something else?"

Steph: "Sure."

With permission to change topics, The Joy's demeanor becomes very formal. "Why Jackson, is that a yard of ale in your hand or are you just happy to see us?"

Jackson mimics her tone, "Why both, of course. I know our broadcast got cut off, but I'm proud of us all, and thought we should celebrate."

Kimi: "By watching you drink a beer?"

Jackson: "A *yard* of *ale*."

Benji: "I wanna see it."

Jackson: "Thank you, sir. Now, someone count me down."

They have nothing better to do. They all chant, "Three, two, one!"

Jackson slowly tilts the long narrow glass up and spins it slightly as he drinks. It's slow going, but he doesn't stop. How is he breathing? Is he breathing? He finally has the round bottom of the glass raised to the ceiling and drains the last drops of golden goodness. He takes a huge breath and daintily wipes his mouth with the sleeve of his smoking jacket. Everyone applauds. Jackson stands and takes a bow. "That was for you, Shad."

Shad: "Thanks, man."

Jackson: "You bet. Fine effort. The donations pretty much stopped when we got preempted, but there is good news to be had. We raised nineteen thousand, one hundred and twenty-five dollars on entrance fees, minus the cost of swag. Plus, we got an additional fifteen thousand in donations. So that's about thirty-five big ones going to restaurant workers."

Benji: "Like me."

Jackson: "Yes. Like our Benji here. Cheers!"

They all take the cue to tilt one back. Jackson continues, "I think that when the current anger dies down, we continue what you started. Perhaps create a Marathon-In-Place foundation."

Steph: "Things aren't dying down. They're heating up. Marches, rallies..."

Benji: "Should we be scared?"

Steph: "It's all wait and see right now. I shouldn't talk out of turn. So, don't repeat this. Inside sources say that the police are gearing up for whatever may come. This could get big. Really big."

There's silent drinking as they all take this in. Until Shad suddenly scoots away from Benji. "Dude, you're killing me."

Benji: "Sorry. Slipped out."

Shad is utterly offended by the stink. "You should be sorry."

Benji: "Hey, can you lose weight by farting?"

The Joy gets excited. "Could that be a thing? Oh my God. Someone look it up. That would be brilliant."

Kimi: "Can't be true. I'd be a fucking rail."

Benji starts searching on his phone for the answer. "Wait for it. Wait for it... Hey, this says you can burn 67 calories per fart."

Steph: "Seriously?"

The Joy: "Kimi, I'm apologizing in advance."

Kimi: "Why should I have a monopoly?"

The Joy: "I could totally live on three-layer bean dip."

Benji: "Wait. Wait. No. It's just a myth. Sorry."

The Joy is devastated. "Why would you set me up for a fall like that?"

Benji: "I said, 'Sorry.'"

The Joy: "You should be, fella. I've had a hard day."

Jackson: "Ok, I have a new topic. How would you all like to celebrate my birthday?"

Steph responds as if she'd forgotten that people ever celebrated birthdays. Or had them. "Oh my God. That's right. Birthdays. Have we missed any?"

There's a long silence as they all look at each other. Seems no birthdays missed. Safe.

Shad: "Dude, what do you want for your birthday?"

Kimi: "Because you already have everything."

Jackson: "I don't have my friends."

The Joy: "Oh. We're right here."

Jackson: "I mean, actually have my friends *here*. Right here. What do you say to coming over? We can still distance. My place is immense."

Kimi: "Fuck you. I live in a chair."

Jackson: "I know that was said with love. Now, we have two weeks. What do you say?"

They all think about Jackson's enticing offer. Steph is the only one who has really ventured out into the world, and that's only been for work.

Shad: "Can we think about it?"

Jackson: "Of course. But, think about this. We can wear fun masks and make it a *safe* birthday bash."

The Joy: "Oh, and wings!"

Kimi: "How do wings make it safer?"

The Joy: "How do you wear a mask without a wings? Or a cape would work. Honestly Kimi, join the party."

Kimi is about to make smartass retort when a dark figure passes in the distance behind Jackson.

Benji startles everyone. He points and calls out, "That's her!"

Everyone turns their heads and looks around their own rooms. What? Who is he talking about? Jackson spots his sister passing way behind him. He seems confused. "You mean Ruby?"

Benji: "Is that what you call her?"

Jackson: "Well, it is her name."

Benji: "Then yes. Ruby. She was there last night, wasn't she? I remember now. Didn't she tell us all to shut the hell up?"

Jackson: "That sounds like her."

Benji: "I want to meet her. Could you give her my number?"

Shad: "Dude, calm down."

Kimi: "Way to play hard to get."

Benji: "I'm not hard to get."

Steph: "Clearly."

Benji: "Jackson, would you do it? Would you give her my number?"

Jackson: "Of course I will."

Steph: "I hate to interrupt young love, but I have an early call. I should really get some sleep or I'll have bags that no makeup could cover. It's in my genes. All the Weiss women are prone to bags."

The Joy: "That match their shoes?" With that quip, The Joy becomes very proud of herself. She muses out loud, "Even hungover, I'm still funny. Cool."

Steph: "Hysterical. Alright then. Till next time, this is Stephanie Weiss, channel 7 news, signing off." She raises her wine bottle and her screen goes black.

Jackson: "Everyone, think about my birthday. No hard feelings either way. But you really should do it." Jackson stands, twirls his yard glass like a baton until it comes to rest under his arm, military style. The group applauds and Jackson signs off.

The Joy: "So, what do we think?"

Kimi: "We think that Steph is on her way to Jackson's to work out her *bags*." She makes air quotes.

The Joy: "Ooh. That. Nudge, nudge. Wink, wink."

Shad: "Ladies, Casanova and I are signing off. Talk to you next week."

Benji likes being referred to as a legendary lover. He smiles at the thought of his potential romance.

The Joy, "Wait! Wait! I forgot. I was going to give an assignment for next week. Crap."

Kimi: "What are we, back in school?"

The Joy: "No. It was going to be fun. Fine, go about your business. I'll text everyone."

Shad: "Can't wait."

Kimi and The Joy lift their glasses: "Cheers."

All screens go black.

LET THE GAMES BEGIN

THE JOY'S APARTMENT/KIMI'S CORNER

Kimi is cross-legged on top of about five blankets and perhaps some rolled-up clothing, all piled up on her La-Z-Boy. She has her laptop out and is trying to get into some kind of working rhythm. She'd hoped that maybe the higher perspective on her little world might help give her a burst of energy. It doesn't. She forces herself to press on, and deal with the administrative side of her fledgling business. She checks the traffic to her face mask website. How long are people staying on the site? How many pages per visit? Which pages are getting the most traffic? And can she do anything useful with this information?

She finally feels that the alcohol is out of her system. She's clearheaded and thinks, I should really take a break from drinking. Her next thought is, Who am I kidding? But even clearheaded, she's having a hard time working. The zeitgeist is too heavy on her mind. Fuck this.

Kimi puts her laptop on top of her cube fridge and ventures over to the front window to check in on the world. On their block is a small supermarket, and since social distancing, the line to get in has stretched down the sidewalk and below their front window. At first, the inane chatter from those waiting to buy provisions was only annoying. Then, it became familiar and better than any TV show. Kimi loves listening in on the conversations of strangers, many of whom have become regulars in her new world. She slides on a mask and sits on the sill.

While her market line is right where she left it, there's something else. People are walking in the middle of the street, chanting. There are homemade signs and lots of fists in the air.

"What the hell!"

STEPH'S APARTMENT

Steph comes in the front door, dressed from work and carrying her briefcase and computer bag. She heads to her dining table/work station and unburdens herself. As she gets her laptop out of her bag and sets it up, her thoughts bounce between how things are heating up and how much she loves carrying a proper briefcase. On the one hand, the marches that are being scheduled for every borough make her feel uneasy. The uncertainty of the time. The not knowing what's coming. On the other, the classic lines of her Louis Vuitton are reassuring and the smell of fine leather is always calming. Just opening it and seeing papers and pens in their proper places is the order and strength she needs.

The moment Steph gets her home office set up the way she likes it, she sees a text from Bill. *Get to the corner of 17 & 8* And just like that, she packs everything back up and heads for her door. As she's leaving, Bill texts again, *Remember, you are not the story*.

SHAD & BENJI'S APARTMENT

Benji is standing at the front window with his phone in his hand with the Citizen app open. He's searching for trouble spots around town, and watching people marching on the street below. On the app, he tracks where incidents are popping up in the city. Is that a siren in the distance? He can feel his anxiety rise. When was the last time he took his medication? He pulls a cotton swab from his shirt pocket and puts it to work with a repetitive rhythm.

THE JOY'S APARTMENT

The Joy comes out of her bedroom and sees Kimi staring out the front window. She calls to her, "Any good chit chat from the market people?"

Without looking at The Joy, Kimi quietly says, "No."

"Not possible." The Joy joins Kimi at the window and sees that the people in line are doing what Kimi's doing, quietly watching protesters pass by. Now The Joy is fixated on the marchers as well. The door buzzer sounds. Neither of them moves. It buzzes again, this time longer. Kimi, in a trance-like voice says, "Buzzer."

"I know."

"You gonna answer it?"

"Maybe it's for you."

"It's not."

The Joy finally breaks herself away from the window and goes to the door intercom. "Name, please."

Over the crackling intercom, "Package Guy."

"Thank God. I need a package, bad." The Joy cracks open her front door to see Vlad, the Package Guy, *her* Package Guy, enter the building and head to her door. If buff put on an extra layer of buff, you'd have Vlad. And The Joy has "had" Vlad. She opens the door all the way for him. Her tone turns flirtatious. "You may enter, Sir Package Guy."

He comes in and hands The Joy a box. She coos, "You shouldn't have."

Vlad lowers his mask, "I didn't. I think it's hair products."

Almost purring now, The Joy says, "Well, you get points for bringing them. Now, how would you like to receive your points?"

"No time to receive points today. The protesters have really slowed me down. I gotta go." Vlad grabs her ass, gives her half a smile, raises his mask and disappears down the hall.

The Joy watches him go. "I hate protesters."

As Vlad leaves, The Joy sees that the apartment door across the hall is cracked open. Mr. Belcher, a short balding guy is peering through the opening, wearing a ratty bathrobe. The Joy squints at his door, which slams shut.

SHAD & BENJI'S APARTMENT

Benji's still at the front window watching the activity in the streets below when Shad walks past on his way to the fridge. "Dude, you're gonna make yourself crazy." Without an actual response in mind, Benji grunts.

Shad can hear Benji's phone get a text but Benji doesn't respond. Shad continues to the fridge. He pulls out a container, opens the lid and smells to see if it's safe. He shrugs, grabs a fork and heads back towards his room. On his way past, he hears Benji get another text. Still, Benji doesn't move. Shad says, "You have a text."

Still no response from Benji. "Sunshine! Hey, Sunshine," Sunshine is the gang's nickname for Benji. It's meant to be ironic and often used to snap him out of his own private world. Shad offers, "Maybe it's Ruby?"

That got his attention. "What?"

"Your text. Maybe it's Ruby."

Benji looks hopefully at his phone, but his hope is quickly crushed. "It's my mom. She says, stay safe." With that, Benji's focus goes back out the window.

Shad feels his own phone vibrate in his back pocket. It's Sandra from work. New Sandra. Sandra D. Hey, at least his text worked out. He pockets his phone and heads for the privacy of his bedroom. While walking he thinks, Benji is so in his own world, taking a call in the living room would have been just as private.

SHAD & BENJI'S APARTMENT/SHAD'S BEDROOM

Shad straightens up his room before calling Sandra, just in case she wants to switch to video. He neatly stacks the papers on his desk and puts his extra shoes in the closet. Then he wonders why he has so many shoes out. He doesn't go anywhere anymore. Shad quickly folds the few clothes that are on his bed, then chucks them into his closet. He'll refold them later. His last move before calling is to smooth his shirt as he stands at his mirror. He feels like his marathon training has him looking tight and toned. He's ready.

Shad stays standing and hits the phone icon. He prepares himself to be casual.

She answers officially, "Sandra Davenport."

"Sandra. Shad." He waits, but she says nothing further. "From work."

"Oh, sorry, my attention is split. I'm watching people marching from my window."

"Yeah. Here, too." More silence. "What did you want to talk about?"

"Yes. Um. Right. Max wanted us to connect on that Krantz Fund. The new dividends. We need to review who we'll be suggesting to join. It's quite a good offer. I'm assuming you're familiar?"

Shad paces while he talks. He tells himself to sound strong. "Yeah. Yeah. I like what I've seen. I have a list ready. Do you want to review the top-line points?"

"Sure. Um yes. I'm sorry. This is so distracting. Are you going to be marching?"

Shad considers this. "I don't know."

"You don't know? This is so important. This is a pivotal time for our country. How can you stand on the sidelines?"

"I mean, I don't know my plans yet. You know. Where. When. You have a plan yet?"

"Of course."

Shad checks himself again in the mirror. "Hey, shall we switch this to a video call to review the Fund?"

"No. I'm good."

Shad looks in the mirror, deflated.

JACKSON'S APARTMENT

Jackson stands on the massive balcony that overlooks Park Ave. He knows that it's his parent's balcony. But they won't be back from the UAE any time soon, so he thinks of it as his kingdom. He cuts a powerful, if not bizarre figure with his arms akimbo and an actual sword strapped to his back. Some people wear hats. He prefers other forms of accessory. From his perch, he's watching the people below and wondering how they all got the message to get out there. So strange that in such a short time it feels abnormal to see that much humanity on the streets of New York City. What should he do? What's his move? As an out-of-work actor, his move is simple. Fill his pockets with as many beers as possible, head out, and treat the whole thing like a giant social event. But now that he's done some charity work and is going to be going to law school, he should probably be more serious. Probably.

He decides to put off deciding. Jackson goes to part of his indoor homemade Ninja Warrior course. The new part with the metal rings hanging from the ceiling. He lays down his sword and leaps for two of the rings. With little effort, Jackson moves like a monkey around his rings course then stops and just hangs. He likes feeling his trapezoids being put to use.

While he hangs there, letting his thoughts leave the outside world and travel around his muscles, his sister Ruby quietly glides past, like a spirit. She's in her usual loose-fitting, flowing top and pants and dark makeup. Everything is black except for the touch of dark gray she uses to break it up. Could they be more different? In her world, there seems to be no room for her handsome, talented, popular, little brother. Well, little by a year. Mommy and Papa said that they had Ruby move in so Jackson would have someone to cook for him. He knew the real reason was because they just don't know what to do with a daughter who's not interested in marriage. And quite frankly, is doing everything possible to ward off any offers in that direction.

Jackson's about to call out to her. See if she'd like him to give Benji her number. She suddenly turns her head towards him. As if coming from somewhere deep inside her, a small trail of smoke seeps out the side of her mouth. Was she even smoking? Jackson decides to not interrupt her path to wherever. Another time.

THE JOY'S APARTMENT

Kimi's in the kitchen area, putting a slice of roast beef between two slices of bread when The Joy comes in with a new orange stripe in her hair. She starts to prep her own meal. "Lunch?"

"Yes."

Excited beyond reason, The Joy responds, "Me too!"

Way less excited, Kimi says, "Great" then watches The Joy prepare her version of lunch. They've lived together for months now, but she still finds The Joy's choices fascinating. Kimi rests her chin on her fist and watches her roommate like she's the subject of a nature show. The Joy reaches into the cabinet for a can of tuna, opens it, runs water in the can, squeezes the now open lid down to drain the water, then does it again. Next, she takes a fork and starts slowly and methodically inspecting the tuna as she flakes it into a bowl. Then comes the mayonnaise. She mixes it in and tastes. Needs more mayo. She mixes and tastes again. This time it passes muster. The Joy turns to the fridge and pulls out a pizza box which contains two slices from the night before. Kimi's about to say that she'd been saving those slices for dinner tonight, but she needs to see where this is going. The Joy puts one slice face up on a plate, then scoops the tuna on top. She takes the other slice and puts it face down on top of that and compresses the structure until the tuna just starts to bulge out from under the top slice. Done. The Joy picks up her plate and heads for the sofa. Once she's appropriately settled she turns on the TV. It's time. She lifts the tuna pie to her mouth and takes a bite. The Joy mindlessly watches news coverage of rallies as she chews. Suddenly she drops her meal, which has some heft to it. It smacks onto her plate. "Oh, my God!"

Kimi, still at the counter, is startled. "What? Something on TV? What's happening?"

The Joy is now flapping her hands like she's got gnats flying by. "Oh, my God, no. Worse."

"What?"

48

"I got a scale."

Kimi is now completely confused. "You got a what?"

"A scale." Seeing no understanding from Kimi, she explains, "A scale. A tuna scale. Now I can't eat this. Ugh." She pushes her plate farther away from herself.

"After all that, you're not even going to eat it?"

"How can I? It's contaminated. Could you eat it?"

"Fuck, yeah."

They stare at each other. The Joy finally gives permission. "Take it."

"You're sure you're not going to eat it?"

"I'm not an animal."

"Clearly, I am." Kimi puts her own untouched sandwich in the fridge and scoops up The Joy's tuna pie.

The Joy says, "But you have to leave my presence. I can't watch you eat that...thing. Waiting to see if you find another scale would be like waiting for the crazed killer to pop up in a horror movie. You understand."

"No one understands." Kimi grabs The Joy's plate and heads to the back window. "I'll be dining *al fresco*." Since lockdown, the most calming part of Kimi's world has been on the back fire escape. She now has a tried and true method for getting her short frame up over all of The Joy's "juju" that lives on the windowsill, and out onto the landing. Even with a plate of food in hand, she doesn't question her new skill. She steps onto a chair, steps over a miniature ship in a bottle except that it's a beauty salon in a bottle, and feels her foot touch down. Then, with her free hand on the bottom of the open window, she lifts her other foot to join the first one and lowers herself until she has achieved ass on metal. Ta-dah! Now in place, she lifts The Joy's concoction to her own face and thinks, Why am I so excited? Right before she can take a bite her phone vibrates. Shit. No. Not stopping. Eating. She takes a big bite, chews. She mentally surveys her mouth to see if she likes what's in it. Damn. Yes. She hadn't seen the capers go in, but damn. It was a genius addition. She thinks, Maybe this will be a good day. But then the thought that her world has gotten so small that a caper could turn things around immediately depresses her.

As she keeps eating, she looks around at the other fire escapes. There are usually other people out, getting a few precious moments of fresh air. Well, air. But not today. To the left, she sees a Black Lives Matter banner hanging from a fire escape and wonders how people get a banner printed so quickly. Maybe they already had it. Her phone vibrates again. This time she pulls it from her back pocket and sees there's a message from her sister Milli reading, *I'm on break.* Milli's one of the few people Kimi looks forward to hearing from. Her one family member she can be herself with. She hits dial.

Milli answers abruptly, "What?!"

This typical greeting from her sister makes Kimi happier than the capers. "What yourself, Dr. O'Gorman. Why are you bothering me?"

Milli becomes herself and lets her guard down. "Just needed someone to complain to."

"I'm your gal."

"Had a bitch of a time getting to the hospital this morning, dodging marchers. How is it by you?"

"Weird quiet. Then, weird loud."

"As I was driving past them, the protesters, I actually felt optimistic that people were pulling together for something good. You know? I mean, something terrible happened, but they're using it to try and effect positive change. Then I get here and it's the same shit. Not enough supplies, not enough beds, not enough help and I think, what's going to be the needed change here? What will it look like? How long is it going to take? And I feel helpless all over again. So many people are so sick."

There's nothing Kimi can say to make it better, so she doesn't try. "How's Shay?"

"Besides going stir crazy being home with the kids? He's OK. It's strained. I try to not talk about my day, which means I have nothing to say. So, he's busy not asking me questions and I'm busy not answering them."

"God. Relationships suck."

"What did Carmen do now?"

Man, Milli knows her. "She said, get this, she said I *make* her needy."

More as a surprise than a question, Milli responds, "Really."

"Yeah. She says that because I never *share* anything with her, it *forces* her to be needy. Because I'm so *closed off* she has to beg. That's bullshit, right? I mean, that's not a real thing. You can't *make* someone needy."

"You could make anyone needy. If you don't make them leave first."

Kimi thinks about this. Could her biggest problem with Carmen actually be her own fault? Fuck! "I suck."

"Knowing is halfway to a cure."

"Halfway is far enough, right?"

"Look at it this way, if you didn't suck a bit, how would we recognize you?"

"Let's go back to your problems."

"I don't have problems. I vented to you. I'm good."

"You're welcome."

"Oh, Mom's worried that you're in the city with everything that's going on and no man. She's working on Mrs. Wang to see if her new dentist son-in-law knows anyone for you."

Over the phone, Kimi can hear the hospital intercom in the background. "Dr. O'Gorman, you're needed in ICU." Milli abruptly shifts to work mode, "Duty calls. Remember, you suck. And thanks." With that, she's gone.

Kimi sits on the fire escape with what's left of her lunch. The dense, edible wedge resting on the plate seems less appealing now. She looks around hoping for one of her fire escape people to show up and create the feeling of neighborhood, but none do. She's contemplating whether to wrap up her lunch and save it for another time or chuck it when she hears The Joy call out, "Oh, my God!" Kimi assumes it's yet another food disappointment. But then, The Joy calls out again, "No!!!"

Kimi leans her head back into the apartment. "You OK?"

The Joy holds up a finger to Kimi. Kimi can now see that The Joy is on her cell.

Into her phone The Joy says, "Well, what did your doctor say? ... Mm hmm... Mm hmm... Mm hmm..."

Kimi can't handle this lack of info. She mouths, "What?" to The Joy, who only holds out her finger again, making Kimi wait. Ugh.

The Joy tightens her jaw and paces as she says, "And how long, did your doctor say? Mm hmm... Mm hmm... Mm hmm... And this is a real doctor?"

THERE WILL BE NO SLEEP

THE JOY'S APARTMENT/THE JOY'S BEDROOM

The Joy lies on top of the pile of everything that's on her bed with her eyes open. She's fully dressed but wearing her ridiculously furry, orange cat-paw slippers that match the stripe in her hair. On her bedside table is a menagerie of her little plastic cocktail swag animals, all staring at her. She turns to them. "This can't be happening." She feels like her world is ending. This gives her a flash of morbid inspiration. She texts a Zoom assignment to the group.

SHAD & BENJI'S APARTMENT/SHAD'S BEDROOM

In his old, worn, workout togs that are his new pajamas, Shad sits in the dark at his computer with Douglas at his feet. He's going back and forth between information on the Krantz Fund and Black Lives Matter. He wants to be able to speak intelligently and have clear opinions on both matters the next time he talks to Sandra. He feels like he's cramming for a test and the class is Sandra D. 101. Shad sits back for a moment. He thinks, Am I in charge here? Am I being led or am I leading? If he's being honest with himself, he's not sure. No. If he's being truly honest, he's letting her call the shots. Not the strong move. He wonders what it is about her that's so appealing. Smart, check. Hot, check. A-type, check. Well, there you have it. What's a smart, self-described handsome, A-type to do? And what harm can come from becoming more informed?

He decides to stop being so honest with himself when a text from The Joy comes in. *Next Zoom call, what do you want on your tombstone?*

STEPH'S APARTMENT

Steph is standing at her wall of windows, looking down on Third Avenue. She's swirling a glass of red wine. This has become her "place." She looks out at the world and muses about the goings on of her day. She'd done a story on the Clappers. The people all over the city who'd spontaneously started standing outside at 7pm and clapping and banging pots for the frontline workers as they'd pass by. People are making deliveries or are on their way home from work at NYU Tisch Hospital. Bill felt it was important to show as much positivity now as possible and she was happy with the assignment. She felt good reporting on people showing support for others. It was like everyone was on the same team.

As she sips her red wine she thinks about how much warmer it's getting. Maybe it's time to switch to white wine. She stands in the dark and enjoys being able to think about nothing important.

Over on the kitchen counter, her phone vibrates. She silently chides herself, *Why didn't I bring it with me? Now I have to go way over there.*

She tears herself away from her spot and checks her phone.

It's a text from Jackson. *Nice piece today.*

She responds, *Can't sleep?*

Want to help me?

Steph smiles and heads back to her spot. This time she brings her phone with her. She takes a moment to enjoy the thought of going to Jackson's place for the night, before she breaks her own spell. *Can't. Early call.*

[Sad emoji]

Me [Sad emoji] too.

Her next text reads, *Next Zoom call, what do you want on your tombstone?*

It takes Steph a moment to realize it's not from Jackson.

JACKSON'S APARTMENT/BEDROOM

Jackson sits alone in the dark, on top of the plush bedding of his parent's California King bed and holds his phone. He'd taken over their huge bedroom about a week after lockdown. Why not?

No Steph tonight. Now what? He feels a text come in and thinks perhaps she's changed her mind. Nope. It's a text from The Joy to the group. It reads, *Next Zoom call, what do you want on your tombstone?*

He texts back, *Cheery* then puts his phone down his pants. Now, even if the next text is equally un-fun, he'll at least get some pleasure from it.

SHAD & BENJI'S APARTMENT/BENJI'S LOFT

Benji's in bed with his feet hanging over the end. He's that big. Or is the bed that small? He's lying on his stomach, propped up on his elbows, playing on his gaming device when he hears the texting start. His eyes briefly dart to his cell, which is lying on his pillow, then back to the zombie onslaught. Another text. His eyes dart again, but he doesn't dare look over too long. This is life or death. So many zombies. When Benji's avatar finally dies at the hands of an undead five-year-old with a chainsaw, he looks at his phone. The texted question, *Next Zoom call, what do you want on your tombstone?* Hmm. He texts back, *Roger that.*

THE JOY'S APARTMENT/KIMI'S CORNER

Kimi is passed out on her La-Z-Boy beneath several afghans. Her phone buzzes. She comes to just enough to look at it. She sees The Joy's text thread. Such bullshit. She texts back, *If anyone else responds to this tonight, I'm stabbing you.*

Kimi pulls the covers over her head and lies there. Shit. She thinks, The Joy, you suck so much. What *do* I want on my gravestone? She listens to several sirens go by, then it's quiet again. Well, quiet for New York. More lying there. Her eyelids start to droop as she begins nodding off. The sound of a cocktail shaker means that sleep is over.

Kimi gets up with her afghans over her like a cape, pulls back her curtain and sees the Joy in the kitchen working her magic. She shuffles over. "Cocktail hour? Now?"

"I guess."

Kimi watches The Joy pour equal amounts of bourbon, lemon juice and honey into the shaker, shake it up, then pour the concoction over ice. She hands the drink to Kimi who stares at the golden concoction in her hand. "What do you call this?"

"It's called a Honey, Life Gave You Lemons." She lifts her own glass and they toast.

"To lemons."

"I can't make myself pack."

Kimi takes The Joy's hand and leads her to her bedroom. "Come on, lemon drop. I'll help you."

CARING IS WORK

THE JOY'S APARTMENT/THE JOY'S BEDROOM

The sun's just starting to rise as The Joy slips into her bright orange swing coat. The coat is one of her favorite garments. It has a tailored, triangular shape that swings away from her body. It usually improves her mood. She fears she's asking way too much of a coat. She picks up her suitcases and stares at Kimi, who's asleep on top of the bed. She shouldn't wake her. But screw it. The Joy opens her hands and lets her bags drop to the ground with a bang.

Kimi blindly thrusts her arms like she's stabbing an invisible attacker. With her eyes still closed she blurts, "I'll cut a bitch!"

"I'm leaving, now."

Kimi slowly comes to consciousness and sits up. "Oh."

"I thought you'd want the chance to say something nice to me."

"Like?"

"I don't know. Like, 'Wow, I'm so impressed with you for risking life and limb to be there for a woman who's never appreciated you. Oh, and, God, you're a beauty.'"

"God, you're a beauty."

The Joy sinks down and sits on her suitcase. Hmm, that was lower than she expected. She almost falls over. "I can't believe I'm doing this."

"It's the right thing to do."

"The right thing is so not me."

Kimi rubs her eyes, now more awake and looks at her friend. "Which is why you're so amazing."

"Ya think?"

"Don't make me say it again. How long you think you'll be down in the land of yacht clubs and hemorrhoid cream?"

"Ugh. A couple of months, more? Ugh."

"Only *your* mother would break a hip on a golf ball. You're doing her a huge solid. I'm sure she'll be nicer to you."

At that attempt at a platitude, they stare at each other and come to the same conclusion. Together, they say, "It's gonna suck."

It's time. The Joy stands, grabs her bags and a cat carrier. Kimi looks puzzled. "Why are you taking the cat carrier?"

"Betty hates cats. It'll drive her crazy."

"But you don't have a cat."

"She doesn't know that." They smile at each other. "Hug my neck."

Kimi stands up on the bed to be tall enough to hug The Joy. She then kisses her forehead and The Joy returns in kind.

"Pray for me."

"I'll pray for Florida."

With her hands full, The Joy somehow manages to pull her mask up. It's one of Kimi's and says, "I'm really a man." She heads out. Kimi hears her calling back from the living room. "No wild parties. And don't get crumbs in my bed."

Kimi sits back on the bed and spots a Charlie's Angels ashtray with a plastic gun in it. She's reaching for the gun when...

"Freeze, mister! Hands off the juju!"

Kimi yanks her hand back. How does she do that?

She hears the front door close, and thinks about how she's gonna miss that crazy bitch. Strange what becomes comforting.

SHAD & BENJI'S APARTMENT

Benji's standing at the front window, wearing a long t-shirt, long shorts and slippers, holding a bowl of homemade ramen and chopsticks. He stares at the marchers as he shoves noodles into his face. Man, his ear is so itchy. Benji uses the non-business end of one of his chopsticks to scratch in his ear. As a siren catches his attention, he leaves the chopstick dangling. Shad walks by, sniffing the air. "Did you make ramen?"

"Yeah."

"Brilliant." Shad, notices the chopstick coming out of Benji's ear. That's new. He chooses to ignore it. He goes into the kitchen assuming that what's left in the pot is his for the taking. He takes it. As he ladles the soup into his bowl, both he and Benji get a text. Only Shad looks at it. It's from Jackson: *Are you gentlemen marching?*

He calls to Benji, "Hey."

No response.

"Benji."

Nothing.

"Sunshine!"

Benji finally breaks contact with the marchers and turns to Shad.

"Jackson wants to know if we're marching today."

"Uh, I don't feel great about being around all those people. Do you?"

Shad acknowledges, "It will be weird. But I want to be a part of it."

"I don't know."

"Come on. You, me and Jackson. We're like our own rainbow coalition. Solidarity, my brother."

Benji considers this. How can he say no? Shad and Jackson are his closest friends. As much as he'd rather stay in his safe little bubble, he knows he should go and support them. "OK."

Shad's excited. He takes a large helping of noodles and heads over to the window. "Thanks, man. Means a lot."

Benji has a new and self-serving thought. "Do you think Jackson'll bring his sister?"

"Ruby, Queen of the Shadows?"

"You're talking about my potential new girlfriend."

"Sorry, dude."

"Forgiven."

Shad raises his bowl. "Taste the rainbow." Benji raises his and they clink bowls and slurp in unison. Benji looks back out the window with concern.

STEPH'S APARTMENT

Steph pushes her way in the front door. Her phone is wedged between her shoulder and her ear, while her hands are occupied with her briefcase, computer bag and her latest wine purchase. She eases her bundles onto the dining table/workstation as she talks. "Fine, Mom."

Her mother's having none of it. "Don't just *fine* me."

"I'm not just *fining* you. I'll be extra careful." Steph know she's better off changing the subject. Ida can be a dog with a bone. "How's Dad?"

"Ugh. Your father's the same. He makes me crazy. It's easier when he has sports to watch. Thank God there's still horse racing."

Steph puts her phone on speaker and sits it in a cradle so she can work while she talks. Or, more accurately, listens. She scans her work emails while Ida continues. "Oh, I almost forgot. You remember Mrs. Golding?"

Steph is reading an email from Bill to all employees who interact with the public about incidents of looting and new safety protocols.

Ida repeats, "Mrs. Golding? ... Hello? ... Are you there? Or are you too big a news star to talk to your old mother?"

"Sorry Mom. What?"

"There you are. Mrs. Golding. You remember her?"

Steph has no idea who her mother is talking about. "Yeah. Sure."

"Well, her daughter wants to be a newswoman and she asked if you would talk to her."

More silence passes while Steph sees an email about how a new wave of her colleagues are sick with the virus. Ida pushes for a response. "Well?"

"Well what?"

"Oh, my God. You're worse than your father. Will you talk to Mrs. Golding's daughter about being a news big shot like my daughter?"

"Is she a drinker? That helps."

Ida's suddenly concerned, "Stephanie, are you drinking too much?"

"Define, 'Too much.'"

"We didn't raise you to be some drunk on a corner."

Steph considers her mother's drinking habits. "No. Most drunks on the corner don't pour Kahlua and cream."

Ida is suddenly wistful, "It's so good. It's like dessert in a glass."

"I like my dessert in wine form."

"What do you want me to say to Mrs. Golding?"

"You're killing me, Mom. Things are crazy. I can't deal with that right now."

"So, I'll tell her to call you next week."

"Oh, my God! How are you not a used car salesman?"

"Please. Sales*person*."

"Oh, we're being politically correct now?"

"Everyone in the *'hood* says I'm very woke."

If Steph was drinking, she'd have done a spit take. She's about to ask Ida to define "woke" when she sees a text from Jackson and takes that as her exit. "Ma, I gotta go."

"I know. I know. You're very important person."

"I'll call you tomorrow."

"I'll tell Mrs. Golding what you said." And before Steph can protest, Ida is gone.

Steph shakes her head. She'd get annoyed if she wasn't so used to it, and a little amused. Then she remembers that Jackson texted. She's ready for something happy. His text reads, *Marching with Benji & Shad tomorrow. Care to join?*

Not what she'd hoped for. She replies, *Can't*

Why not?

Steph lets herself think about how great it would be to see her friends in person. She remembers how they parted on the sidewalk in front of their favorite dive bar almost three months earlier. If she'd known that this would last so long, would she have given her friends more time to speak? She knows the truth. She'd still talk about herself. But they love her anyway.

I can't become part of the story

Bummer.

Steph is bummed, but she doesn't dare join her friends. Hey, Jackson's birthday's coming up. Shouldn't she be looking for a gift? That's what a girlfriend would do. Is that her role? Steph navigates away from email and starts looking for gift ideas. What do you get a guy who could buy whatever he wants and does? Ah. Wait. Lightbulb moment. She Googles, "Ninja Warrior Gifts." She finds t-shirts with sayings like, "Never Never Never Give Up," "Show Me Your Kettle Bells," "Inspire," "and "Quit is a four letter word." There are tote bags, hats, towels, it's all pretty expected stuff. Then, she sees it. Something totally unexpected. She thinks, Now, that's just stupid enough to be perfect.

THE JOY'S APARTMENT

Kimi stands in the middle of The Joy's living room. It's quiet. Not that The Joy was always talking, but there's a sound to someone else being in a space, and now that's gone. Kimi feels the "whoosh" of her own movements being absorbed by no one and bouncing back to her. So weird. She has the place to herself. Her first thought is to rearrange all the juju. Her next thought is to fear her first thought.

She goes to the music corner and considers what would be appropriate. She puts on Beyoncé's *All the Single Ladies*. Damn, that's good. Is it cool? Who cares? Kimi starts to dance by herself. Is she good? Who cares? Kimi lets the feeling of freedom wash over. She wants to leap up onto the sofa but fears her lack of coordination so she steps up and keeps dancing. She joins Beyoncé singing about all the single ladies. God, this feels good. There's a flash of seeing people in old movies standing on chairs, putting a foot on the chair back and slowly tipping it over. Dare she? Fuck it! She puts her foot on the back of the sofa and slowly shifts her weight more and more singing, "Dah, dah, dah... Dah, dah, dah, dah..." Over the sofa goes and Kimi with it. She loses her balance and rolls on the floor, coming to a stop face down in front of a shallow chest of drawers by the front door. She asks herself, What did I expect? Lying there, she sees something on the floor. From under the chest of drawers she pulls out a cat toy with a bell on it in the shape of Fred Flintstone. What the fuck? Was there a cat here? Does a cat called The Fred really exist?

Kimi's phone vibrates. It's a text from Jackson. Kimi rolls onto her back and reads, *Shad, Benji and I marching tomorrow. You in?* Holding Mr. Flintstone and her phone, Kimi considers this. Would it be worth going outside to march? It might. She hates that she's suddenly nervous. More correctly, frightened. In an attempt to be strong, she looks Fred in the eye and texts back, *In.*

Jackson responds, *Brilliant. Tell TJ*

She's gone.

What?

WELCOME TO THE SUNSHINE

TAMPA AIRPORT

The Joy pushes a luggage cart holding her two large bags and cat carrier through the front doors of the Tampa airport. The moment the hot, humid air hits her masked face, she feels like she's traveled to a strange new land. It's no longer just Florida, land of her disapproving mother. It's a bright, shiny place where people act like nothing is wrong in the world. They aren't wearing masks. No one. Wait. That guy over there has a mask on and it's under his nose. So, one guy and he's doing it wrong. Never one to mind standing out, The Joy suddenly feels self conscious. Should she lower her mask?

Her whole trip down had been like a contest for who could be safer. The marchers in the city that her Uber driver passed were all masked up and no one seemed to be standing closer than eight feet apart. Her Uber driver's car smelled like a Purell factory had exploded inside it right before she'd gotten in. At Newark Airport, what few people were actually there were masked up. And onboard, everyone was in a constant state of wiping. But now, because everyone acted the way they did before lockdown, it felt foreign.

68

While still trying to figure it all out, a powder-blue Cadillac pulls up in front of The Joy and the passenger window goes down. The tan, trim, gray-haired driver who has his mask hanging from the rearview mirror, leans over and calls to her. "You have to be Joy." The Joy bends down a bit to respond, "Well, if I have to. And it's *The* Joy."

"It's me. *The* Nathan Waxman. But you can call me Nate. Hold on. I'll pop the trunk." The trunk of the Caddy rises up and The Joy rolls her bags to the back of the car. As she's about to lift the first one in, Nate meets her behind the vehicle. He's not even as tall as he seemed sitting down and The Joy towers over him. "Where are my manners? Let me help you with that." She lets Nate load her luggage, though in truth she feels she would be way more capable than this skinny, little man. She just smiles, not that he can see it behind the mask. They get in the car, which smells like coco butter, and pull away.

Nate leans his head to The Joy without actually looking at her, as he talks. "Don't worry *The* Joy, Betz, *The* mother, is going to be just fine."

The Joy cautiously lowers her mask and answers flatly, "Oh, I'm not worried."

"Sure you are. Hey, want to stop for a quick bite? You must be hungry."

"If I must be."

"Great. There's a little deli on the way. You like deli? Of course you do. You live in New York, land of deli. Am I right?"

As they ride, The Joy watches the sunshine dancing on the water and wonders what she's doing here. Why did her mother want her to come? It's just going to be a festival of backhanded remarks and frosty looks. That can't be fun for Betty. Or, maybe it is.

After an indiscernible amount of time, Nate declares, "Here we are." He drives his Caddy to the front of a brightly lit deli in a strip mall looking like it's been stripped of all personality. Or maybe it was built that way.

The Joy leaves the thoughts of her mother that were swimming in her head and looks out. "Oh, Nathan."

"Please, call me Nate."

"Nate, I'm not actually hungry."

Nate's not put off in any way. He's like a puppy who you push to the side and keeps coming back undeterred. "Sure you are. And keep your money in your pockets. It's on me. As a welcome to Florida."

She acquiesces to this tiny Jewish force. It seems the easier choice. "Thank you, Nate." She overenunciates his name.

"Please. Don't thank me. It's just a sandwich. Someday, I'll buy you a meal and you can thank me then. Don't thank me for a sandwich. What is it? Some bread, some meat, a pickle... When I buy you a meal, you can thank me then."

The Joy suddenly thinks, I believe I love this little man.

BETTY'S HOUSE

From the outside, Betty's single-level home is an ode to stucco. The Joy stands at the front door thinking, The longer I stand here, the longer I'm safe from this reunion of the damned. A horn honks and she turns to see Nate wave and motion to her to go inside. Ugh. Fine. She'll do it. She pulls out a key, lets herself in and carefully announces, "Betty! It's Joy."

There she is. Betty. Or "Betz," as her friends call her. She's in a wheelchair by the sliding glass door that looks out onto the Florida room, which looks out onto a golf course. Betz looks as crisp as ever. Nothing is out of place. She turns to her daughter.

"There you are. Look at you. Oh, dear. Is that orange?"

The Joy touches her hair. "Oh, *that* orange. It's a Crayola original. Nate's nice."

"Yes, he is. You'll have to write him a thank-you card. Are you going to ask how I am?"

The Joy puts down her bags, walks over and gives the woman who birthed her an uncomfortable kiss on the cheek. "How are you, Betty?"

"Honestly? I feel like a fool. A golf ball. Really? Now look at me."

"You look great. You always look great."

"No, I don't. I look like an old lady in this wheelchair. I'm not old. Mrs. Baker had to help me get dressed this morning. So embarrassing. Honestly."

"Well, I'm here now. You don't have to be embarrassed. You look...young." And she does. Betty is an attractive woman who only "needed" a minimal amount of work done to stay fresh looking. And her personal style is impeccable. She's not large-framed like The Joy. That came from The Joy's father, who left decades ago. Betty's look is sporty, elegant and enviable.

Betty lets out a long sigh. "You can put your things in the guest bedroom. I had Carol put new sheets on the bed and there are fresh towels in the bathroom. You'll want to wash up."

The Joy gets up and collects her things. Betty looks over in horror. "Is that a cat?!"

"Oh, that's just The Fred."

"Joy, I can't have a cat here. He'll stink up everything with cat smell."

"Oh, The Fred doesn't smell."

Betty is incredulous. "Joy, the second I smell that cat, he's out."

"Got it." The Joy smiles to herself as she heads to her sanctuary.

BETTY'S HOUSE/THE JOY'S ROOM

The Joy is lying on the bed of her new, temporary home. The room is bright with zero personality. Everything is shades of yellow with white rattan furniture. She's going to have to do something to make it bearable. So far, the only touch of The Joy in the room is the arrangement of plastic cocktail swag animals on the bedside table.

She pulls out her phone and sees several texts from Kimi. The first reads, *You get there?* The next text says, *Where the fuck are you?* The last reads, *Fuck you!* The Joy smiles. She misses her sarcastic friend already. She's about to text back and thinks, Not enough. She hits the dial icon.

Kimi answers abruptly, "Where the fuck?"

"Sorry."

"You said you'd text when you landed. I checked. You landed hours ago. Not cool. Not cool!"

The Joy is touched. "I love you."

Kimi's tone changes. "You know I don't believe in the "L" word, but I "L" you too. How was it?"

"When I left the apartment, I felt naked. Like the disease could walk up and slap me on the ass. So, I imagined myself in my own bubble, and that was cool, being a bubble girl. Ever see that old movie, *The Boy in the Plastic Bubble* with John Travolta?"

"No."

"Well, if you did, you'd know what I'd look like if I was a bubble girl. You can Netflix it."

"OK, Bubbles. What else?"

"The airport was empty. Like a future-y sci-fi movie. And then, there were like five people on my flight, like a future-y horror movie. Oh, oh, this was truly horrible. No booze! They're not serving liquor now. How can they get away with that? It's un-American."

"There's your future horror movie."

"Exactly! Thank God I had on my Wine Rack."

"I'm sorry. The Russian judge needs clarification on that. Wine rack?"

"My Wine Rack. Do I have to teach you everything?"

Sarcastically, Kimi begs, "Take pity on me."

"Ugh. Fine. A Wine Rack is a bra with bladders in the boob cups you fill with wine. And there's a nozzle you can drink from. It's all very discreet."

"Very."

"And here's the genius part. You don't even have to fill it with wine. I had gin in my right boob and tequila in my left. I didn't know what I'd be in the mood for so... be prepared."

"You're like a giant, blond Girl Scout. In a bubble."

"Oh, almost no one is wearing a mask down here. It's a sea of full faces."

"No shit!"

"Complete shit."

"Which mask did you wear down?"

"I started with 'I'm really a man,' then over Georgia I switched to, 'I'd rather have something else on my face.'"

"A classic."

"Nate didn't even mention it."

"Who's Nate?"

"That's the little Jewish guy Betty's seeing. Not that she'd admit it. He's so cute and tiny. I want to put him on a charm bracelet. He drove me to Betty's."

"The big question. How was the reunion?"

"Ugh. Just...ugh." The Joy thinks about how challenging this is all going to be. "The cat carrier was an inspired move. Even for me."

From the living room Betty calls out, "Joy. Joy. Can you get my binoculars?"

"Well kiddo, gotta go help Betty spy on her neighbors. Or as she calls it, 'Caring.'"

"You're my hero. Oh, I'm going to march with the guys tomorrow. Wish me luck."

In a bit of a whine, The Joy says, "Noooo. I wanna protest. This sucks."

THE WIDE WORLD

SHAD & BENJI'S APARTMENT/OUTSIDE

Shad and Benji are standing in front of their apartment building. They're watching hordes of people passing in the street, wearing masks and holding signs. Shad holds his arms out. Through his mask he says, "O.M.G! Air!" Even though the air still smells like New York, it smells like victory. He feels energized. He's almost jumping. Benji, on the other hand is swinging his arms about himself like people do when they step out into the snow. "Dude, what are you doing? It's warm out."

"The wind on my arm hair is tickling me."

Shad just stares at his roommate and reminds himself that there are some things about this guy he'll never understand. Then he hears a familiar voice call out...

"Gentlemen!"

He turns to see Jackson bounding towards them. God, he's fit. And somehow, simultaneously, Jackson's clothes look insanely casual and stupidly expensive. Of course, his mask is coordinated with his scarf. His arms are out, as if to hug them, but he stops several feet away.

"Gentlemen. I'm air hugging you."

Both Shad and Benji mimic the move. Shad says, "Dude. I missed you."

"I missed you guys, too."

Benji looks behind Jackson. "I thought Ruby was coming."

Jackson laughs. "My sister's not much of a joiner." He sees that Benji is dejected. "But, if you come to my birthday party, she'll be there." Benji perks up at the thought. Jackson asks, "Any word from—"

"From that hot bitch Kimi? She's right here." They turn to see Kimi walking up. Huge smiles all around. The air hugging is repeated. A feeling of happiness washes over all of them. It almost hurts not to hug. They're bordering on giddy. The far side of the border. Kimi looks around at her friend's faces. "Hey, Jackson. Nice not-my-mask."

Shad says, "We missed you, too."

"I'm an acquired taste, but once you've had me, you crave more."

To Kimi, Jackson apologizes. "Forgive me. For my first foray back into the world, I chose to coordinate."

She just shrugs.

Shad says, "Shall we do this?"

With that, the foursome turns, heads into the crowd and starts walking north with the rest of the marchers.

STEPH'S APARTMENT

Steph stands staring into her open refrigerator. As she looks at its sparse contents, she considers the ramifications of each item. Yogurt? No. She's not feeling the dairy love at the moment. Better to save that for dessert tonight. There's that leftover tomato soup. Hmm. Acid. No. Sliced turkey? Does she need protein right now? Maybe. How would she have it? She knows that bread is out. Bread. When was the last time she enjoyed bread? That would just be crazy. She thinks, maybe on one of those crispy, whole-grain flatbreads. But that would add about 95 calories. Does she really need the cracker? It's just for the crunch. She could put the turkey in lettuce. Is there lettuce? She checks the drawer. Yes. OK, turkey, lettuce. God, she'd love mayo. Mustard would be smarter. What else? She could slice up some red pepper and add sprouts. That might make it more filling. She stands there staring for a full minute. It all seems like so much hassle. Finally, she grabs the pickle jar, takes out a spear and heads back to her computer.

As she reviews the notes on a story about protesters, pickle juice runs down her arm. She licks it before it can contaminate her computer. Her mind wanders to her friends who she cannot be with. Sacrifices.

BETTY'S HOUSE

Betty is sitting in her wheelchair in the Florida room, watching her neighbors golf. Her binoculars are on her lap. She raises them periodically and looks at their golf games. The Joy comes in with a tray of food and puts it down on the folding table next to Betty. "You might want to be more discreet with those."

Betty reviews the finger sandwiches on the tray. There's a look on her face that says she's just smelled something bad. "I'm watching golf. I'm doing nothing wrong."

"Mm-hmm."

Mother and daughter sit in silence.

Betty looks at the tray again, "What's that?"

"Turkey and Swiss."

"No, that." Betty gestures to the cocktail giraffe on the tray.

"Just some cocktail swag to make lunch more festive."

"Don't be ridiculous."

The Joy picks up her plastic giraffe and discreetly whispers to it, "Don't pay attention to the mean lady" before slipping it into her pocket.

Betty continues looking outside. More silence. The Joy's not good with communal silence. "Who's that guy?"

"Which guy?"

"The one in the banana-colored pants."

"That's George Marx."

"Tell me his story."

"There's no story. He and his wife Mindy are lovely people. They're from upstate New York. He was in paper bags."

The Joy is about to make an in-the-bag joke when Betty stops her. "Before you make your inevitable smart remark, don't. We've heard them all."

The Joy shuts down. Betty finally adds, "Horrible bridge players. Don't tell them I said that."

"It's safe with me. How about those women over there?"

"Kate Brown, Jackie Bishop and Denny Jeffries. They have a daily threesome."

The Joy opens her mouth and Betty cuts her off. "Don't say it." She doesn't. Betty continues, "Denny's husband James passed two years ago. Such a shame. He was a very nice man. Now we're left with Denny. She thinks she's funny."

"Is she?"

"Merely tedious." More sitting. More not talking.

The Joy waits for the next group of golfers. "What about her?"

Betty is suddenly annoyed. "What about her?"

"Who is she? What's her story?"

"Not everyone has a story."

The Joy audibly deflates and takes a sandwich. Betty gives in. "That's Franny Banks. She's a dear friend."

"I never heard about her."

"Why would you? Do I know about your friends?"

The Joy considers this. "Would you like to?"

"Not really."

The Joy gets up. "Well..."

"You're leaving me?"

"Did you want me to stay? It's hard to tell."

Turning her attention back to the green, Betty raises her binoculars.

WHAT THE ZOOM

THE JOY'S APARTMENT

Kimi's in the kitchen mixing herself a cocktail for the group call. With the temperature outside getting warmer, she thought a gin and tonic was overdue. She stirs and tastes. There's no way around it, The Joy is just a better bartender. She misses her friend. But now, seeing the curtain to the corner that her life had become, and how it's now wide open, she considers her new freedom. She has to admit, she likes it.

OK, let's do this. Kimi has her laptop on the kitchen counter. She clicks the hosting button and...

Waits.

Nothing. Did she do something wrong? She looks all around the screen. Shit. This was never her job. Shit. Damn it. Which buttons? Argh. She starts clicking at random. Finally, there it is. OK. Oh, shit, she has to accept everyone into the call. Shad and Benji are first. They're on the sofa with beers and nachos.

Shad: "That took a while."

Kimi: "Shut up, you."

Benji: "I think you're doing great."

Kimi: "Thank you."

Shad turns to Benji: "Suck up."

Next, Kimi gets Steph on the call. She's in her usual pose with a raised wine glass. "Hey, gang."

Kimi's frustrated. "Wait. Hold on. Shush up."

Steph: "Remind me again, why aren't you in the diplomatic corps?"

Jackson's screen pops up. He's wearing a helmet that covers his entire face.

Benji: "Dude! Mandalorian. So cool."

Jackson: "Right."

Benji: "Where'd you get it?"

Kimi: "At the Who-The-Fuck-Cares Mart."

Steph: "She's in a mood."

Jackson raises the helmet so it sits on top of his head like a crown. "What's wrong my friend?"

Benji: "I was hoping Ruby would be joining us."

Shad: "Is that why you bathed? You know, she can't smell you."

Jackson: "I was actually asking our friend Kimi."

Kimi: "I hate all this social coordinating shit. So not what I'm built for."

Steph: "Which begs the question..."

Kimi: "Don't. Just don't. Listen. All of you. Before I get The Joy, we have to be extra nice to her."

Jackson: "We're always nice to her."

Kimi: "I mean it. Her mother is making her crazy."

They all think about that for a moment. Then, they each think about their own mothers. Then they think, Thank God I don't have The Joy's mother.

In unison, they all overtalk their own versions of, "You got it." "OK." "Sure."

Kimi: "OK. Here we go." She clicks The Joy onto the call and... There she is, looking upbeat and perky in her incongruous surroundings. She's holding a shiny pink cocktail. Except for the libation, it's not the picture they were expecting.

The Joy: "Hey gang! Does the city suck so much without me?"

Shad: "So much."

Kimi: "All day long."

Jackson: "Indeed. What is that cocktail?"

The Joy: "Oh, I just made it up. It's got equal parts vodka, grapefruit juice and baby aspirin. I'm calling it a Drunken Toddler."

Perhaps a bit too caring, Steph asks: "Seriously, how are you, girlfriend?"

The Joy: "So good!"

Kimi: "My god. You're such a liar."

With that, The Joy breaks. "I am. I'm a big fat liar. It's awful here. And not like, I-cut-my-bangs-uneven awful. It's like, I don't know." She takes a big swig of her drink and continues talking through the ice cube in her mouth. "It's so awful, I can't even think of another 'awful' that's awful enough to compare it to."

Steph: "Oh, baby. I'm sorry."

The Joy: "How do you talk to your mother so much?"

Steph: "I... I just always have. Oh, and she loves me."

The Joy: "Stop showing off. Quick. Someone talk about something else."

Kimi: "Epitaphs?"

The Joy: "Yes! Good."

With a heavy dose of sarcasm, Shad adds: "Yes. Gravestones are so much cheerier."

The Joy: "Oh, my God, Shad. Just work with me. Don't go to your downer side. Now, what do you want on your gravestone?"

Shad: "I'm not a downer."

The Joy: "Fine. No. But you are." Looking for any support, she turns to Kimi. "Kimi girl. Don't let me down. What do you want on your gravestone?"

Kimi: "'Best lesbian ever!!!' With three exclamation points."

The Joy: "See, Shad? That's how it's done!"

Kimi: "I was going to have it say, 'Best Asian lesbian ever,' and then I thought, Why should I add the qualifier? Just be the best."

Jackson: "Atta girl. OK. Me next." Jackson raises a sword, seemingly from nowhere. "Died in battle."

Benji: "That's so good."

Shad: "Why?"

The Joy: "Shad, don't make me tell you again. Benji, you next."

Benji: "I don't think I can top that."

Jackson: "It's not a competition."

The Joy: "Well, a little, it is."

Jackson: "Oh."

The Joy: "Benji, what's on your headstone?"

Benji: "I want mine to read, 'Where'd he go?'"

The Joy claps with delight. "See? Now you're winning." Benji sits up straight. He's visibly pleased at taking the lead.

The Joy: "Steph?"

Steph: "Oh, I'm allowed to talk now? Well thank you, Madam Chairwoman for allowing me the floor. My epitaph will read, 'She Enjoyed.'"

The Joy: "No. I don't like that one. Benji's still leading."

Steph: "I think Florida is making you mean."

The Joy: "I'm ignoring you."

Steph throws her hands in the air. She decides to just let The Joy blow off her Florida steam. For now. She tops off her wine and waits for the next opening.

Kimi: "So, what's your headstone going to say?"

The Joy: "Nothing. It's just going to be blank."

Shad: "That's cheating."

The Joy: "My game. My rules."

Kimi: "Is that what you want it to say?"

The Joy thinks for a moment. It wasn't what she meant. It does seem prophetic. Not that she'd use that word. But she loves the thought and loves Kimi even more for noticing it.

"Yes! That's what I want on my gravestone. And it's my new life motto. 'My game. My rules.' See? I told you this was a great game. I feel so much better." She lifts her glass. "Cheers!" They all cheers her back.

Steph: "Well, if we can move on..."

Shad: "I haven't gone yet."

Steph: "Oh, sorry."

Shad: "No problem. Mine will have an arrow pointing up and to the right."

The Joy: "I don't get it."

Benji: "It's a stock market thing. It just means that you're winning."

Shad: "Thank you, Wingman."

Benji: "No problem." The roommates high five.

The Joy: "Whatever."

Steph: "OK, moving on. How was the march, my little protesters?"

Shad: "So great. So glad we did it."

Benji: "It was weird to be outside."

Shad: "He's been taking his temperature on the hour since we got back."

Benji: "I think something's wrong with my thermometer."

Shad: "Because you don't have a fever?"

Kimi: "Gotta admit, I thought it was great, too. I felt like I was part of something. Well. No. It felt like everyone one else was a part of something and I was there. Does that make sense?"

Shad: "Totally."

Jackson: "It was stirring. And positive. Very positive."

Shad: "Yes! I didn't know what to expect. But it was like a giant street party with purpose."

Envious, The Joy whines: "Oh. I'm missing everything."

Kimi: "Don't go back down the hole."

Jackson: "I suppose this would be a bad time for me to bring up my birthday party."

The Joy: "No. it's OK. I'll pretend to be happy for you."

Jackson: "Thank you. So, who's coming? I have big plans."

Shad: "I think I'm in. I've had a taste of freedom. Now I'm like a man with a drug. Benji, you coming?"

Benji hesitates.

Jackson: "Ruby will be here."

Benji: "I suppose I could try and make it."

Kimi: "Smooth, Casanova. I'll be there."

Jackson claps his hands together. "This is going to be so good. Steph, you're coming, right?"

Steph: "Well..."

Kimi: "Drop the act. We all know you've—" she makes air quotes "—been there."

The Joy: "Nudge, nudge. Wink, wink."

Steph: "It's just... I'm not there while there's a gathering."

Kimi: "So come, stand in the corner and we'll throw cocktail onions at you."

Jackson: "You have to come. It's my birthday."

Shad: "Don't be a party pooper."

The Joy: "Do it. Act as my second."

Finally breaking down, Steph agrees, "Fine. Fine. I'll come. I'll be The Joy's second."

Benji laughs to himself. "She said 'come.'"

Shad shakes his head: "You're an idiot."

Benji: "Ask me if I care."

Jackson: "Here are the rules."

Kimi: "There are rules?"

Jackson: "Yes. Rule one. No presents."

Kimi: "Done."

Jackson: "No negativity."

Kimi: "And I'm out."

Jackson: "Seriously. Rule three. Bring an overnight bag. I plan on this thing getting lit."

The Joy is back to whining: "Oh. I want to get lit. I don't think I can be happy for you after all."

Jackson: "You can join via video."

The Joy considers the proposition. "Hey. I've never been lit long distance." She thinks some more and looks around her yellow and rattan room. "I may have to put down a tarp."

Kimi: "Safety first."

Steph: "Well. I hate to be that girl but..."

Kimi: "We know. You're too important to slum it any longer."

Steph: "It's not that. It's...well yes. I guess it's that. I have an interview with Miss Molly at 8am."

Benji gets nostalgic: "Miss Molly? I love her. I watched her every morning. I always waited for her to say my name. She never did. She said, Benny once. But I knew she didn't mean me. Remember her signoff? 'Remember kids...'"

They all join in with Benji, "Happy is a choice. And I choose happy."

Shad: "I didn't know she was still alive."

Steph goes into fast-talk mode: "They tell me she is. The network's doing this big two-part special on the best of children's programming. It's a feel-good. They're trying to balance all the bad news that people are overconsuming. Seriously, some people are news-bingeing all day every day. I don't know how they do it. I can't watch that much and it's my job. Anyway, there you are. And, of course, I'm relegated to a three-minute segment with Miss 'I didn't know she was still alive.' All very exciting stuff except completely not. My star is clearly on the rise."

Kimi: "Just go already, you successful piece of shit."

Steph: "Love you, too. The Joy, keep your chin up and come back to us soon. Yes, Benji. I said, 'come.' The Joy, remember, my hair will look like shit until you get back. Bye all." She raises a glass.

The Joy: "Wait, wait! You need your assignment for next week."

Steph: "Make it fast."

The Joy: "Ah. I hate pressure! Wait. I forgot it. You know you can't put me on the spot like that. Wait! Wait! Yes! Regret. Everyone has to share something they regret."

Steph: "I regret that I waited for that. Cheers." And she's gone.

The Joy: "OK. You all know that didn't count."

Jackson: "We know."

The Joy: "I miss you guys so much."

Shad: "You can call any time."

The Joy: "Really?"

Shad: "No."

The Joy smiles and raises her glass. "To next week."

They all cheers: "To next week,"

And all the screens go black. Kimi sits in her apartment and looks around. That was good. And this is good. But quiet. What does she need?

ANOTHER WORLD SHIFT

JACKSON'S APARTMENT

Jackson has pulled his Peloton bike out onto the balcony. With the weather warming up, he'd hoped that being out in the air would give him a sense of freedom and drive him to work out harder. Steph had already recorded her workout at 5am. Jackson admires her discipline, among other things. But the increasing sound of sirens during his workout is breaking the spell. There have been reports of looting all over the city. He wonders, what's wrong with people? Why can't they be more like Miss Molly and choose happy?

SHAD & BENJI'S APARTMENT/SHAD'S BEDROOM

Shad is at his computer on a video conference with the office. He wonders why he still thinks of it as "the office." No one has been in an office in months. It's "the team." He decides to just think of it as "the team." And today, Max is bordering on giddy as he shares what would seem to an outsider a horrible event. But Max is Max and this is what he lives for. Max declares, "Dive! Dive! We're in another dive! And do you know what that means? Anyone? Anyone?"

Shad's used to this scenario and decides not to fall for it. Not wanting Max's spotlight on him, he says nothing. Seems Collin and Old Sandra have the same strategy. While Shad waits out the silence, he thinks, Yep, she's Old Sandra now and forever more. But Sandra D. is new to this dynamic. She pipes up, "It means opportunity."

Max delights, "Yes! Opportunity! Thank you, Sandra D. It's nice to finally have someone on the team with balls. And because we all prepared our people for this by... By... Come on, New Sandra, don't leave me hanging. By...?"

"By managing expectations."

"And New Sandra, two for two! Yes, managing expectations. By managing expectations, our people see that what we told them would happen *did* happen, and what we tell them *will* happen will. And now, we buy! Who else here is excited?"

As the cheer fest goes on, Shad sees a text come in from Christopher, his old office—slash that, his old teammate. As stealthily as possible, Shad's eyes shift to his phone. The text reads, *Dude, I'm on the golf course.*

Shad responds, *You suck!!!*

So much!!!!!!

Shad tries to catch up to Max's discussion of technology stocks. Christopher texts again. *How's the new girl?*

Fine

You love her

What?

Collin told me
Collin's full of shit
[*Kiss emoji*]

Shad looks up at the team. What is Max saying? He has no idea. Oh, shit, it's his name. Shad feels like he's been caught looking out the window by his math teacher, which happened a lot. Think fast. Think fast. He decides to try a Crazy Ivan. He's gonna zag. "You know, I was wondering, what was the price of Home Depot in January?"

Max is stopped by this. Who knows what his original topic was, but Max is now connecting the dots from where he was to Shad's question. Of course, there were no dots, but only Shad knows that. Max goes on a long rant about supply chain and what a boon it's been for them and will likely continue to be. Shad looks over at Sandra D.'s square. She's smiling at him. Did she catch his misdirection? She must have. Shad gets another text from Christopher: *Birdied the 9th! Enjoy your meeting.*

THE JOY'S APARTMENT

The sound of the door buzzer causes the pile of blankets on Kimi's La-Z-Boy to shift. Her curtain is open to the rest of the room. The buzzer sounds again and Kimi tosses aside the blankets and rubs her eyes. Her first movements of the day are stiff. Her joints take a moment to lubricate. She gets up and shuffles to the front door, still rubbing her dry eyes. There's just no need to wake up early anymore. Hours of the day mean nothing to her. Days of the week mean even less. Before she reaches the door, the intercom buzzes one more time. She presses the button and says, "I hate you."

"Package Guy."

"Oh, you" She buzzes him in and opens the door. Vlad stands there with a large box. They just stare at each other. Finally he says, "You're Kimi Chu, right?"

"Yeah."

"I guess this is for you." Vlad stands there holding the box, not making a move.

"Do I get to have it?"

"Oh. Here." He hands her the box and looks over her head, scanning the apartment.

"She's not here."

Vlad is visibly dejected. "Oh." He just stands there.

Kimi finally decides to take pity on The Joy's man-slave. "She's in Florida. With her mother."

"She hates her mother."

"Word gets around."

After a bit more standing there, Vlad turns and leaves without another word. Kimi calls after him, "What, no sex?" And he's gone.

Kimi sees the apartment door across the hall slam shut. Whatever. She looks at the box in her hands and remembers what she ordered. When The Joy went to Florida, she'd continued sleeping in her corner. But after about a week she thought, why? There's an entire bedroom that's going unused. She stripped all of The Joy's bedding, trying not to think about the things it has seen. She considered using the spare bedding and thought, no. Order new. And here it is. New sheets.

She scoots into The Joy's bedroom and makes the bed, smoothing out her new powder blue purchase. They feel almost silky. She'd justified going for the higher thread count based on her projected mask sales. She's selling a bit more each week. And Steph said people could be wearing masks well into 2021. Kimi lies across her sheets and thinks, It was totally the right move. Tonight she'll sleep in a real bed for the first time in forever.

STEPH'S APARTMENT

Steph is on her sofa with bottle of Pellegrino, still dressed for camera. There's a glass on the coffee table, but she drinks directly from the bottle. Why dirty a glass? She puts her feet up on the coffee table, pulls a coin out of a pocket in her blouse and begins turning it in her fingers. After her interview with Miss Molly—real name Mellissa Feinstein—Molly handed Steph a Susan B. Anthony silver dollar. In the interview, she'd told Steph that when she'd first gotten the call for the children's show, she was down to her last seven dollars. Six bills and this coin. It was only a one-day gig with the possibility of more. If it worked out. Molly decided to roll the dice on success and used the six bills to take a cab to the studio, which meant she was down to this one coin. If the job didn't last, she would be flat broke. But the show was a hit from day one. Molly put the coin in her purse and told herself that as long as she kept that coin, she would never be down and out.

Steph hadn't planned on liking Miss Molly. As a kid, she'd always found the TV show saccharine and slow. But this is a woman who's sharp and smart and easy to be with. Like that aunt you always wanted. After the interview, Molly shocked Steph by giving her the coin. She told Steph that it's her turn now, and to not let go of the coin until it was time to pass it on. Molly wasn't preachy. She just made Steph feel like she wanted to be better. How did she do that? Steph continues turning the coin in her hand and considers her not-yet storied career. Who will she benevolently pass this coin on to? She thinks, And, why me? Am I anything special? My parents certainly think so, but that's their job. I think so, but I have a huge ego. Steph doesn't mind having a huge ego. She feels she needs it for the job. Jackson thinks I'm special. Jackson... Jackson... So complicated. But she's getting more and more comfortable with the thought of it lasting. She knows she's dropping her guard which makes her proud of herself. Doesn't take much.

BETTY'S HOUSE

As The Joy passes through the living room on her way to the kitchen, she sees Betty and her friend Franny sitting in the Florida room with iced tea, which may or may not be enhanced. Of course, neither of them is wearing a mask. They're laughing like old friends laugh. The Joy is only used to seeing her mother laugh with other people. Betty spots her and calls out, "Joy, what are you eating now?"

Feeling caught in the act, The Joy calls back, "Nothing."

"Then get out of the kitchen. You'll only get into trouble."

Embarrassed, The Joy heads back towards her room. She's stopped by Franny, "Joy. Come here. Let me see you."

After a deep breath to ready herself for whatever nitpicking may come, The Joy joins them in the Florida room. She stands, feeling herself tower above them. "This is me."

Franny's style mimics Betty's although Franny is a bit stockier. "Sit with us."

The Joy looks to her mother for a cue that it's OK to join the inner circle. She gets a raised eyebrow and supposes that's as much of an "all clear" as she's going to get. She sits. Franny puts a friendly hand on The Joy's leg.

"I was just telling Betz that, now that she has you to help, she should have a little cocktail party. She's been too isolated in this house."

Betz protests, but not really, "I don't think Joy is interesting in throwing a cocktail party."

Franny asks, "Joy, would you do it?"

The Joy hesitates. No one back home is doing in-person parties. What a crazy world she's stepped into.

Betty rolls her eyes. "See? I told you she's not interested."

"I'm always interested in a cocktail party. But, there's that pesky pandemic. It's all the rage."

Franny laughs, "Relax. You're not in New York anymore, dear. Things are different down here. What do you say?"

The Joy's mind goes into cocktail mode, "Well, I am quite the bartender."

Franny claps her hands. "See! There. It's settled. What do you like to mix?"

The Joy gets a crafty smile. "What do you like to drink?"

Franny turns to Betty, "Oh, this girl is a keeper." Betty doesn't respond. "We can have the Marxes, the Willsons, Nate, of course. Denny?

Betty protests, "Oh, please."

"Betz, don't be a stick in the mud. She's alone. You don't have to talk to her."

"Fine."

Franny turns to The Joy with the gleam of gossip in her eyes. "Did Betz tell you about what happened last year at the Christmas party?"

The Joy leans in, "No. Do tell."

Betty protests, "Franny, no." They both look at Betty who clearly does not want to revisit this topic. The moment of fun has been shut down. The Joy has seen this dynamic too many times.

Franny finally turns to The Joy. "So, orange?"

The Joy touches the streak of orange in her hair. "Do you like it?"

Franny smiles at Betty, "Maybe I should try it."

The Joy jumps in. "I can make it happen. I brought a few extensions with me for just such an emergency."

"Oh Joy, Franny's just trying to be nice." And there goes whatever chance there was to get the fun back.

The Joy stands, "I think I'll go check on my cat."

SHAD & BENJI'S APARTMENT/BENJI'S LOFT

Benji's on his bed, knees up and under headphones. He has several cookbooks laid out open around him. What should he make to bring to Jackson's birthday? He's been on an everything-Asian kick, but thinks he should find something Middle Eastern for Jackson. And Ruby. Something with lamb. He tries to get in the appropriate food mood by switching out his most recent music go-to, the Japanese garage-punk band, Sakuran-Zensen for Middle Eastern pop. He immediately misses the rebellious feel of his old selection, but tries his damnedest to like what he hears. It's not working. He decides to try Middle Eastern rock. More better. He actually likes it. So different, but compelling. He thinks about how much music is out there in the world. How will he ever have time to hear it all? With the new rhythms in his head, he continues his cookbook search. He smiles as he thinks about bringing a delicious offering. His new exotic and intense music soundtrack makes him feel like a badass chef.

THE JOY'S APARTMENT/FIRE ESCAPE

The world outside is gray. Kimi is sitting on a bright yellow cushion that she has pulled out onto the fire escape. It makes her outdoor office space more comfortable. Should she have checked with The Joy before she did it? Would this be considered messing with the juju? She thinks, This is why I didn't check. She has her phone in her hand and looks like the cat that swallowed the canary. She thinks about what she just did. So ballsy. So not her. Moving the cushion pales in comparison.

After another moment of phone staring, she calls Milli and waits. Milli answers, "What?!"

"That's right, what?"

"What?"

"Ask me what I just did."

"What did you just did?"

"I invited Carmen to come stay with me while The Joy is in Florida."

"No you fucking did not!"

"I fucking did. And watch your language."

"God, you bring out the worst in me. But holy F-word, Kimi. I am stunned."

"Me, too. So grown up, right? Are you so proud of me?"

"You know, you didn't invent moving in."

"Just say you're proud."

"I'm proud."

"Thank you. It seemed right. You know with The Joy gone and Carmen's business temporarily closed, and me finally making bank, I feel like such a big girl."

"You are a big girl. A five-foot-tall big girl." Milli's tone changes from mocking to caring. "I'm really happy for you. I think it's the right thing."

"It is, right?"

"Don't start second-guessing yourself."

"No. I wasn't much."

Back to mocking, "There's the Kimi I know."

"Don't tell Mom and Dad."

"I'm not going to out you. But…"

"But what?"

"If this works out, and I really hope it does, you're going to have to come clean at some point."

"I actually believe I could hide my sexuality until they die. Or hey, maybe I'll die from COVID and that'll be that."

"Don't even."

"Mom almost blew an artery when you told her you were dating an Irish guy."

Milli laughs. "Yeah, that was fun. She asked if I was prepared to throw my medical career away and live on potatoes. But, she got past it. Now she loves Shay."

"That's because he came with a firm handshake and sperm."

"Well, one thing at a time. Congratulations on your big grownup move."

"Thank you. What am I keeping you from?"

"Not much. Just the dead, the dying and the defibrillating."

"God, you're important."

"I know."

"Go. I'll talk to you later."

"Love you."

"Love you, too."

Kimi hangs up and lets the inevitable trepidation wash over her. What has she done? She looks around, and spots Stella hanging wet towels over the railing of her fire escape to dry. Since moving in with The Joy, Stella has become one of Kimi's few "in-person" connections. She enjoys the mix of familiarity and distance. Kimi calls up, "Hey, Stella!"

Stella looks down.

"Carmen's coming up from Miami."

Stella smiles and yells back, "Welcome to domestic life."

"Thanks."

"I could loan you a kid. For practice."

"I'm good."

"I'd give you the nice one."

Kimi just laughs at that, then salutes Stella. After a moment, she folds herself down into a fearful, almost fetal ball. "What have I done?"

PARTY PREP

SHAD & BENJI'S APARTMENT/BATHROOM

Benji's at the sink with a towel around his waist. He has to stoop to check his hair in the mirror. It's gotten long. He likes it. It's far from the look he kept as a mathematician. Being an out-of-work cook has a plus side. But he wants to do something extra to make an impression at the party. He doesn't see his height as remarkable, which, it is. But he's been taller than everyone else since he was in junior high. So, nothing new there. He opens an overstuffed vanity drawer and digs out an electric razor. He's about to plug it in. But first? His ears. They're making him crazy. He hits the cotton swabs hard. Yes! That's better.

There's a banging on the door. Shad calls in, "Come on man. You've been in there forever. Douglas and I have to go to the can."

"Give me a minute." Benji raises the razor to the side of his head.

THE JOY'S APARTMENT/BEDROOM

Kimi is dressed in her best industrial floral chic, a glass of vodka in her hand. She checks her look in The Joy's makeup mirror and decides to add a bit more hair gel. Without it, her hair just sits flat to her head. She leans in to do the job and thinks about all the women who have their hair straightened. What's wrong with them? Out of the corner of her eye she spots a perfume atomizer. Should she wear perfume? She thinks, Hey, it's a brave new day. Why not? She sprays two squirts on herself and quickly learns why not. Fuck. How do you get rid of this shit? Ugh. Back to the shower.

SHAD & BENJI'S APARTMENT

Shad's standing outside the bathroom door with Douglas on leash. Benji opens the door revealing his new look. Tons of full black hair on top that's gelled and sculpted to cover one eye. The sides and back of his head are shaved down tight. Total anime. Shad and Douglas look at him.

"What? Like it?"

Shad shakes his head and walks Douglas past his roommate. The dog goes right for the litter box. Shad's about to sit on the commode and stops halfway down. "A little privacy?"

Benji shrugs and leaves the two to their business. Shad sits on the can and holds Douglas's leash as the two enjoy their tandem constitutionals.

JACKSON'S APARTMENT/BATHROOM

Steph is putting the finishing touches on her makeup for the night. She'd gotten there early, knowing that Ruby would be no help in the party prep department. What a strange individual she is. Steph finds it easiest to just avoid her. And Ruby doesn't seem to mind, or even notice. With everything in place, it's time to doll up. Jackson is now used to seeing her not made up, but why spring that on everyone else? And if she's honest with herself, Jackson still doesn't see her totally undone. She now has her own drawers in this palatial bathroom. She started with one drawer for her barest essentials; eye liner, mascara, and foundation. But she quickly expanded to a second for brushes, a flat iron and other haircare tools. She does a final face inspection and deems herself ready.

As Steph turns to leave, she sees Ruby standing there and jumps back. Fuck! She thinks, How long has Ruby been there? She doesn't want to offend Jackson's sister, but the chick is flat out creepy. Steph asks, "Can I help you?"

"No."

JACKSON'S APARTMENT

Jackson surveys the scene. It's perfect. He feels like it's not only a gift to him, but to his friends. We need this. It's going to be the best birthday. He takes a moment to breathe in the space and center himself, then checks his watch and decides to make a pre-party cocktail. But from which country?

BETTY'S HOUSE

The Joy is doing the final prep for Betty's cocktail party. She's made a pitcher of Arnold Palmers and a pitcher of gin and tonics to cover both the drinking and non-drinking guests. The Joy is positive that everyone is a drinker, but having a choice lets them pretend they might opt out. She tries to balance what she'd normally do with what Betty will deem acceptable. No cocktail swag. Although she does have a monkey in her pocket. It's just nice to know he's there. She thinks this would be a good time to believe in God, because this would definitely get her into heaven. Then she remembers that time when she'd "borrowed" Betty's car, got pulled over and pretended to be deaf to get out of the ticket. She did get a date out of it. But, she had to fake sign language the entire night and eventually had to fess up after she automatically burst into song to Adele's "Someone Like You." No. Not believing in heaven is probably safer.

The Joy hears Betty calling to her from her bedroom. Damn. She calls back, trying to stay light. "What's up, buttercup?"

"Don't make me yell."

The Joy goes to Betty's bedroom door. Her mother is sitting up on the bed. She'd taken a nap, as she always does before a party. The Joy sees the rolled towel on Betty's pillow and remembers that putting it under her neck is her mother's trick for keeping her hair just so while napping. "There you are. I need help getting into the chair."

"Your *wheel*chair?" The Joy knows that Betty hates saying "wheelchair."

Pained, Betty says, "Yes."

They've developed a system for transferring. The Joy pulls the chair over to the bed so she can raise her mother, pivot with her and put her down in one motion. She bends her knees and stoops in front of Betty. Holding her hands out, she asks, "Ready?"

"Hold on." Betty scoots herself closer to the edge of the bed, moaning just a bit. "Okay."

The Joy gets her hands under her mother's arms. "You know the drill. When I feel your head on my shoulder, I'll stand." Betty takes a moment, then lays her head on her daughter's shoulder. And for that moment, they get lost in each other's perfume. They both let the hold last just a tick longer than needed. Then, The Joy raises her mother, turns and places her in the chair.

LET THE GAMES BEGIN

JACKSON'S APARTMENT

Steph emerges from the bedroom, wearing a little black dress. Of course. With a drink in each hand, Jackson turns to see her. She looks fantastic. He says, "Happy birthday to me."

"Happy birthday to you." She comes over and kisses him as she takes the drink she assumes is for her. It is. Out of the corner of her eye, with her lips still pressed to Jackson, she sees Ruby sitting in a wingback chair and staring at them. She now has her head covered. Men are coming this evening. "Your sister is staring again."

"Ignore her."

"Can't we find her a hobby?"

"Staring *is* her hobby."

The door buzzes. Ruby is closest to the intercom, but everyone knows that she won't be getting up. Jackson goes over and pushes the buzzer. "Yes, Maurice?"

Over the intercom, Maurice, the night man announces, "I have a Mr. Benji, a Mr. Shad and a Mr. Douglas here for you."

"Brilliant. Send them up, please."

"Certainly. And happy birthday, sir."

"Oh. Thank you, Maurice. I'll have Ruby bring you down a piece of cake."

Maurice responds, "No need, sir."

Jackson says, "She frightens you, doesn't she?"

"A little bit, sir."

"She's less scary with cake in her hands."

"If you say so, sir."

From his pocket, Jackson pulls a facemask that coordinates with his shirt. He opens the front door and waits for the elevator to arrive. And, there they are. Benji and Shad in masks. Douglas not so much. Shad is looking fabulous in slacks and a fitted green sweater that tells the world he works out. Benji's hair is beyond. He has on a graphic, black, Boba Fett t-shirt. Even Douglas looks spruced up. Benji hands Jackson a covered bowl. "It's a lamb curry. Happy birthday."

"Oh, thank you, my friend."

Shad holds out a small box. "You said no presents, so here."

"Gentlemen. I'm touched. Welcome to my home." They step inside the grand apartment not knowing where to look first. Shad shakes his head in approval, "Holy shit, man."

Steph walks up, "I know, right."

Shad offers her a huge air hug. "Hey. We finally meet again. Great to see you, girl. You've been busy."

"The news never sleeps."

Jackson calls out, "Ruby, come! We have guests." Everyone turns to the dark presence in the large chair. She pulls on a black mask that matches her head cover, gets up and glides over with her eyes down. Shad gives Steph a look that says, "What's up with her?" Steph shoots him a look that says, "Don't."

Benji sees nothing but the object of his desire. He takes the dish from Jackson and hands it to Ruby, "I brought lamb curry."

Ruby looks at it, "I'm allergic to lamb." But then, she looks all the way up at Benji. He smiles at her. And she... Is that a smile? Hard to know, but it's the closest Steph has seen to date. The intercom buzzes again. The sound does nothing to break Ruby's gaze. Jackson smiles, "Guess I'll get that one, too."

Maurice informs Jackson that a Miss Kimberly is here and sends her up. Jackson stands leaning in the open door with his arms folded, waiting for the inevitable smartass remark. The elevator opens as does Kimi's mouth. Wide. Jackson smiles, "Get it out. Come on. Just say it."

Kimi enters spinning, making each step an umbrella step. "Oh, my God, you suck so much more than I thought!" Steph approaches in all of her attractiveness. Kimi looks her up and down. "And *you* suck." She looks at Ruby. "I don't know you, but I bet you suck, too." Ruby grins. She immediately takes a shine to Kimi. "Jackson, this place. It's like Lady Gaga ate gold leaf and threw up! Oh, here." She thrusts a brown paper bag at him.

He reaches in and pulls out a scented candle. "You shouldn't have."

"I didn't. I stole it from The Joy."

Jackson laughs. Then Kimi pulls the real treasure from her back pocket. It's one of her masks. He puts it on, "How do I look?" Everyone leans in to read the mask. It says, "Fuck sexy. (BTW, that's me.)" Benji laughs.

Jackson announces, "And now that you're all here, allow me to give you the tour of what I'm calling, 'Jackson's B-Day Bar Crawl and Ninja Course.'"

Steph leans quietly to Kimi, "Are you wearing perfume?"

Jackson has turned each room of his parents' Park Avenue palace into a different bar theme, each with a specialty cocktail. First up: the kitchen, which is a Mexican cantina. There's a donkey piñata and bright orange, red and green scarves draped all around. "*Bienvenidos, amigos!*" He hands a frozen margarita to everyone except Ruby, who grabs a juice box. Jackson motions to them all, "Follow me." They take their festive drinks and do as instructed.

Jackson leads them to the entertainment room slash sports bar. Playing on the big-screen TV is a rerun of the 2018 Super Bowl.

Sitting on a mahogany side table are pint glasses of stout and shots of Bailey's Irish cream. Shad asks, "Dude, are those for car bombs?!"

"They are."

"This is a dangerous room."

Jackson says, "You brought an overnight bag, right?"

"And a vomit bag," says Kimi. "Hey, be prepared."

Jackson smiles. "But wait, there's more."

Playfully Shad says, "Goody. More."

They head to the library, which is set up as a sophisticated cigar bar, offering an array of whiskey, vintage port and fine cigars.

Benji picks up a cigar and rolls it in his fingers next to his ear as if he's a connoisseur. "Nice one." The gang all looks at him, wondering if their friend is bullshitting or if he actually knows of what he speaks. With Benji, it's always a toss-up.

Along the way, the gang gets to see all of Jackson's homemade Ninja obstacles. They seem even crazier in person. Shad looks up at the rings hanging from the ceiling. "Dude, I may need to try this."

Jackson says, "Oh, you will."

They finally make their way back to the living room. "And that's it." Suddenly, Jackson rushes over to the balcony. "I almost forgot. Come. Come." They follow his lead. The large balcony is lit up like a Tiki bar, complete with a large bowl that has something flaming in the center. Against the New York night skyline, it's magical. Shad goes to shake Jackson's hand, then realizes that they're not doing that and pulls back. "Man, I gotta hand it to you. You know how to birthday."

Kimi looks at Jackson. "You're like the Martha Stewart of overkill. The Joy would have loved it." The Joy...

BETTY'S HOUSE

The cocktail party is in full swing. No one is wearing a mask. No one is staying socially distant. They're all speaking loudly at each other. All The Joy can see is wet-word projectiles flying from their faces. She can't believe that she's the most careful one in the room. Well, careful-ish. Everyone's dressed like they could be at "the club." And, no surprise, they've all opted for the gin and tonics. The Joy watches her mother holding court. You'd never know this woman is in pain. But what she clearly *is* in is her element.

A large woman wearing a larger print approaches The Joy and puts out her hand. "Carol Baker." The Joy looks at Carol's hand. Is she going to shake it? She looks around the room of close talkers and thinks, Fuck it. She shakes Carol's hand. "The J... Um, Joy."

Carol sips her cocktail. "I hear you made these. You're quite the bartender."

"Happy to serve."

"I just think it's lovely that you're helping our Betz like this."

"Well..."

"Well, indeed. That one can be a pistol."

"Mmm."

"I hear you're a hairdresser?"

"Guilty."

Carol looks around The Joy's head. "Where's that orange I heard about?"

"Oh, I got rid of it. I think it made Betty uncomfortable."

"Betz? Uncomfortable? Pish tosh. She's a crazy one."

The Joy stares at her mother and thinks, Betty? The crazy one? She doesn't notice Carol drift away. When she turns back, Carol is already across the room. Just as well. The Joy is about to start her third gin and tonic. That usually means she'll soon say something someone will regret.

JACKSON'S APARTMENT

The music is pumpin'. Benji has piped his phone into the huge stereo system. Chunky, glorious, Arabic heavy metal fills the apartment. Benji and Ruby are dancing. If you can call it that. Their movements are jerky and spastic. Kimi is fascinated by this. Standing there with a big, tropical cocktail in her hand, she yells over the din to Shad. "It's like watching people trying to escape angry bees."

Jackson calls Kimi and Shad over to his salmon ladder. "You guys have to come try this." They head over. Kimi looks at the ladder. "By 'have to,' you mean…"

Shad says, "I'll try it." He turns to Kimi, handing her his giant tropical cocktail. "Here, hold my drink."

"The opening line to so many great tragedies."

Steph watches all of this and figures it's time. While no one's paying attention to her, she goes and calls down to Maurice.

Moments later, the doorbell rings. The sound of the bell is grand, audible only as one element of the pumping soundtrack. But Jackson hears it and looks around, not knowing who it could be. Everyone is here. Steph scoots to the door. "I'll get it." Jackson watches her go. Maurice is on the other side of the door, struggling to keep something in the hall at bay. Steph reaches around and takes the first large object from him, turns back to the room and announces, "Everyone! Everyone!" No response. She puts two fingers in her mouth and makes a loud whistle. That got their attention. Everyone looks to Steph. Who knew she could do that? Jackson finds her whistle talent skill bizarrely sexy. She calls out, "And now, for the man who *needs* absolutely nothing, on his birthday…"

Steph reaches out the door, comes back in with a huge rubber ball. It's almost three feet in diameter and has a rubber handle. Steph does a full-on basketball chest pass to Jackson. He catches it and looks at the American Ninja logo on its side. What the hell is it? She starts grabbing the other balls from Maurice and tossing one to each of the partiers. She keeps the last one for herself and hands Maurice a small roll of bills. He thanks her, steals a look over at Ruby, then leaves. Benji calls out, "I know what this is!" He sits on his ball, holds the handle and starts hopping around the room.

Delighted, Jackson takes the cue and gets on his ball. "I absolutely love this! It's perfect." Jackson bounces up to Steph and kisses her. "You're brilliant."

"All for you."

In a matter of moments everyone, including Ruby, is bouncing around the Park Avenue apartment like children. So much fun. Jackson yells, "First one to the cigar bar and back wins." And they're off.

BETTY'S HOUSE

The Joy grabs the empty gin and tonic pitcher from its tray on the piano and heads to the kitchen to refill it. She's impressed with how much these people can imbibe. It makes her optimistic for her future. As The Joy watches the gin pour over the ice, Franny comes up behind her holding out her glass. "Just pour it right in."

The Joy asks, "No rocks?"

"Rocks are for weenies."

The Joy cocks her head, reconsidering this woman. She pours gin into Franny's glass. "I like your style, lady."

"Why, thank you." Franny tips the straight hooch to her lips and drinks it down. "Another."

The Joy does as told. "Why, you are a little hellion."

"I am. I am." Franny puts her arm around The Joy, "So what's being single in New York like? You must have so much fun."

"It's a requirement."

"You must have so much sex."

"Define 'so much.' Oh, don't bother. I do."

"I knew it! Down here it's all widows and old men. Nothing exciting. It's a never-ending loop of tennis, cocktail parties, golf, cocktail parties. The same people all the time. Your mother sure kicked this place in the pants when she moved in."

"Do tell."

Someone calls out from the living room, "Hey, where are the drinks?!"

Franny leans in to The Joy, "Another time. Let's go water the lions." The Joy smiles at Franny and they head out to the thirsty guests like new girlfriends. The room applauds as they re-enter with the liquid bounty. The Joy can feel herself start to loosen up. "I love the roar of a crowd."

Most of the cocktailers are now around the piano. Someone calls out, "Nate, play something." Nate does the obligatory, 'Oh, no. I don't want to be the center of attention' as he steps up to the piano stool. Mr. Harris rolls Betty over. Nate takes a seat and asks, "What do you want to hear?" A flurry of songs get called out. After a moment, ignoring the suggestions, Nate looks at The Joy and says, "Wait. Wait. I got it." He begins. The intro is familiar. What is that? He sings, "One, singular sensation, every little step she takes..." It's the big number from *A Chorus Line*. His voice isn't amazing, but it gets the job done. He looks at The Joy and it's clear that song is meant to celebrate her. As he continues, the rest of the room joins in. The Joy can feel all of their eyes on her as they sing. She's the singular sensation and for the first time since arriving, she's feeling accepted. Yay. She looks over to Betty wondering, how's she taking this. Catching her mother's eye, Betty winks at her. A wink? Is she drunk or is she actually happy that her daughter is here? Who cares. The Joy knows this won't last. My game. My rules. She *chooses* to be happy.

At the end of the song, everyone applauds. Carol calls out, "Now Betz. Sing something." Nate turns his head to Betty as his fingers take on the next tune. She rolls her eyes, but doesn't protest too much. He starts slowly, "Another bride, another groom..." Betty joins, "Another sunny, honeymoon. Another season, another reason, for making whoopie..." Again, the room joins in. The Joy delights in this side of Betty.

Franny whispers to The Joy, "I wish they'd just have sex already and get it over with."

The Joy shivers, "Ugh. I can't think about that."

"Don't you want your mother to be happy?"

"I could go either way."

"Well, I'd like to see my friend happy. And it's good gossip."

"I do like gossip. Although we call it tea."

"Tea? I like that. I'm you're tea date." Franny looks around the room and spots George Marx. "You see that man, in the pink pants?"

"The bag man?"

Franny laughs. "Yes. The bag man. Well, he has a thing for lady's shoes. Wait till later in the evening. He'll find a reason to slip on Carol's mules. Carol has a larger foot, you know."

"I wear a ten and a half."

Franny gets a sly smile. "Oh, my God. You have to sit next to George and slide your shoes off. Please?"

"Like you had to ask."

JACKSON'S APARTMENT

Shad and Jackson are shirtless, racing from one end of the hanging ninja rings to the other. The gang cheers them on. "Go! Go! Go!" Jackson gets to the end first and hangs there waiting for Shad to finish. He reaches out a hand to Shad. "Well done, my friend." Jackson shakes with Shad. "Thanks, man." They both drop down and Steph hugs Jackson. "I'm so proud of my he-man."

He hugs her back. "To the victor, the spoils."

"I'm the spoils?"

Kimi says, "Well, you're *spoiled*." She sips her third cocktail. Fourth? Whatever.

"Kimi, you're so not nice to me. I could sic my man on you."

"He's afraid of me." At that, Ruby high fives Kimi.

And with that, Steph pulls her dress off over her head and tosses it on the floor, which leaves her in black sport-cut undies and a back sports bra. Damn, she's ripped. She points at Jackson, "Come on big guy, you and me."

Jackson's loving this. "As you wish."

They both jump up to grab rings. Steph calls out, "Kimi, you sorry excuse for a friend, count us down." Kimi, Shad and Benji all look up, admiring Steph's form.

Kimi says, "As you wish. Three, two, one, go!"

Jackson and Steph take off, swinging from ring to ring. He's got all kinds of reach on her, but she makes a good show of it and is smiling when she finishes second. Still hanging, Jackson wraps his legs around Steph. "God, you're sexy."

"I know."

The heat between the two radiates down to the onlookers. Kimi snaps a picture on her phone. Finally, she can't take it. "God, I hate you both. I'm going to Mexico." She heads for the kitchen.

Jackson and Steph finally drop down and she puts her dress back on. Jackson turns to Shad, "Salmon ladder?"

Shad grabs his shirt from the floor, "I'm in. Benji?"

Benji scoffs, "Child's play."

Jackson asks Steph, "You in?" She's proven her point. Once was plenty. "Just go show off to your friend. It's your birthday."

The three guys head to their next challenge and Ruby and Steph follow Kimi to Mexico. For the first time since they met, Ruby smiles at Steph. "You're kinda badass."

"Let's keep that our little secret."

BETTY'S HOUSE

People are no longer walking straight. It's like the floor has been tilted three degrees off level. The Joy is sitting next to Mr. Marx on the cream colored sofa. The Joy looks over to Franny, slowly slips off her shoes and pretends to be interested in the conversation Betty and Nate are having about Christmas wreaths. Betty is trying to explain that they're just decoration and not religious.

"I'm not going to put one on my door. *Genug* already."

"I don't see why not."

"How many times do you want to go around about this? It's not even Christmas time yet. Let it go."

"My point is—"

"I know your point. I've heard your point. I hear all of your points, Betz. Here a point. There a point. Everywhere a point, point." With that he gets up to refill his drink. But not really.

When The Joy steals a look down at her shoes, they're on Mr. Marx's feet. She looks over at Franny with delight. Mission accomplished. They both applaud discreetly to each other.

Just then The Joy feels her phone vibrate and finds pictures from Kimi. It's her gang having a big time without her. It all looks like so much fun. Way more fun than catching an old man wearing your shoes. She sees cocktails being raised in the different theme rooms, a race on bouncing balls, and Jackson and Steph hanging half naked from the ceiling in a steamy embrace, and a group selfie with masks dangling from ears. It's totally lit and she's missing all of it. Suddenly, feeling more blue than before her mother's party, The Joy gets up and heads over to the drink pitcher. Nate looks lost in thought. She holds out her glass and says, "Hey bartender. Fill a girl up?" He looks over and smiles.

CLEAN UP ON AISLE 5

JACKSON'S APARTMENT

Jackson is one day older. He stands in the kitchen over the eight-burner cooktop. Last night, there was alcohol. This morning there's alcohol and pork. He thinks, *Haram*-on-*haram* action. He's got all manner of breakfast going. Eggs, bacon, lattes are in the works. Steph is at the island, arranging a large wooden platter with a pile of croissants as well as different cheeses and jams. They're each wearing parts of the same pair of pajamas and easily move by each other as they perform their tasks. No words are needed, though he does grab her ass as she passes on the way to the fridge for orange juice. She grabs his ass on the way back.

The smell of bacon wafts out from the kitchen. The first one it hits is Douglas. He licks Shad, who's stretched out on the sofa in the living room. The smell lifts Shad's head, nose first. So good. He rubs his eyes and thinks, Hey, I survived. He's impressed with his ability to recover from the epic antics of the night before, until his hand travels over his face. Ow! What the hell? He carefully feels his mouth. He has a fat lip. He feels it with his tongue and can taste the dried blood.

Shad tries to remember what happened. After a moment, it comes to him. In his zeal to show off his fitness to his friends, he misjudged his timing and took the pole from the salmon ladder to the mouth. Oh well. Battle scar. In a different time, he'd explain it away with the phrase, "Bar fight." But who's going to bars now? He'll need a story. But not at the moment. He takes a deep breath of bacon air and gets to his feet.

When Shad and Douglas enter the kitchen, Shad notes how domestic and perfect Jackson and Steph seem. Will he ever enjoy this kind of connection with a woman? This ease? His mind drifts to Sandra D. He tries to picture them in his kitchen making breakfast. But then he pictures Benji muscling past in an old, stained anime t-shirt. The picture loses its luster. Steph sees Shad standing there. In a hushed tone she says, "Good morning, Starshine."

Shad's back in the present. "Smells great in here."

Jackson turns. "Good morning. Ow. Sorry about the lip."

"Yeah, well. Bar fight."

Jackson smiles. "Looks like you won. Latte?"

"Like it's a question."

Jackson turns to Steph, "Would you serve our guest?"

Shad slides onto one of the island stools and Steph slides a latte in front of him. He grabs a croissant, smells it, and takes a bite. With his mouth still full, Shad says, "May I?"

Steph smiles, "You just did."

"So good." Shad reaches for another to give to Douglas.

Jackson chides him, "Don't fill up. I made eggs."

"And bacon?" They all turn to see Kimi standing at the kitchen door, wrapped in a gilt-edged bedspread with her red bucket hat low on her head. Her eyes are open just wide enough so she doesn't bump into things.

Shad pulls out a bar stool for her. "You're gonna want to get in on this."

"You don't think I know that?"

Steph puts a latte in front of Kimi and Jackson puts full breakfast plates in front of both Kimi and Shad. He stands back proudly. Steph snuggles next to him and they watch their guests eat. Kimi looks up from her grazing at this perfect couple. "Can you move your blinding brilliance elsewhere. I'm trying to eat."

Suddenly self conscious, Jackson and Steph separate. They each fix themselves a plate and grab a stool at the island. There's a stretch of silence as the foursome basks in their feast. Before going for seconds, Shad turns to Jackson. "Great party, man."

"Glad you enjoyed."

Kimi notices Shad's lip. "Damn, you enjoyed your lip wide open."

Shad feels his lip. It still hurts.

More silence. More eating. Jackson finally pushes his plate forward. "Well I, for one, am thrilled with my party. I thank you all for making it a night to remember. And I do remember most of it." He leans over and kisses Steph.

Before Kimi can make a smart remark about the lovebirds, Benji and Ruby bounce into the kitchen on their ninja hopping balls. Kimi immediately re-aims her focus. "It's Mr. and Mrs. Pacman."

Receiving that as a huge compliment, Benji and Ruby high five. Jackson's thrilled to see his sister happy. This is truly a great morning. He looks at Steph and winks. She rises to get lattes for the new arrivals. Jackson asks, "What can I get you two?"

Benji responds for both of them like they're in a fine restaurant. "I'll have the eggs and bacon. And the lady would like a croissant with a little bit of butter and jam." Ruby seems fine with the order. The other four look at each other. Jackson assembles the request and gives each their plates. "Here you go Benji. And for the lady." He tries not to smile too hard at Ruby for fear of breaking the spell Benji has cast on her.

As everyone eats, Steph is suddenly slapped in the face with a truly horrifying thought. Oh shit! She transitions into fast-talk mode. "Listen guys. I have to ask you a huge favor. Well, I'm not really asking. I'm telling. None of you can say anything about last night to anyone. I mean, that I was here, at a non-essential gathering, with a bunch of people I don't live with, inside, and that no one was wearing a mask and that no one was distant. That shit would ruin me. No one can know. I could lose my job. You have to promise me. Do you promise?" She looks at all of them. They all nod and say their agreements. "Sure." "Yeah. "Of course." All except Kimi who's looking into her lap.

Steph spots this. "What? ... What?"

Kimi responds sheepishly, "So, I suppose sending a few pictures to The Joy was a bad idea?"

BETTY'S HOUSE/THE JOY'S BEDROOM

The covers are pulled up, but the bed's not made. It's still in use. The Joy's phone rings. It's Steph's ring tone, the Meredith Brooks hit, "Bitch." A hand reaches out from under the covers and grabs the phone from the rattan bedside table. The Joy pulls it under the blanket and hits the "ignore" button. A moment later the phone vibrates with a text. It's Steph again. *You can't post any of the pictures Kimi sent you. DELETE! DELETE! DELETE!* The Joy thinks, Too late.

A man's voice says, "Is everything OK, beautiful?" The Joy pushes back the covers and sees Nate lying next to her with a big smile across his tanned, wrinkled face. Fuck! Again, The Joy thinks, Too late.

SHAD & BENJI'S APARTMENT

The front door opens. Douglas leads Shad and Benji into their apartment. Shad's holding the leash and is pulled into the bathroom, where Douglas goes right for the litter box. Shad's incredulous. "Dude, we were just outside. You're turning into such a pussy." Shad stands there while Douglas does his business. "You should be embarrassed."

When the task is completed, Douglas prances into the living room. Shad follows. No prancing. He sees Benji curled up in the armchair, texting.

"Who you talking to, already?"

In trance mode, Benji responds in a monotone without looking up. "Ruby."

"Dude, we were just there. You should be embarrassed."

"Unh."

Shad stands there for a moment and chooses to leave his pathetic roommates to their peculiarities. He heads for his bedroom. Maybe there's a message from Sandra D.

BETTY'S HOUSE

The Joy is wearing a colorful, flowing robe and trying to push a very rumpled Nate out the front door. But he keeps adding one more thing to their stealth goodbye. "That was nice. I really did enjoy myself."

"Good for you."

"Didn't you? I'd like to know that I at least made it nice for you."

"Just shush. Now get."

"Can we do it again?"

"No. I was drunk and you're a dirty old man. Scoot. Scoot."

Nate lets himself be pushed forward. With a gesture of playful acquiescence he says, "Fine, I'm scooting." Then wagging a finger at her he adds, "But I know where you live."

The Joy continues shoving him out the door. "You. Go. And when you get home make a date to have sex with my mother."

Done. She's finally able to close the door. She turns around and leans her weight on it, as if he may try to push his way back in. He doesn't. What a mess. Even for her. Things were so much simpler with Vlad. They were discreet-ish. Shit. She wonders how discreet Nate is. Did anyone see him leave? She goes over to the Florida room and looks for Betty's binoculars. Grabbing them from a side table, she scans the back yard looking for Nate. No sign of him. Maybe he made a clean escape. He moves fast for an old guy. She continues making sweeps of the area. Then, CRAP! There's Franny across the way on her back porch with her own binoculars up and staring right at The Joy with a sly smile on her face. What does she know?

THE JOY'S APARTMENT

Kimi sits on the front windowsill, watching the street and not seeing as she thinks about last night. She has to admit, she had fun. She was out. She laughed. She bounced. She relaxed. She had a great breakfast that came with a bonus to-go bacon bag. She even liked Jackson's sister. What an odd one. But she likes making room for odd.

As she looks out on the people standing in line for the supermarket, she feels a bit guilty for having fun. They're all in the day-to-day drudgery of lockdown and she just partied in a palace. Well, they don't know that. She even has her mask back on, which makes her feel like a hypocrite. She certainly didn't have one on for the better part of last night and she was way closer to people than she is now.

She spots a guy by himself in line with a blank look on his face. As if no one can see him, he picks his nose and flicks it out to the world at large. It's like if he doesn't make eye contact with anyone, he's invisible. Kimi thinks about giving him shit for littering, but snot is biodegradable. Behind him in line is the little old Chinese lady who's one of Kimi's regulars. They exchange a familiar head nod. Kimi wants to warn the woman about nose-picking man, but what can she say? More staring into space.

Farther back in line are the Lemon Ladies. The ones who never seem to be in a sweat, but are always dressed in the best, most expensive Lululemon workout gear. Even though they're farther back in line, Kimi can hear Lemon Lady #1 as she calls her, talking into her cell. She's holding the phone, not at her ear, but in front of her mouth as if it were an hors d'oeuvre tray.

Lemon Lady #1 says, "Patti, you're just going to have to ask her yourself. You know me. My lips are sealed." She makes a shrug motion to her friend, Lemon Lady #2, as if to say, "I'm in the right, right?" Her friend nods in agreement. The call continues. "Patti... Patti... No. I'm not sharing information about someone else's nose job... You ask her... Bullshit, it was purely cosmetic. But I'm not talking... Because... My lips are sealed."

Kimi calls out to her, "Then you're a goddamn ventriloquist."
Lemon Lady #1 flips Kimi the bird. Her friend follows in kind.

Kimi thinks she liked last night but it's nice to be home.

JACKSON'S APARTMENT

On his new ninja ball, Jackson hops around the living room, picking up red go-cups from the night before. They made quite a mess for only six people. But he doesn't mind. It was completely worth it. Perhaps his best birthday ever. His mind travels to the different parts of the evening. One more enjoyable than the last. As he does sweeps of the room, he passes Ruby multiple times. She's planted herself in a throne-like chair and has her head in her phone. Jackson can only assume that she's texting Benji. But why not be nosy?

"Are you texting Benji?"

She doesn't look up. "Maybe."

"I don't mind."

"Why would you?'

"I don't."

"You shouldn't." She still hasn't looked at him.

"I'm just letting you know that—"

"Don't say it. You'll ruin it."

"Fine."

"Fine."

"Well, have a nice day." Jackson takes the trash he's collected, bounces it into the kitchen and adds it to another huge, swollen bag he'd already started. Steph had helped pick up the kitchen before she left. He was thankful for the extra hands but she was pretty upset. He thinks, She's probably making something out of nothing. Then he starts to extrapolate what could happen if photos of her being unsafe hit the social shamers. It's not a pretty picture. But, it's probably nothing. He starts feeling protective. What would he do if she needed him to stand up for her? Of course, he would. But she's strong. It's one of the things that's attractive about her. She doesn't need him.

STEPH'S APARTMENT

The feeling of dread is palpable. It fills the room like a gigantic marshmallow. Do marshmallows rot? Steph's does. She sits in front of her computer. Her elbows are on her dining table/desk and her hands are in her hair. They seem to be all that's holding her head up. Her worst fears are on the screen in front of her. Pictures of herself unmasked and partying. The worst one shows her with an unidentifiable man hanging from a ceiling, half dressed, and completely entangled. How did she let this happen? Why hadn't she warned people before the night started? Why did she even agree to go? Why are these people still her friends? Ultimately, she's mad at herself for being so careless, but it's easier to blame others. She can feel her heart simultaneously racing and sinking. Like it's pushing her torso forwards and back with each beat. It's hard to breath. Maybe she has COVID? No. She's not that lucky. The only thing dying is her career. She lets herself get absorbed in the dizziness of it all. And then, her phone rings.

She doesn't have to look. She knows it's Bill and she knows she can't duck it. In the short moment between the phone ringing and answering it, Steph has a million thoughts about how she should play her greeting. Should she pretend she has no idea that images of her without a mask or dignity are circulating the Internet? He'd never buy it. Should she sound contrite? Lead with apologies? No. Never lead with an apology. Murry, her dad, had taught her that. He was a heck of a salesman in his day. That was before he made a bundle on parking lots in Atlantic City and retired. Maybe she should leave the news and buy parking lots. Who's she fooling? She's not going to get the chance to leave the news. It's about to leave her. All she can do is take her medicine. She answers the phone. "Yeah, Bill."

Bill's voice is even and reveals nothing. "Good morning."

The following silence lasts too long. They're both playing chicken. Steph's not going to give. Bill finally dives in. "Here's the bottom line. Mason wants you out. He said, and I quote, 'I don't want the stink from that careless bitch on my network.' I went to bat for you. I said, we've all been careless bitches in our time. Then I reminded him of something he'd rather not remember. That bought you a little time. Maybe enough time for the inevitable news cycle to wipe you from the spotlight and replace you with someone dumber. Someone dumber. Imagine that. You get no on-camera time. Jackie's moving up to take over your assignments and you're doing research. Jim doesn't want to hear from you. He's afraid of any association, so you're sending your stuff to me to pass on to him. There's no guarantee that the hammer won't come down at any time, but this is how we'll proceed for now."

There's more silence. Bill finally says, "Say, 'Thank you, Bill.'"

Steph can barely choke the words out. "Thank you, Bill."

Bill goes into more of a fatherly mood. "Really Steph, what did I tell you?"

"Don't become the story."

"Yet, here we are."

"I know. I feel sick."

"You should. What a waste. I haven't seen a career on the rise like yours in years. And you pissed it away."

She's afraid to ask, but does, "Did I piss it away?"

She can feel Bill shaking his head. "I don't know. Probably."

Finally she whispers, "Thank you, Bill."

"You're welcome." He hangs up and Steph goes back to her position of hands in hair. But now she has even more to think about. At least the first shoe has dropped. Just then her cell rings. It's Ida.

Steph answers cautiously, "Yeah, Mom."

"Your father and I would like to know, who is this Sheik of Araby you're swinging half-naked with?" And there's the sound of that second shoe...

BETTY'S HOUSE

Betty's now dressed for the day, in her chair in the living room where The Joy left her. The Joy enters with a tray that has two drinks. Betty's skeptical. "What have you got there?"

"Bellinis. Perfect for hangovers."

"For curing them or causing them?"

"Curing, Silly. I make them with Champagne and kombucha. Here, try."

Betty reluctantly takes her drink from the tray and sips it. "Not bad."

"Good." The Joy sits across from her mother and sips her own drink.

"I have to admit, I can use a little hair-of-the-dog after last night. It all went down so easy. You're quite the bartender."

Was that a compliment? The Joy doesn't want to make too much of it and break the spell of civility between them. She quietly accepts the offering. "Thank you."

Betty looks around at the aftermath of the party. Things are somewhat picked up. Somewhat tousled. "It was fun, wasn't it?"

"It was."

"You seemed to make a few friends."

"Well... Hey, swell singing last night. Didn't know you had your harmonies so tight.

"There's a lot of things you don't know about your mother."

"Tell me one."

"Oh Joy, don't put me on the spot."

The Joy realizes she pushed too hard and backs off. Can she save this? "You do have a lovely voice. Very Bernadette Peters."

"Thank you. We used to sing show tunes, you and I."

"I remember. I just didn't remember what we sounded like."

"You were pretty bad. I was pretty good. I like singing with Nate." At the mention of his name, The Joy is at a loss for conversation. That was a big eff-up, even for her. But Betty doesn't notice. "He wants to get me in bed, you know."

The Joy tries to sound shocked, "Really?"

"Don't be so surprised. A lot of men want me."

Being overcomplimentary, The Joy says, "And they'd be lucky to have you. And by 'have' I mean—"

"I know what you mean. It's been awhile, but I'm pretty good between the sheets."

WHAT? What did Betty just say? The Joy can't contain her smile. She raises her glass. "To hidden talents."

Betty pauses for a moment, then raises her glass. "Hidden talents." They both drink. Then, "I got the strangest call from Franny while you were in the kitchen. She's like the cat that swallowed the canary. I wonder what gossip she stumbled onto."

The Joy tries to maintain outward composure as her head spins. Crap! What does Franny know? She can't *know* know. And Nate wouldn't say anything. Would he? He might. A night with The Joy *can* be epic. Maybe he's a bragger. Crap, crap, crap. Divert! Divert! "Oh, did you see George tried on my shoes last night?"

"He has pretty feet."

"Does he?"

"You didn't notice. I think I can identify everyone in this community by their feet. So many sandals and flip flops. And so many people who shouldn't be wearing them. Honestly, do they never look down? Jackie Bishop has *the* worst hammer toes. And she makes us look at them. If I were her I'd swim with boots on. Oh, one time Kate Brown's husband Buster—"

"Buster Brown?"

"You can't make this stuff up. Anyway, we were all poolside and there's Buster, sitting with his legs crossed. And under his big toenail is a piece of blue string. Just hanging there. And, of course, Buster was bouncing his foot, so the string was waving around. Well, I couldn't look away. From then on, I gave him the rapper name, Lil String."

Who is this woman? The Joy asks, "You gave him a rapper name?"

"I can be hip. The point is the footcare down here is abysmal. You have to stay on top of your feet as you get older."

"Noted."

Betty looks critically at her daughter. "Let's see 'em. Whip them out."

"You want to see my feet?"

"What were we just talking about? Yes, show me your feet."

The Joy slips her feet from her ultra-furry orange slippers so Betty can inspect. She's glad her pedicure was recent.

Betty seems pleased. "Look at you. What pretty feet you have. That nail color is ridiculous, but your feet are well shaped and your toes go in descending order, as they should."

"I worked hard on that."

"Very nice."

The Joy sits up straight. "Thank you, Betty."

"You're welcome."

They sit quietly enjoying their morning-after beverages. It's nice to be without their usual tension. Is this what it's like to get along with your mother? Then Betty adds, "I wonder what Franny knows."

THE JOY'S APARTMENT

For once, the place is completely picked up. Without rearranging the juju, Kimi has made the apartment neat and inviting. The curtains are all pulled back and the sunlight does what the older furniture cannot. The apartment is cheery.

Kimi sits in a tight ball, on top of the cube fridge in her corner with her arms holding her knees. She's making herself as small as possible as she waits for her guest. No, not guest. And not friend. More. She's told herself that she'll know whether she's done the right thing the moment she sets eyes on Carmen. But will she? She knew when she first saw Carmen that something was different. They were at her friend Tanya's for a deck party and had both been hungover from separate outings the previous night. They sat under a tree and spoke easily about, well, everything. They hadn't noticed the pin lights wrapped around the tree trunk turn on as the sun went down. Hours had gone by. Good hours. And without making a formal plan, they saw each other exclusively until Carmen got the job offer in Miami. The "no formal plan" part of the relationship worked for Kimi. No pressure. Life just moved in the right direction all on its own. That's the best. Now what? She's made a commitment to this woman. Kimi knows herself to be highly susceptible to buyer's remorse. Fuck. She thinks, I'm an idiot. Carmen's not a car. I can't just—

The doorbell buzzes.

Kimi takes a deep breath, makes herself smile and slides off the fridge. She shakes her muscles out like an athlete prepping for a race before she goes to the door. Right before she gets to the intercom she has a sinking thought: Damn it. I didn't shave my legs. It has been weeks, at least. That's a fine welcome. Hey baby, wanna pet a monkey? Too late now. She hits the intercom.

"Speak."

A woman's voice answers. *"Digame, bitch."*

That's it. That's all it takes. Kimi's heart leaps. She buzzes in Carmen.

SHAD & BENJI'S APARTMENT/SHAD'S BEDROOM

Shad's at his computer. His team video has barely started, but Max is already deep into ribbing him. Shad's just nodding and waiting for this to pass. "I hope the other guy looks worse than you. Holy shit, Shad. I haven't seen a split lip like that since I was in the Navy."

They all pause at that. Does Max have a military background? Collin says what they're all wondering. "I didn't know you were in the Navy."

"I wasn't. That's how long it's been. Since never. Shad, you could sell ad space on that thing. I mean, get a sponsor and monetize your pain. Does that at least come with a good story?"

With a straight face, Shad says, "Bar fight."

"Bullshit."

"That's my story."

Max stares at Shad's straight face and decides to leave it at that. "Fair enough." Shad feels like he made a strong show of it and smiles to himself. Ow. He sees Sandra D. looking at him. Let her look.

Max moves on to a new target. "So, Old Sandra, what can you tell me about the Moore family?"

Sandra bristles slightly at her new Old name. "Well, I think they're going to bring their son-in-law into their account. I think he's worth about two point five."

"You think or you know?"

"Well..."

Max goes into lesson mode. "People, don't tell me what you think. I don't give a shit what you think. Tell me what you know. 'I think' is worthless. There's bank in 'I know.' So, let's try this again, Old Sandra. What do you know?"

Snap! Old Sandra has had enough. She explodes. In her thin voice, it's not quite as potent as it could be. "You really want to know what I know? I'll tell you what I know. I know that my name is Sandra M. Wiley. My maiden name was Sandra M. Stratford. The M. stands for Molly which was my great grandmother's name. She was the first woman in my family to graduate college and she finished third in her class in 1952. She went into banking and taught me that *she* who controls the purse strings controls the world. She advised me to not let myself be bullied and I think—correction, I *know* I'm taking her advice right now. I've stayed with your team because you have a sense for finance like no one else, and I can learn a lot. But here's the deal. You can call me Sandra, Sandra Wiley, Sandra M Wiley, Sandra Molly Wiley or OG Sandra. But if you call me Old Sandra ever again, I'm out." Even in her soft-spoken tone, it was an impactful speech. And no one saw it coming. Max's eyes are wide, but no wider than anyone else's. He smiles and nods his head. "OK, OG Sandra, what can you tell us about the Moores?"

Like nothing happened, OG Sandra shares all the intel she has on the extended Moore family including what assets, goals, other potential connections and investment opportunities they're bringing to the table. Not bad.

Shad can feel himself be proud for his teammate. He wonders if he can slyly text Christopher about this while attention is elsewhere. But just then he gets a text from Sandra D. *Hey tough guy. Marching tomorrow. Join?* Shad thinks, Damn, this is a great meeting.

ZOOM – YOU LOSE

BETTY'S HOUSE/THE JOY'S BEDROOM

The Joy is propped up on her bed by a bounty of new and colorful pillows. The personality-less bedroom now has a few hits of flair. Just enough to make the entire space seem out of balance. The Joy tells herself that it's a work in progress. She has her laptop open and resting on the spot for which it was named: her lap. The bedside table has her cocktail, which is clear. Her plastic animals all sit out facing away from her. She can't handle them staring in judgment.

Should she put on a brave front for the call? She decides to try. She logs in to find Jackson and Shad waiting for her. "Hey guys!"

Shad seems preoccupied. He's looking over his shoulder at his front door and offers an absent, "Hey."

Jackson is a bit brighter. "From the Empire State to the Sunshine State, I say, hello." He raises his beer to her. "Shad, where's your compatriot?"

With a hint of nervousness in his voice, Shad says, "I'm sure he'll be here in a sec."

Jackson: "Did he go out?"

Shad: "You know. It's Benji. He could be anywhere."

Jackson looks at him quizzically and the three sit in silence. Waiting. It's germaphobe Benji. He wouldn't be just anywhere.

After what seems like forever, Kimi's screen pops on. She's not alone. "OK everyone, best behavior. See: Don't be a dick. I want you all to meet Carmen."

There's a moment of wide-eyed, what-the-fuck as they all see Carmen for the first time. Jackson's the first to break through his shock. "Carmen. Lovely to meet you. So glad you can join our little group."

Carmen, a stunning Latina with large, dark eyes and notable curves, responds, "Thank you for having me." Her slight accent makes her even more appealing.

Shad: "Jesus, Kimi!"

Kimi: "I know, right?"

The Joy is incredulous, "You're what a Carmen looks like?!"

Kimi: "Thought I said don't be a dick."

Carmen: "Kimi's told me so much about you all."

The Joy: "Well, she left out a few things about you." Carmen just laughs quietly, taking it in stride.

Kimi: "What are you saying? That I can't have a beautiful girlfriend?"

Shad: "Of course you can."

The Joy: "You have to admit, you are stepping up in class. And you'd think it might have come up. Once."

Carmen: "Like after you two slept together?"

Damn! Apparently, Carmen is not a beautiful pushover. There's bark in this not-a-dog. The Joy backs down. "Touché. You're right. I'm a horrible person."

Jackson: "I wouldn't say horrible."

The Joy: "You will when I share my regret."

Kimi: "You didn't know you weren't supposed to share those pictures of Steph. Well, you should have. But you hadn't been told specifically. I should have never sent them to you. There. That's my regret. I regret sending you the pictures."

Shad: "Where is Steph? Is she joining us?"

Jackson: "I texted her, but..."

Kimi: "But what?"

Jackson: "But nothing. She didn't respond."

Kimi: "And you stopped at that? Go over there. You're the boyfriend, right?"

Jackson: "I don't want to impose if she needs time."

Kimi: "Bullshit. Someone back me up."

Shad: "I'm not an expert, but maybe Kimi's right."

Carmen: "She is." Carmen kisses Kimi's forehead.

The Joy, unable to take it anymore, whispers: "I slept with my mother's boyfriend."

They all strain to hear her.

Shad: "What was that?"

Again, The Joy whispers, "I slept with my mother's boyfriend."

Shad: "What?"

The Joy loses it. She yells: "Oh, my God! I slept with my mother's boyfriend!"

Kimi: "Oh, my God. You *are* so bad. So, so bad."

From the living room Betty yells, "Are you okay in there?"

The Joy yells back: "Shut up, woman!" She immediately realizes the misstep and calls out, "Shutting...up the window. Got cold. Fine now. Have a nice day." Back to the group she says, "I'm such a bad person."

Kimi: "Does Betty know?"

The Joy: "Does a bear shit in the sink?"

Shad: "Are you going to tell her?"

The Joy: "Are you going to drop acid?" Now she's enjoying her own banter. "Hey, I'm good at this game! And no, I'm not going to tell her. But it gets worse."

Kimi: "How? Did he stroke out mid orgasm?"

The Joy: "Betty and I are starting to get along. You know, bonding. Well, bonding-ish, for us. Get this. She told me I have pretty toes."

Kimi: "You *are* bonding."

Just then the front door opens in Shad's apartment and Benji bounds in. There's a look of relief on Shad's face. Benji, sporting a facemask and a new black eye, sits down next to him. He pulls out a pocket-sized hand sanitizer, puts it to work and cheerfully addresses the group. "What have I missed?"

Kimi: "Who wants to field that one?"

Carmen: "You must be Benji."

Benji takes in this new person: "You must be Carmen. You're even prettier than I expected."

Shad looks at his roommate. "When did you become Mr. Suave?"

Jackson: "Dude, nice shiner. What happened?"

The Joy blurts: "Benji, I slept with my mother's boyfriend!"

Kimi: "Old news."

Benji: "Damn."

The Joy: "And now you all have to say something you regret so I don't feel so awful."

Kimi: "Trust me. No one's gonna top that."

The Joy: "Oh, my God! You have to try."

Kimi: "Fine. I regret waiting so long to ask this one to come to New York." With that, she kisses Carmen's forehead again.

Carmen: "You're forgiven."

The Joy: "Serious. That? That's supposed to make me feel better?"

Kimi: "It's not all about you."

The Joy: "Sometimes. Sometimes it is. Someone else, go."

Jackson: "OK, I'll go. I regret that Steph is in such a bad position because of something that happened on my birthday."

The Joy: "No. That's me being awful again. Someone, regret something that I didn't do."

Benji: "I regret that I didn't know Ruby could be on the call. I mean, are we adding girlfriends now?"

Jackson: "Oh, you're officially a couple?"

Benji: "Yeah. That's OK, right?"

Jackson: "Sure. Sure. It's OK."

Shad: "It's weird."

Benji: "What part?"

Shad: "It's just that she's..."

Jackson: "Careful, my friend."

Kimi: "We almost got a new regret."

The Joy takes a drink. "That would have been nice."

Jackson: "What are you drinking? That's not water is it?"

The Joy: "God, no. It's straight vermouth. It's part of my penance. I'm not allowing myself fun flavors."

Kimi: "Since when are you Catholic?"

Carmen: "She doesn't have to be Catholic to be penitent. She did a very bad thing."

The Joy: "Thank you, Carmen. I think." The Joy suddenly has a new thought. "Wait. You two aren't sleeping together in my bed are you?"

Kimi: "I'm not sure how much sleep we're getting." Kimi and Carmen share devilish grins.

The Joy: "Oh, no. Oh. No."

Kimi: "Relax. I bought new sheets."

Shad: "Hey, I have a regret."

Jackson: "Do tell."

Shad: "I regret that I didn't ask Sandra D. if she had a boyfriend before I agreed to march with her. And I further regret that her boyfriend is a dick and nowhere near good enough for her. And I even further regret that I told him so."

Kimi: "You did not!"

Shad: "I did."

Jackson: "What did he do?"

Shad: "He chased me down the street yelling 'Stop that man! He stole my wallet!'"

Kimi: "Oh, shit."

Shad: "Yes, shit."

Jackson: "And?"

Shad: "To hear the rest of the story, you'll have to buy my book. I'm calling it, *Saved by the Roommate*."

Jackson: "Does that shiner have anything to do with it?"

Benji: "I'm not at liberty to say."

Kimi: "This is so weird."

Benji: "Hey, where's Steph? Did I miss her?"

Kimi: "Ask her boyfriend."

Jackson: "She's in a mood."

Kimi: "That's it? She's in a mood? Dude, 'in a mood' is when your roommate eats that last slice of pie you were saving. This is epic."

The Joy: "I said I was sorry. It's just pie. God!"

Kimi: "Steph's life just turned to shit. I mean, my life had turn to shit, but it just wasn't that big of a turn. Her life was great. Now it's, well, worse than mine."

Carmen: "Thank you."

Kimi: "You bet."

Benji: "Should we text her?"

Jackson: "Let's let her be for a while."

Benji: "I'm texting." While the gang watches, Benji slowly speaks his text while he thumb types. "You're missing it. I have a black eye and The Joy screwed her mom's—"

The Joy: "TMI! TMI!"

Benji looks up: "Too late."

They all further drain their respective drinks as they wait for a response from Steph. They get nothing. Shad gets up and turns back to Benji, "Another beer?"

Benji: "Sure. Hey, can Ruby join us next time?"

Jackson looks pained: "I don't think—"

Benji: "Not fair. Kimi gets to have a girlfriend."

The Joy: "Well she didn't ask."

Benji: "Fine. I'm not asking. Wait. Text from Steph. She says, 'I'm in hiding.' This is sad."

Kimi: "Sad, yes. It's completely nuts. Listen, Carmen and I are going to go. We have dinner plans."

Carmen: "We do?"

Kimi: "Never you mind."

The Joy: "Wait. Wait. We need an assignment for next time."

Shad returns with beers. "Maybe we should pass on the assignments for now. They haven't been working out real well."

The Joy gets stern: "You're not the boss of these calls, fella."

Shad: "And you are?"

The Joy: "Thank you for recognizing it. So, I want good news. Next week everyone needs to share good news. It can be about you. Or me."

Jackson: "I like that one. It's cheery." Jackson raises his glass. "Here to getting back to cheery."

Everyone follows his lead and toasts to returning to cheery.

Shad: "We'll see you all next week." He and Benji disappear. The rest talk over each other's goodbyes and their screens go black.

The Joy's left sitting alone on her bedding, wondering if she'll be found out before she cracks and 'fesses up. She shakes her head defiantly. No. C) None of the above. She decides that, barring being revealed, she'll take her indiscretion to the grave. That's the mature thing to do. She takes a sip of her vermouth and shudders. "I hate the taste of penance."

COMES THE FALL

STEPH'S APARTMENT

Steph is on her Peloton bike. She's already put in almost 38 miles and has no thought of stopping. Maybe she can just pedal until someone more famous commits a bigger offense and knocks her out of everyone's minds. Her cell vibrates. No sound. She turned the sound off after the first dozen messages shaming her for being "A stupid, stupid girl." People said things like, "Wear a mask, bitch!" She got lots of those. She also got, "Not everyone's life is a fucking party." "People are dying and you don't care." "You deserve to burn in hell." She even got one "Filthy Jew!" She'd thought that one had gone out of fashion years ago, but apparently not. She looks at the caller I.D. and sees that it's Ida. Her mother's been trying to reach her for hours. Ugh. Fine. Steph hits speaker and keep pedaling. "Yeah, Mom."

"There you are. I've been calling and calling."

"Sorry."

"Your father and I were so worried. You could have been at the bottom of a stairwell with your head cracked open."

"That's why I take elevators."

"I'm glad you can joke."

"Me, too."

"I was kidding just there."

"Me, too."

"So?"

"So, what?"

"So, do you want to tell me who this young man is with the muscles and the hair?"

"Seriously? My career is in the toilet, Mom. A toilet everyone is standing in line to flush, and you're focused on who the *guy* is?"

"I'm your mother."

"Sorry. Forgot."

"Well?"

"Well, what?"

Ida sounds fed up. "First, get off that damn bike. I know when you're not paying attention."

Steph stops peddling. She sits up, reaches for the towel hanging over the handle bars and wipes her face. "Fine. I'm paying attention."

"Thank you. Now, tell me about this new gentleman. Is he a gentleman?"

"Yes."

"Is he American? Or am I not allowed to ask that?"

"Yes, he's American. Does it matter?"

"Yes, it matters. I don't want some *gentleman* coming along and taking my baby away to some *country*."

"By *some* country, do you mean some Middle Eastern country?"

"When you're a mother, you can tell me what I'm allowed to worry about. Until then, it's your job to set my mind at ease."

"That's a big job."

"You don't think I know that?" With that, Ida gives a small laugh, which breaks the tension. "How about that? I'm halfway to a cure."

Steph smiles, despite herself. She always loves when Ida catches herself being ridiculous and owns it. After a beat, she shares, "He's a nice guy. Er, man." It's still strange to think of Jackson as a man. He's so much more playful than most men. "I've known him since high school. He comes from a good family and—oh, you'll like this. He's going to law school."

"So?"

"So?"

"Do you love him?"

"I don't know. I like him a lot." Steph's not ready to admit the depth of her feelings just yet. Too much is up in the air and saying how she feels makes her vulnerable. More so than she already is. "We're still in the beginning. We'll see."

"Well, your father and I—"

"Set a very high bar. We'll see, Mom."

Steph's phone vibrates. Should she beg out of Ida's interrogation? She looks and sees that it's from her old boss, Janis. Janis, who'd been fired for drunk-texting ageist remarks. No. Steph's not ready for that exchange. She decides to stick with the devil who birthed her.

THE JOY'S APARTMENT

Carmen is sitting at the kitchen counter drinking coffee when Kimi shuffles out of the bedroom, laptop under her arm. Kimi's mostly dressed for the day, which right now means dark top and pants, furry slippers and her red bucket hat.

Carmen looks up. "Are you just waking up?"

"No. I've been working in the bedroom. Did you make enough coffee for me?"

"What do you think?"

Kimi shuffles into the kitchen, puts down her laptop and fills her mug. She's grown attached to a pink mug with a white skull on it. It makes her feel like she's making a nod to girly while still being badass. She takes a sip. "I think I should never doubt you."

"I'll thank you to remember that."

Kimi kisses Carmen's head as she passes on her way to the sofa. She settles into the corner and adds, "I got so used to working on my Lay-Z-Girl in the corner, that I just started working in bed. I looked up and an hour was gone. Pathetic."

Carmen just smiles and lets Kimi rant.

"I'm not maximizing my momentum. I've been looking at business videos, but they're all so much bullshit. Everyone has *the* answer. Fuck them. No one has *the* answer." She lists all the must-dos that she's being bombarded with. "I should use this online store. No, I should use that one. No, I need a squeeze page. No, I need to be blogging. I need a YouTube channel. I should be tweeting. Ugh! I hate all of them. What am I missing?"

"A sense of humor."

"Fuck you. But with love."

Carmen raises an eyebrow. "Language." After a moment, they hear clarinet music from outside. Carmen looks around. "Is that live?"

Kimi has an idea. "Hey, I want you to meet someone."

"Really?"

"Sure. Of course."

Kimi shrugs, gets up and heads towards the window at the back of the apartment. Carmen follows. On the way, Carmen spots one of The Joy's pieces of juju. A baby doll with a white body and black head and picks it up. She says nothing. Lifting it is her way of asking the questions.

"Oh, that's Pinchy."

Enough said. Carmen puts down the doll and joins Kimi at the back window. Kimi's already pulling over the armchair. "There's a method to this. You go from the seat of the chair, not that arm. That arm could spell disaster. Then, while holding the window frame, scissor-step over the salon-in-a-bottle till one foot lands on the fire escape. Then, slowly, carefully bring the other foot over. Got that?"

Carmen gives the thumbs up. Kimi takes it as a dig.

"Humor me."

"I thought I was."

Kimi demonstrates how it's done. After she's in place, she turns back to Carmen. "Now you."

Carmen gracefully executes the process with little effort. She has at least eight inches on Kimi which makes stepping over things a nonissue. Half disgusted Kimi says, "Show-off."

Carmen just smiles. "Now what?"

The clarinet music is louder. Kimi points to the man seated on a stool across the way. "There. That's Clarinet Man." She fires a small wave in his direction and he offers a small nod back without stopping his tune. Kimi says, "He's gotten better. Used to suck out loud." She calls to him, "This is my girlfriend, Carmen." He nods again.

"Over there. You see the windows with the blue curtains?"

"Yeah."

"That's Billy and Bob. I know, right? They're new. Nice guys but loud talkers. And up there is my girl, Stella." Kimi puts her hand next to her mouth and calls up. "Hey, Stella! Stella!"

Carmen looks at Kimi. "I don't even know you."

After a moment, Stella comes out onto her fire escape with a baby in her arms and looks down. "You rang?"

"Stella, I want you to meet my girlfriend, Carmen."

Stella looks genuinely happy for the introduction. "Carmen, I've heard so much!"

Carmen's surprised. "Really?"

"No. But Kimi told me to say that."

Kimi calls up, "You're a traitor, Stella."

Stella's baby starts crying. "Duty calls. Nice to meet you, Carmen."

"You as well."

Stella disappears into her apartment. Carmen turns to Kimi, "You have a whole world back here."

"Great, right? Wanna meet the assholes out the front window?"

"Let's not rush things."

Kimi's deflated. She was feeling proud of her personal growth. She'd said girlfriend twice. Then she realized that she didn't say fiancée. Did she fuck up?

SHAD & BENJI'S APARTMENT

Shad's on the sofa, not finishing what's left of his lunch. Or is it dinner? He's lost in thought. Douglas is on the sofa beside him, staring at Shad's plate as if to say, "You gonna eat that?" Shad wonders why someone with as much potential as Sandra D. would settle for a jerk like her boyfriend. *Blaze?* What kind of name is *Blaze?* And that's coming from a guy named Shad. He thinks, I bet the guy's real name is Brad, or Brent, or Bernie. No, Barney. Shad decides to name her boyfriend "Barney." And why does he care, anyway? This is New York. There are way more women than men. He could have his pick. But it's effing lockdown. Who is he going to pick from? Is he just attracted to Sandra D. because he's meeting absolutely no one new? He tries to be as honest with himself as possible. No. She's that special. Barney's a fuck face. Shad's not done with the fight. He stands and quietly declares to himself, "I'm not done with the fight."

OK, time to get back to it. He dumps his plate in the sink, then heads to his room. He can hear Benji in the loft laughing and stomping his feet. "Hey, Benji! I'm going to work. Keep it down!" No answer. "Hey!" Nothing. Shad shakes his head, goes into his room and closes the door.

SHAD & BENJI'S APARTMENT/BENJI'S LOFT

Benji is sitting on the edge of his bed, hunched over his phone. He wears earbuds as he plays an online game. There are Asian zombies on surfboards with chainsaws. But the audio seems off. Like he has his head in a can. He takes one of the earbuds out and swallows hard. He then works his jaw, trying to pop the problem away. Nothing. He thinks, It'll pass. Benji keeps the one earbud out and tries to refocus on his game. But the time he wasted thinking about his ear has caused him to fall behind. Too many zombies. Too much carnage. His avatar is replaced by a blood slick on the water as a female avatar surfs up onto shore, victorious. He gets a text from Ruby reading, *Drink my wake, surfer boy!* He's been out-surfed. He doesn't actually mind.

JACKSON'S APARTMENT

Wearing just tech pants and a necktie, Jackson is working his way up the salmon ladder. He can now usually make it to the top rung without crashing to the ground. With that done, he has to decide what to do next. He goes into the long hallway, figuring he'll work on his leg strength. With one quick bounce on the mini tramp, he launches himself to the top of the hall, catching himself and bracing up there with both arms and legs. Once he feels he has his purchase, he grabs his phone from his pocket and looks at news of the world. Damn, Steph's picture is still towards the top of his newsfeed. He feels bad for her, but what can he do? He chooses to try and focus on good news. He'd rather be happy. Jackson looks at the Marathon-In-Place site. The total amount raised hasn't gone up much since the event. Should he be doing something? Leverage their success to create other events? School doesn't start for a while yet. He has time. Could he let other people license the Marathon-In-Place name? What should his business model be?

While he ponders what the smart move would be he gets a text. Good. He was tired of thinking, anyway. The text is from Steph.

Hey, Mister.

He replies, *Hey, yourself.*

Long pause. *Want to come over? I shouldn't be seen going out.*

Jackson had told his friends that he wasn't pushing Steph because she needed her space. And she did. But what he didn't say, or perhaps didn't admit to himself, was that he was uncomfortable with her now. It had stopped being him pursuing her and became her needing him. Why was it so different? The whole thing had a new gravity. He's already blown her off twice. Finally, he texts back. *Sorry. In the middle of something.*

Crickets. Finally, *k*

Jackson stays wedged in the hall, suspended off the floor. He knows he's being a dick. He can hear Ruby laughing in another room. He doesn't understand women.

BETTY'S HOUSE/BATHROOM

Betty's on a plastic hospital stool in the shower, washing herself as best as she can. The Joy is standing by in case Betty needs her, hoping that she won't be needed. She leans against the bathroom vanity, trying to see her phone's screen through all the steam. It's not going well. Ugh. She puts the phone down and looks around the bathroom. Would she understand this woman better if she knows what she keeps in her medicine cabinet? Hmm, medicine cabinet. Let's look. As quietly as possible, The Joy opens the mirrored door and peeks around. It's all pretty standard stuff. Aspirin, throat lozenges, nail clippers... Tampons? Seriously? The Joy thinks, Betty must have had these since before *Law & Order* was in reruns. She searches the box for an expiration date. Damn. These things might turn to dust if touched.

"Joy!"

The Joy is startled. She throws the box. Tampons fly everywhere. She quickly bends to pick them up and tries to sound as nonchalant as possible. "That's my name. Don't wear it out."

Over the running water Betty calls out, "What did you say?"

"What? Nothing. What did you say?"

After a long pause, Betty calls out, "I was thinking. I'd like to have my ladies over for drinks. No men. They're a pain in my ass."

"Okay."

"Would you like that?"

The Joy has to think about this. "You want me to join?"

"Isn't that what I just said?"

"Okay."

"You can be the bartender."

The Joy wonders if Betty means, "I just want you there to serve drinks," or if she means, You're that super-fun gal everyone likes to have around because in addition to a winning personality, you also pour a mean-ass cocktail. Today, The Joy chooses to go with that second one.

STEPH'S APARTMENT

Christina Aguilera is belting one out at top volume. Steph's sitting on her bike, but not working out. She's gazing out the wall of windows at her city, and slowly spinning the pedals. In the cupholder is a sports bottle. It's filled with wine. Steph thinks she may go stir crazy. She's used to going out for work and getting to interact with people. She wonders if she's just starting to experience what everyone else has been dealing with during COVID. But her situation is way worse. She's now day-drinking a lockdown cocktail with a shame chaser. And what the hell is with Jackson? Is he ghosting her? Or is being locked in causing her to overthink things? Her father always told her, "If you think long, you think wrong." Is she wrong? No. Something's changed. She listens to Christina, thinking, That woman gets me. She knows my pain. Steph idly spins the pedals some more as she takes a hit from her sports bottle.

There's a text. Jackson? No, Janis. Shit. Steph never read the previous message. Too many messages were going back and forth from work and she'd forgotten about it. But here it is again. What could she want? Steph looks with one eye. It says, *Stop avoiding me. I'm not contagious.* She scrolls up to see what the original message said. It reads, *Welcome to the club. Call me.* Steph doesn't want any part of this club.

SLEEPING WITH ONE'S SELF

SHAD & BENJI'S APARTMENT/SHAD'S BEDROOM

Shad's in bed in the dark with the sheet pulled up to his waist. Hands behind his head, he lets his thoughts swirl. He considers pleasuring himself while he thinks of Sandra D. What's a scene that would be the most exciting?

He imagines having the apartment to himself. There's a knock at the door. He goes to the buzzer and asks, "Who is it?" The response is a female voice, muffled just enough by the bad speaker to be unidentifiable. "It's me," says the voice. He buzzes the woman up. A moment later, there's a knock at the door. He looks through the peephole and sees Sandra D. standing there in a trench coat. No, a fur coat. White and fluffy. It sets off her dark skin. He slowly opens the door, careful to only show a half smile. She slinks in.

"Thanks for making me wait."

He's cool. "Anything worth having is worth waiting for."

She stands looking out the window with her back to him. "A gentleman would take a lady's coat."

He comes up behind her and pulls her coat back from her shoulders, letting it drop to the floor. She's nude. Her skin is flawless. He steps forward and kisses her neck. She lets him fondle her from behind before turning to kiss him. He whispers, "What about Barney?" She purrs, "I killed him."

Shad moves his hand from behind his head slowly reaches down to feel himself. Yes. This scene is exciting enough.

THE JOY'S APARTMENT/BEDROOM

The space has been redecorated to the point of being almost unrecognizable as The Joy's bedroom. No colorful scarves, piles of pillows or heaps of clothing which may or may not be clean. The room is picked up and the soothing colors are all very tasteful. There is still a stylist's chair in front of the floor-length mirror, but it now faces the room and has one light blue throw pillow that matches the bedding. Kimi is sitting in it with her chin on her knees. She's watching Carmen, who's in bed, fast asleep. Carmen's breathing is causing the new white comforter to slowly rise and fall. Kimi's wondering if it was all really that easy. If all she had to do was agree to move in together to have happiness follow. If her fighting it was the only real obstacle. It's like in *The Wizard of Oz*. Kimi had always been angry at the ending of *The Wizard of Oz*. The part where Glinda, the Good Witch of the North, tells Dorothy that she had the power to go home all along, but Glinda didn't tell her because she didn't think that Dorothy would have believed it. Kimi had always thought, Christ bitch, I would have tried! Look what you put her through. She could have died! Kimi thinks, I'm fuckin' Dorothy. I had the power all along and I didn't believe it. She sits there watching Her Happiness sleep.

Then...

Did Her Happiness just let out a hairy-man burp? Was there burping over the rainbow?

JACKSON'S APARTMENT/DEN

Jackson's asleep on the leather sofa. The blue light from the TV flickers in the space. There's an empty energy drink and two empty beer bottles on the floor next to him. His eyes are darting back and forth beneath his eyelids. Dream time.

In his dream, Jackson is stepping up to the starting line for his first run at the city Ninja Warrior course. He's jumping up and down in his satin track pants and matching necktie, trying to pump himself up. The crowd cheers and waves signs reading, "Park Avenue Ninja." On a large screen next to him, a short film on his backstory is running. It's the "feel-good" piece on Jackson Asghar. There are pictures of him as a boy in the United Arab Emirates, surrounded by his sisters. He's adorable. An old teacher says, "We always knew Jackson had untapped potential. We just didn't think he'd ever tap into it." His parents talk about how proud they are of him. His father says, "Jackson is a very smart boy. He can order in and calculate the tip right on the calculator on his phone. Usually." His mother adds, "He has a good heart. That's what matters. Just ask any of the girls he's left behind." Jackson watches thinking he's not coming off as well as he'd hoped. Shit, there's Ruby. What will she say?

Ruby adds, "My brother's a dick."

Jackson's head falls to his chest. The video stops. They didn't say anything about his charity work. They didn't mention that he got into law school. What the hell? He stands there feeling like he's just had his pants pulled down. In the distance he hears, "...two, one, go!" It's started. But he's not going. Why not? He can't move. Steph is at the announcer's podium. "You should have come over, asshole."

Jackson wakes with a start. He grabs the back of the sofa and peers over, as if someone might be there taking notes on his dream. But, of course, he's alone.

SHAD & BENJI'S APARTMENT/BENJI'S LOFT

The light is on low. Benji is sitting up in bed with his guitar in hand. He's composing a song. If it's good enough, he'll sing it to Ruby. He thinks, This is what you do. You put it on the line and let the chips fall where they fall. A lifetime of being odd man out has made him impervious to embarrassment. He wonders if that's his super power. He's beyond embarrassment. The thought makes him smile.

STEPH'S APARTMENT/BEDROOM

Steph's bedroom looks like she's been living in there and only there. And except for her cycling sessions, she has. Her bed has become like her little island. She's in Jackson's pajama bottoms and her own tank top, asleep on top of the covers. Surrounding her are magazines. *Southern Living, Expat Living, Australian Life, Belize & You, Welcome to The Dark Continent.* On her bedside table are the barely touched remains of a Chinese takeout dinner and the thoroughly touched remnants of a bottle of wine. All electronics are off.

BETTY'S HOUSE

The Joy comes out of Betty's bedroom. She'd taken Betty in earlier and helped her into bed. They sat up watching a dancing competition show and judging the performances as if they knew what they were talking about. They'd agree on things like, "That's not good extension! Please!" and, "She never finishes her movement. That's why she'll only ever go so far." Finally, Betty fell asleep.

Now, The Joy has this quiet house on a golf course to herself. She goes to the Florida room, sits in a lounge chair, puts her feet up and reaches for the binoculars. As she scans the darkness, she wonders what her friends in New York are doing. She feels like she's left her life and is now living in some alternate universe. And not a fun one with hot aliens. Who would pick an alternate universe with all this rattan?

Then, across the way, she sees movement. There's a small light from a house to the right. It blinks three times, fast. The Joy wonders if she saw that right. There it is again! It's a signal. But to whom? A dark figure scurries across the grass. Well, what passes for scurrying down here. Whoever it is slips into the screened porch. A secret tryst! Fun. She thinks about the secret life of older people for a while, wondering what fun her later years will hold. Then, across the way, she sees a similar pattern. But this time, the light flickers five times. And there goes the scurry across the lawn and into the home. Fascinating. She has to wait a full fifteen minutes to see it again. Blinking across the way. One long, three short. Again. One long. Three short. And, as expected, someone is scurrying into the house. Hey, that's Franny's house. Who just went in? The Joy can't tell. This is great.

Watching the indiscretions of others lets her feel a bit better about herself, until...

The Joy is startled by a quick tap on the screen door.

In a stage whisper, Nate says, "May I come in?"

The Joy whispers forcefully, "No, you may not."

"Why?"

"Because."

"That's not a reason."

"Oh, I think it is, fella."

"I brought you a cookie."

"I can't be bribed. What kind of cookie?"

In his most tempting voice, Nate says, "A black and white cookie."

Damn it. It's The Joy favorite. Telling herself that this is just a snack, she looks back to Betty's quiet bedroom, then goes to the screen door. "Hand it over."

Nate pushes his way in. "Wanna get crumbs in the bed?"

ZOOM OF DOOM

STEPH'S APARTMENT/BEDROOM

Steph's sitting cross-legged on the bed with her laptop, her back resting against multiple pillows. She checks to make sure that her wine is within arm's reach. Her hair and eyeliner have been prepped. The rest of her is rather tousled but she figures hair and eyes can carry you through. The call started about five minutes ago, but she felt that waiting out the inevitable moments of people monkeying with their volume and cameras is worth any shit she might get from The Joy. Her level of patience is rather low these days. Finally, she clicks join. And there they all are. They don't notice her screen come up, at first.

Shad: "I'm just saying, it's being seen out of context. She's not a slut."

Kimi: "A woman does something, anything and she's a slut. They never call the guys whores. It's bullshit."

The Joy spots Steph's arrival. "There you are!"

Steph: "Here I am." They all snap-to and stop their conversation, which was clearly about her.

The Joy: "OK. I told everyone to be nice to you."

Steph: "Did they have other plans?"

Kimi: "I always have other plans."

Steph spots Jackson in the upper right frame on her screen, but says nothing directly to him. She hasn't heard much from him, and when she had, all he said was, "S'up?" S'up? Seriously? She wonders what he's thinking. Fuck him. That's what *she's* thinking.

Kimi: "Steph, you haven't met my super-hot girlfr—er, fiancée. This is Carmen."

Carmen: "Nice to meet you, Stephanie. I've heard a lot."

Steph: "You and everyone else on social."

The Joy forces a laugh and says in a generic Asian character voice, "You so funny."

Kimi: "Oh, are we Asian slurring now?"

The Joy: "Can't I make a joke?"

Kimi: "No."

The Joy: "My game. My rules."

Shad: "OK. Break it up. Steph, good to have you back."

Steph: "Thanks. And Carmen, you *are* super hot."

Carmen: "I know." Kimi smiles. She likes that if she can't be the hot one, she's with the hot one.

Benji: "Welcome back, Steph. We missed you."

Steph: "Thanks. Is your cheek swollen?"

Benji: "What?"

Steph: "I said, is your cheek swollen?"

Benji touches his face. Once the black and blue had faded, he almost forgot about it. "It's nothing. But I look badass, right?"

Steph: "Always."

The Joy takes over: "OK, OK. Steph, I was gonna pick a group cocktail for tonight, but I thought you needed your wine right now."

Steph: "Need is such an ugly word."

The Joy: "Hmm. Ugly and true. Anyway, we're all drinking freestyle. Cheers." They all raise their glasses of whatever and drink.

The Joy: "Now that the niceties are past, let's get to our assignment. Steph, you weren't here last time, and you didn't acknowledge my texts, no hard feelings, but perhaps a little, so you'll go last. I'm going first. Ready, set, go!" She leans towards her to share her tasty secret. "People down here are having secret sex all over the place!"

Kimi: "Didn't you die and go to heaven? Which, for you is hell."

The Joy: "Ha, and ha. But listen, they're sneaking around in the dark like cats."

Kimi: "Like real cats, or like The Fred cats?"

The Joy: "Kimi, you're sucking the fun out of random sex. Now listen. There's a whole system. You flash your lights a certain number of times, then flash again. A back door opens and the special someone runs in. I haven't figured which people are assigned what flashing sequence yet. But it's, you know, like Morse code for booty calls. Way more fun to watch than TV."

Shad: "So, let me make sure I have this. Your good news is that other people are having casual sex."

The Joy: "That's what I just said. Honestly, Shad. Keep up. OK, who's next?"

Kimi: "And have you partaken in said casual sex?"

The Joy: "Ignoring. Next."

Shad: "I'll go. I got a raise."

Jackson: "From Max-a-billion? Fantastic! Shocking, but fantastic."

Steph: "It speaks."

Jackson: "What?"

Steph: "*What*, what? Shad has the floor."

Shad: "Thank you. And yes, it was a little shocking. But we're doing well and he appreciates the extra effort I've been putting in."

Kimi: "So, what you're saying is, in an extra effort to bag the new, hot chick, you got a raise."

Shad: "Don't say 'Bag.'"

Kimi: "I was going to say 'Bang,' but I'm trying to be polite." Kimi nods to Carmen.

Carmen: "It's OK. You do you." Kimi smiles and kisses Carmen.

The Joy: "Do we have to watch this?"

Kimi: "Yes."

Shad: "Can I continue?"

Jackson: "Please."

Shad: "It's more than just a Sandra effort, which I admit to. Thanks to the habits of a certain roommate..." Benji raises his hand. Shad nods. "...I started investigating home-gaming stocks. OMG. Score. That led me to online betting stocks. *Huge* score. So, hard work, skirt chasing and a roommate who won't grow up equal raise." They all applaud him. "Thank you. Next?"

Benji: "Me. The immature roommate will go. I had good news, but this is better. I got a call from Patrick yesterday. The restaurant is going to open up for takeout and they want me back."

Shad: "Dude, you didn't tell me."

Benji: "I was saving it."

Everyone's excited for Benji's news. There's lots of overtalking and congratulations.

Benji: "Yeah. My folks are kinda bummed. They're still hoping I'll move home till this blows over. But, a man's gotta do, right?"

Jackson: "Right."

Steph: "Seriously?"

Jackson: "What?"

Steph: "*What*, what?"

Kimi: "You two realize this is playing out in public, right?"

Steph: "Benji, what was your original good news? You said you had other good news but this was better."

The Joy: "Good catch."

Steph: "Thank you."

They all wait for Benji to answer, but he just sits there.

Steph: "Benji!"

Benji: "What?"

Steph: "Are you having hearing problems?"

Benji: "No."

Steph: "I asked you what your original good news was going to be?"

Benji: "Oh. Yeah. It's just... I wrote a song for Ruby."

The Joy gets excited. "Oh, oh. Sing it! Serenade us."

Benji: "Not yet. I haven't sung it to her yet. Maybe after."

The Joy: "I can't wait."

Benji: "You'll have to."

The Joy deflates and moves on. "OK, Jackson? Regale us with good news."

Jackson takes a deep breath and thinks. He's got nothing. Should he make something up? No. He's many things, but he's not a liar. He has his standards. Wait. He's got something. "I have one. Maurice, the doorman, you met him. Well, he's not afraid to talk to Ruby any more. Benji, I think you're having a positive effect on her. I thank you."

Benji: "Most welcome. Hey, you should do a video hang with us. It'd be super fun."

Jackson: "Oh, no. I couldn't intrude on your time."

Kimi: "What a polite way of saying, hell no."

Benji: "Well, if you change your mind..."

Jackson: "You'll be the first."

The Joy: "Ok Steph. You're bringing up the rear."

Steph: "Honored."

The Joy: "Come on. There has to be something good. It can even be stupid, like Jackson's was." Jackson puts his hand over his heart as if she wounded him.

Steph sits up straight and takes a swig from her bottle of wine. "OK, I have two. One, I showered today."

Shad: "Impressive."

Steph: "Thank you. And B, the cost of living in Croatia is surprisingly low."

Kimi: "Where the fuck is Croatia?"

Carmen: "The Mediterranean."

Steph: "It's where the Italians go to vacation. And as of now, it's one of the few countries letting in Americans."

Shad: "Would you really leave the country?"

Steph: "If I can't leave my apartment."

They all sit and drink for a while. Steph's finally had enough: "Well, that's as depressing as I care to be in public right now. I thank you all for humoring me, and for not asking me about work or my personal shame."

The Joy: "Oh, I was just going to ask you—"

Steph: "I love you all. Goodbye." With that, Steph clicks off the call. Let them fumble around without her. It was good to see them, but that was enough. She thinks Jackson's worse than a dick. He's a coward.

She's about to turn on *The Morning Show* with Jennifer Aniston, one of her favorites. But she feels that lately, it just depresses her. She takes a swig of wine and goes back to her travel magazine.

FUMBLING IN THE DARK

JACKSON'S APARTMENT/BALCONY

Jackson's asleep in the sun. His computer is open on the stone dining table and his chair is pushed back. He'd come out on the balcony with the idea of working in the fresh air and natural light, but after just ten minutes researching restaurant charities, he fell asleep.

His arms are folded and he seems at peace. And he is, for a while. He dreams of being at an audition for a mouthwash commercial. None of the other guys auditioning are anywhere near as attractive as he is, not that he would say that out loud. He waits for his turn with confidence. He's going to land this gig. A woman with a clipboard leans her head into the waiting room and calls him to come in. Jackson flashes his charm at her as he passes into the room. She shyly smiles back and announces to the panel of three people sitting behind a table that Mr. Jackson Asghar is here. He stands before them. A squat woman with glasses on her head says, "Whenever you're ready."

Jackson takes a breath to center himself. "Ready."

Squat Woman leads him in, flatly reading the other part from her script. "Something's different about you, Chris."

Jackson starts his line. "I just ate five onions, but no one will ever know, because I use Mouth Fresh Mouthwash."

Squat Woman puts her glasses on her face, looks at her script and looks back at Jackson. "Stop. Stop. That's not the line."

Jackson pulls his rolled up script from his back pocket. All of a sudden, what was a script for Mouth Fresh Mouthwash is now a script for Dick Fresh Douche. Shit. He tries to cover. "All apologies. I have it now."

Squat Woman is starting to seem impatient. She begins again. "Something's different about you, Chris."

Jackson, now reading from his new script says, "I just did five guys but no one will ever know because—" He stops.

Squat woman is put out. "What's wrong now?"

Jackson looks up. "I can't say this."

"Sure, you can...Something's different about you, Chris."

Jackson takes a deep breath and tries again. "I just did five guys but no one will ever know because I use Dick Fresh Douche. Great for dicks and it even works on dishes."

"Perfect. You're our Mr. Dick Douche!"

With that Jackson wakes from his dream, looking around to see if someone might have witnessed his audition. But, of course, the scene played out for him and him alone. For a moment, he listens to birds and his own breathing. Man. So odd. Maybe he should try to go back to work. He sits and pulls his chair back up to the computer screen, but his mind is now on other things.

STEPH'S APARTMENT

Steph's surfing the web, doing research for Jackie's piece on the growing rodent problem in the city. With the rat's usual diet of restaurant trash greatly diminished, they've gotten bolder. They're now coming out of the sewers and going through residential trash. Steph tells herself that she should be happy she's not doing this particular story on the street. But soon, the thought of Jackie leapfrogging over her for on-camera time trumps the horror of going toe-to-toe with Ratzilla. The world is one nightmare news story after another and she's missing all of it. "This sucks!"

She sits with her head in her hands for a moment rethinking the night of Jackson's party. She imagines herself being strong and telling him that for professional reasons, she can't be there. Then she pictures herself saying she'd go, but stopping at her front door, throwing her coat off and staying home. Lastly, she sees herself in the Uber on the way over to the party and declaring to the driver, "Turn this bad boy around. I'm going home!" But she knows that she did none of those things.

She has to move on. Maybe there's something exciting in the fridge. She knows there isn't, that she's just giving herself an excuse to leave her computer, but she's happy to let herself be fooled. Steph stares at everything she already knew was in there, walking through each item and coming up with a reason why she shouldn't eat it. But are those reasons valid? She's not on camera. Who gives a shit what she looks like sitting alone in her apartment? Fuck them all. She's goin' in! She grabs the cheese slices and the mayonnaise out of the fridge, then reaches to her freezer's way-back for the hidden stash of pound cake. She cuts two thick slices of the golden cake, slathers mayonnaise on both slices and places a slice, no, two slices of Havarti between them. With her sandwich of defiance in hand, she opens wide. At the precipice moment of rebellion, Ida's ringtone sounds. Steph pauses for a moment, puts down her indiscretion and answers. "Yeah, Mom?"

"Hello, New York."

Steph walks her cell out of the kitchen and over to her wall of windows. "You're timing is genius."

"That's your mother. I'm a genius. It must be where you get it."

"Oh, I'm a genius." After a stretch of no words, Steph lets out a large exhaust of air. She can feel a tear come to her eye as she looks out on the city she's not allowed to be part of.

"This will pass."

"Will it?"

"Everything passes. The bad stuff passes, and the good stuff passes."

"Cheery."

"That's life. Not always cheery. How's the gentleman?"

"He's a dick."

"Oh, that reminds me, your father wants to talk to you." Steph laughs despite herself. "See, your mother can be funny." Ida calls out, away from the phone. "Mur! Mur! I have your daughter. Come. Talk."

Steph can hear Murry in the background. "Hold on. I'm coming. Hold on. They're coming around the clubhouse turn."

Ida informs Steph, "You father's watching the horses." They both wait in silence until, "OK. Here he is. I love you."

"Love you too, Mom."

"Oh, and Mrs. Golding said to tell you she doesn't want you talking to her daughter." Ida then speaks away from the phone, "Here, talk to your daughter."

And just like that, Ida is replaced with Murry. "Hello, my daughter."

"Hey, Dad."

"I have advice for you."

"Great." Steph waits for the wisdom, not expecting much.

"Your mother told me that you haven't returned Janis's calls. Mistake. Never burn a bridge. You don't know what this woman will be doing in the future. She could get another big job. That's a good connection."

"I don't think—"

"Listen. Here's the thing."

"There's a thing?"

"There's always a thing. The thing is people have short memories. This woman, this Janis will sit and wait. What else has she got to do? She'll wait, and when someone needs what she can do, they'll justify giving her another chance. Maybe they can get her for less money. And, here's another thing."

"A bonus thing."

"People fail upwards. Once someone has had success, they see themselves as a successful person. They project that, so it's how everyone else sees them too."

Steph considers all of this and she can't disagree. As much as she'd like to avoid Janis, she should call. "OK."

"Good. Oh, and don't lead with an apology. Never lead with an apology."

"Hey Dad, how did you get so smart?"

Playfully, Murry says, "I'm a genius. Didn't you know that's where you get it?"

Steph smiles. She can feel the tear has dried on her face and there isn't another to take its place. "Thanks, Dad."

"Of course. You're my baby girl."

"Love you."

"Love you, too. Now, I gotta go talk to a man about a horse." And the line goes dead. Steph continues to look out her window.

THE JOY'S APARTMENT

Kimi's at the kitchen counter with her head in her computer and her earbuds pumping trance music. She'd never planned on becoming an entrepreneur, but here she is. Of the many things she'd considered taking on to promote her online mask venture, the one she chose was blogging. It felt the most natural and comfortable to her. She could keep the attitude from her masks and write little rants with that same smartass point of view. She thinks of it as long-form smartass. The blog title is "On & In Your Face." Her newest entry will be about kissing with a mask on. She'd made the mistake of mask-to-mask kissing Carmen when she'd first arrived. It was like kissing a damp towel filled with her own wet breath. Kimi's thinking that this is really a public service piece. Between being deep into writing and having her music flowing directly into her brain, she doesn't hear the door buzzer.

Carmen calls from the sofa, "Door! Kimi? Door!" No response. Carmen looks up from her book and sees that she might as well be alone. She unfolds herself from the sofa and goes to the intercom. "Yes?"

"Package Guy. I have something for Kimi."

"Okay." Carmen hits the buzzer, then heads out the door and down the hall. Vlad stops halfway in the front door. He stares at Carmen, clearly taken with her lovely Latina looks. She waits then asks, "That's for Kimi, yes?"

"Yes." He just stands there.

"May I have it?"

"Yes."

But he just stands there. She reaches to take the box from his hands. "Thank you...?"

"Oh. Vlad. I'm Vlad."

Almost as if she's speaking to a child, Carmen says, "Thank you, Vlad."

"You're welcome." He turns to leave and turns back. "Have a nice day."

"I always do." Off he goes. Carmen laughs to herself. She's aware of the effect she has on some people. Sometimes she minds. Sometimes not. She thinks, Kimi was never too intimidated to talk to her. She likes that. Just then, Carmen notices the apartment door across the hall is open. A disheveled-looking older man in a robe stands staring at her. But not in the way that Vlad stared. This man is looking more critically. Carmen takes the lead. "Can I help you?"

He reaches into his pocket, pulls something out and thrusts it forward. In a gruff voice he asks, "Stick a' butter?"

Carmen looks in the man's hand. He is indeed holding an unopened stick of butter. She smiles. "That's so sweet, but I already had lunch." She walks back down the hall and into The Joy's apartment, closing the door without looking back. Once inside, "Kimi, I met the neighbor."

BETTY'S HOUSE

Dressed in head-to-toe daisy print and wearing a white head scarf, The Joy practices her putting on the lawn outside the Florida room. She has a glass cup lying on its side, set about twenty feet in front of her. The Joy puts her large Jackie O sunglasses on top of her head, sizes up the task, then swings the putter. The ball rolls across the perfectly manicured green grass and comes to a stop about an inch before its target. Nuts. The Joy walks over, looks around and gives the ball a small kick into the glass. Yay. She claps.

From inside the screened room, Betty calls to her. "Joy!"

The Joy's first thought is that she was caught cheating. She answers innocently. "Yes, Betty?"

"Joy, I just got the strangest call from Franny."

Again, as innocently as possible, "Oh?" She looks over at Franny's house and sees a little man waving. Shit, It's Nate. She looks away, but he keeps waving. In her head she yells, 'No. Don't wave. Stop waving.' The Joy swats at him to stop, as if he were a distant bug. He finally continues on his senior way. Is it about to hit the fan?

SHAD & BENJI'S APARTMENT

Shad's on the sofa with his feet up. He's looking at his phone and scrolling through the market's closing numbers from the day. He already knows what's there for the most part. This is just a relaxed review and a new part of his daily routine. He likes to be able to start his day with messages to his clients. Some little piece of good news. His clients feel good, he feels good and Max loves it.

He looks at his watch. This is probably a good time to call home. His mother is likely to pick up. Avoiding his dad is always preferable. But with lockdown, their schedules are less predictable. Is he feeling lucky? Doesn't matter. He has to call. He sits up and straightens his shirt, not that they'll see him. OK, let's do this. Just as he dials, Benji comes down from the loft and walks by on the way to the can. As he passes, he lets one rip.

The smell hits Shad immediately. "Christ, man!"

"Think of it as a free COVID test."

"What?"

"If you couldn't smell it, that could indicate that you have COVID. Say thank you." With that, Benji goes into the bathroom and closes the door behind him.

"Swine!"

A woman's voice asks, "What did you call me?"

"Sorry, Mom. It's just...never mind. Happy anniversary."

"Oh, thank you my Shad. You're so sweet."

"Just how you raised me."

"That *was* my doing, wasn't it?"

"All you. So, you guys doing anything special?"

"Well, let's see. Your father is taking me out for a lovely dinner and then a night of dancing at that new jazz club. Oh, and he bought us matching ponies. The kind with the long horn on their foreheads. We're going for a ride over that nice new rainbow in the back yard."

"He's a true romantic."

"Isn't he! It's either that or we sit home with something I made a week ago and froze, and re-re-watch *Invincible*. Which is about as romantic a movie as your father can handle."

"The one about the walk-on football player for the Eagles?"

"That's the one. He watches it every year, right after the Eagles are out of contention. It's his way of getting in a win. There *is* a love interest, so technically, it counts. Now, tell me, how are you doing? How's the world of high finance?"

"Well, if you must know, I got a raise."

"My man. That's wonderful! Your father will be so proud."

"I didn't get a trophy. Just a raise."

"Now, now. That's the man I love."

Shad decides to end this line of conversation. It's his mother's anniversary and he doesn't want to make this another conversation about himself and how he can't connect with his father. Or more accurately, how his father refuses every effort to connect with him. "Chad or Joe coming over?"

"I see what you're doing. And yes, Chad is coming with Shanna and the kids on Saturday. They're getting so big."

"Chad and Shanna?"

"You're so bad."

"Just how you raised me."

She laughs. "Would you like to wish your father a happy anniversary?"

"I'll let you pass the message along."

"Oh, Shad. He's just not good at showing his feelings."

"Unless you're running with a football." Why did he say that? "I'm sorry. That's my fault. You two are such opposites."

"That's what keeps it fun. Why would I want to marry me? I already know the stupid things that I'm thinking. I want to hear someone else's stupid things."

Shad considers this. "Well, tell Dad I said happy anniversary."

"I will."

"And tell Chad I said, Hey."

"I'll do that too. Any other assignments?'

"That should do it."

"Thanks for the call, baby."

"You bet. Love you."

"Love you, too."

Shad hangs up and sinks back into the sofa. That's done. Not done well, but done. He sees Douglas on the floor, burying his head into his paws. Shad takes a whiff and calls out to Benji, who's still in the can. "Hey, Sunshine! Looks like Douglas doesn't have COVID either!"

Sounding troubled, Benji calls out, "Houston, we have a problem!"

Never something Shad wants to hear from someone in a bathroom.

THE JOY'S APARTMENT

Carmen's in her spot on the sofa, reading. The clanking of Kimi moving in the kitchen makes her look up from her pages. She sees Kimi gathering seemingly unrelated food items into a bowl, a habit she picked up from The Joy. But for Carmen, seeing it for the first time, it seems odd. She asks, "What are you making?"

Kimi's not used to being watched. Even when they were in the same space, The Joy was always in her own world. "There's not really a name for it. Let's call it, a bowl of crap."

"Mmm."

Kimi suddenly realizes that she's serving herself without thinking of Carmen. She might be hungry. Kimi's used to, and good at, not thinking of others. She liked not thinking of others. God, she sucks at this. "It's not good. You want some?"

"You're quite the saleswoman."

"I know, right?"

"I think I'll wait for dinner."

Kimi brings her bowl over to join Carmen on the sofa. She sits on the opposite side and brings her feet up so they're resting on top of Carmen's feet. She notices that Carmen has something green in her teeth and gestures. Carmen tilts her head, not understanding. Kimi gestures again. Carmen shakes her head. "Use your words."

"You have something in your teeth."

"Oh." Carmen retrieves the piece of "who knows," examines it, then puts it in her mouth, presumably swallowing it. Kimi's a bit confused at how this lovely woman could do something so repellent. She checks with herself. 'That was gross, right? Yes, that was indeed gross.' She tries changing topics to get that picture out of her head. She asks, "What's for dinner?"

"You tell me."

"Oh. It sounded like you had a plan."

"Me? It's your town." In mock-complaint Carmen says, "You never take me out to nice places."

Kimi looks up from her bowl of crazy. "There is no out."

"A girl can dream, no?"

They sit on their private island of a sofa staring at each other. Kimi thinks, What can I do? I should be doing something. Carmen came all this way. What am I bringing to the party? What have I got? She takes a spoonful of the newly dubbed "bowl of crap" and looks deep into Carmen's eyes. She has an idea. "Hey, let me show you New York."

Carmen sits up. "Really?"

"Really."

"But, the pandemic."

Kimi puts her bowl on the coffee table, gets on her feet and reaches out to Carmen. "Come with me." She sees Carmen's face light with intrigue. This is good. She walks Carmen to the front window, grabbing two masks from her old corner along the way. They're new. She was waiting for the right time to present them. This seems the right time. Kimi hands a mask to Carmen. "Here." They both don their face covers. Kimi's reads, "She's with me." Carmen's says, "I'm with her." It's clear that, behind the masks, they're both smiling.

Kimi then lifts the window sash. "Here. Sit here." Carmen sits on the sill and Kimi stands just behind her. There is the line of people waiting to get into the supermarket. "There it is. These people are New York. Let's listen, shall we?" Carmen leans out just a bit and tries to pick out a conversation from the colorful lineup. At first the sounds all seem to blend, but then she can hear a mother and young son who are just below. The mother is white and wearing bold, solid colors. Her son is mixed race and wearing a BLM t-shirt. He's saying, "So I told Bruno he didn't bring his manners with him."

His mom rolls her eyes. With a slight Southern accent she says, "Baby, it's not his fault. Bruno comes from a long line of no manners. Ever hear his father suck his teeth and pass wind at the same time? The man's like a double-ended flute." The boy laughs. "Don't worry, baby. You just keep bringing your manners and you'll be A-OK." The boy smiles at his mom and gets a small hug in return. Carmen turns to Kimi with a look that says she loves what she just saw.

Kimi smiles. "Good, right?" Kimi scans the line to see if any of her regulars are there. Hey, it's Leather Vest Guy. She points him out saying, "See that guy down there in the Leather Vest? I named him, Leather Vest Guy."

"How obscure of you."

"Come on. You remember. The video? The fight. The one that got all the attention for my masks. That's him. Kimi raises a hand to him. Leather Vest Man nods his head in return.

"I was hoping the Lemon Ladies would be out here. They really hate me. You have to meet them."

"I look forward to it."

Two rather round men walk past the line in mid argument. Both look to be Middle Eastern and in their mid-sixties. One is a head taller than the other. The people in line all turn to listen in on the passing fight. Tall Round Man says, "You have to boil them first, you putz."

Short Round Man is defiant, "Don't use Yiddish when you're talking about pork. It's disrespectful. And I'll slap the shit out of you if you boil just one of my back ribs, you fuck." The tall man laughs at him.

Short Round Man: "What, you don't think I can?"

Tall Round Man: "I'd like to see you try."

Short Round Man: "Don't push me."

With that, the tall man slaps the short man on the side of the head, causing his hairpiece to go askew. The people in line gasp. The short man quickly rights his hair, "You just wait till Ma hears about this. You're so screwed." The short man shoots ahead and the tall man calls after him. "You're such a baby!"

As the short man disappears around the corner he yells back, "Rubber and glue, my friend. Rubber and glue!"

The tall round man takes chase, yelling, "Not applicable!"

Carmen turns wide-eyed to Kimi. "That did not just happen."

Kimi does her best cowgirl impression. "Happens all the time in these parts, little lady."

Carmen smiles. She's delighted. "I could sit here for hours."

"Be my guest. I'm going to get back to the high-powered world of face masks. Gotta see what I can do to lower overhead. My margin is crap."

"I was thinking, what if you—"

Kimi the Cowgirl cuts her off. "Now don't you worry your purty little head about it." Not seeing Carmen's displeasure at being shut down, Kimi kisses her on the forehead. As she looks up, Kimi locks eyes with the old Chinese women she knows from the supermarket line. The old woman squints at the sight of the kiss. Is she judging her? Is she displeased? Will this woman who's become a part of Kimi's life without actually exchanging words now ghost her? Is this the end of their head nods? Kimi now thinks of her own mother and how unhappy she knows her mother will be at the thought of her marrying another woman. Well, only if Kimi tells her.

SHAD & BENJI'S APARTMENT

Shad's got his laptop set up on the dining room table. Now that Benji's once again leaving the apartment for the restaurant, Shad figures he'd let himself out of the cage of his bedroom to work. He'd tried working on the sofa with his feet up. And while it felt comfortable, even decadent, it ultimately felt too informal. He likes sitting up straight. Good posture makes him feel powerful. He thinks, I am powerful. Sharing good news with his clients makes him feel even more so. He'd spoken to one of his favorites this morning. He got to tell Janet that her fantasy football gaming stock was about to double. She was, of course, delighted. Shad considers how most people don't understand the good he does for the world. They think that stocks and investing is for a select few. But here's a woman who was not a millionaire when she started working with his team. She is now. And his analytics were pivotal in her being confident about her future. Shad sits up even taller.

As he scans his office mail, he sees a report from Sandra D. and shakes his head. As he speculates as to why great women are attracted to dicks, Benji bursts through the front door. He has a mask and a neck scarf on.

Shad looks up. "How's life out in the big, bad world?"

Benji just holds up a finger to pause any chat, and makes a beeline for the bathroom. A moment later he returns with a thermometer sticking out of his mouth and his hands on his hips. He looks like a sick superhero.

Shad smirks, "Tell me, Captain COVID, what battles did you fight today while you kept the world safe for white clam sauce?"

Benji is playing it serious. He looks at his watch and holds up another finger to pause the conversation. He nods at his wrist as the necessary time ticks by. Finally, Benji pulls out the thermometer and checks his temperature. "Ninety-seven point two."

"That's low, right?"

"Actually, my natural body temperature is lower than the average human's. Also, my resting heart rate is low, forty-four to forty-six, which is more atypical except for distance athletes, and my blood pressure varies between—"

"Dude, if I was your doctor, I'd be bored by now."

Annoyed, Benji heads for the kitchen. "Thanks for caring."

Shad throws his head back. He's really been enjoying his time away from Benji. It's crazy to complain about wanting time alone during pandemic lockdown, but...what a treat. He thinks he better right this ship before it snowballs. Then he thinks, Wow, I just mixed metaphors, big time. Oh, well. No one heard it. Safe.

Shad follows Benji into the kitchen and stands next to him in front of the open refrigerator door. Both men are now shoulder to shoulder and bathed in white light.

Shad says, "The maintenance gal came to work on the toilet today."

"Yeah?"

"Yeah. It's fixed. For now. But she gave me a raft of shit. No pun intended. Said we use too much paper."

"Both of us?"

"She didn't specify."

"Paper amount is personal."

"Mm-hm. What looks good?"

"Hunh?"

"What looks good?"

Benji shrugs. "I don't know."

They stand there for some time. Benji mumbles, "You hungry?"

"No. But if you put it in front of me, I'll eat it."

"Ravioli?"

"Sure."

"Or ramen?"

"Sure."

"Which?"

"Ramen?"

"How about pizza? I'm working on my crust."

"Perfect."

"What?"

"Seriously man. I think you need to get your ears checked."

Benji keeps looking in the fridge, then glances to Shad. "You know, in this light, you look like a little Negro angel."

"You're a dick."

"The better to see you with." The two roommates smile, but not at each other.

STEPH'S APARTMENT

Steph's lying on the floor, wearing a matching jog bra and yoga pants. Her good friend, Christina Aguilera pumps through her earbuds. She's on a workout mat next to her bike. There's also a new rack of hand weights. At the moment, Steph's using fitness bands to work out her quads and hamstrings. She counts out each move in the sequence. Fifty per leg. At times, this workout can be almost meditative. But she's been adding new movements every few days and it's gotten to the point where all the counting just feels tedious. Steph stops mid-count and lies flat on the floor with her arms out, looking straight up. Is that dirt on her ceiling or is there a crack? Maybe the whole thing will give way and come crashing down on her. But probably not. More lying there.

Then, in a quick move, she rolls over onto her stomach, grabs her cell, which was on the floor next to her, and punches in a number. Band-Aid, ripped!

The voice that picks up is snarky. "If it isn't Steph Unmasked."

Steph knew she'd be in for more than a bit of shit. "Come on. Get it all out."

"Oh, I will. Margaret and I had a bet. She didn't think you'd call. But I know better. Quite the fall you took. Welcome to the inner circle of celebrity shame. Great headlines. 'Hanging from ceiling/Falling from grace.' 'Unmasked and Unforgivable.' 'Boozy Newsy.' Margaret's favorite was the clean and simple, 'Nice Underwear.'"

Steph waits. Is that it? Can she get away with changing the topic? "So, you and Margaret haven't killed each other yet?"

"We did, but I revived her. Put me on video." Steph knows that Janis loves video calls. She has no idea why. "Come on. I wanna see it."

"See what?"

"I wanna see how disgrace has ravaged you."

Steph hits video. And there's Janis, her old boss and one of the most obnoxious people she's ever known. She looks even worse than the last time she looked worse. Yet, because of working so closely, she feels oddly like family...the family you try to avoid.

Janis bellows, "You bitch! You, absolute bitch!"

"Good to see you too."

"Look at you. When a career woman's career shits the bed, especially when it's her fault, she's supposed to look like it. Overeat. Live in pajamas. Break her hairbrush because she finally tried to brush her hair after not brushing it for a week. What the fuck? Are those hand weights?"

"Yeah."

"God, I fucking hate you."

After seeing each other every day and some nights for the last few years, Steph hasn't seen Janis since her own career demise. They spend a moment just looking at each other. As the ice starts to melt, Steph asks, "How are you doing?"

More calm now, Janis says, "No apology for not returning my calls?"

"A wise person told me, never lead with an apology."

"We're well past the lead. You can apologize now."

"I'm sorry."

"Thank you. How am I doing? Look around." Janis turns her phone and pans her living quarters for Steph. It's a mess. Crap everywhere. Just then a little girl of about five runs in and jumps on Janis, almost knocking her over, then runs out again. Janis yells after her, "Brook, I'm gonna kick you till you bleed!"

Brook yells back, "No you won't. You love me too much."

Janis looks back into the phone. "I fucking hate that kid." But Steph can tell that she doesn't mean it. Margaret walks past in a t-shirt and pajama pants. Janis calls to her. "Margaret." Margaret keeps walking. Sarcastically Janis tries again. "Margaret, my heart." That stops her. It's clear that this is part of their home ritual. Margaret walks over. "I want you to meet Miss Nice Underwear." Clearly excited, Margaret comes over and leans into frame. Damn. She and

Janis could be twins. She's a mirror of what Janis would look like if she hadn't let herself go.

She waves at Steph. "Hey. Nice to finally meet you. We've had so much fun at your expense."

"Glad I could provide a service."

Margaret waves it off. "If you can't laugh... Am I right?"

Janis shakes her head. "Margaret fucking sunshine, here."

There's a crashing sound in the next room. Margaret looks behind her. "The call of the wild. I better go make sure my kid's not bleeding out." She waves again. "Bye. Don't be a stranger." And she's gone.

Janis watches her leave. "She's always happy. Like she swallowed lightbulbs."

"I like her."

"You would. I like her too. So, what's your next move?"

"I don't know that I have one."

"If you're not dead, there's always a next move."

Interesting. "Okay, what's your next move?"

"You don't think I have a move? I have a move. I'm just not going to tell you."

"So why should I tell you my next move?"

"Because you don't know enough to have one."

"And you're going to help me?"

"Maybe. If you'll stop working out and eat a box of Twinkies."

JACKSON'S APARTMENT

Jackson is in front of his computer wearing a long white robe and holding a lightsaber. He bows to the screen. "Till we meet again, young Filbert."

On the screen is his cousin's thirteen-year-old son, Filbert. The boy is similarly dressed. They've been playing together this way since well before lockdown. Filbert lives in the UAE. "I look forward to your next defeat, Jack Strong."

"I'm sure the pleasure will be all mine." Playfully, Jackson adds a devious laugh.

The kid flashes Jackson his best menacing look at the screen. "He who laughs last..." Filbert does his own menacing laugh. The screen goes black.

That was fun. Or at least a distraction. Jackson lays his weapon down on the floor and sits at his computer. He looks at the Marathon-In-Place account. He's been doing his best to focus on something important and, along with Shad and Benji, has worked on expanding their charity's efforts to launch races around the country. Shorter races that are more accessible to the average person. He's pleased with how well he's doing, not letting thoughts of Steph hold him back any more. But, of course, now he's thinking of her. Why is she so mad, anyway? Of course, he knows the answer. Were his actions so egregious? Ugh. He hates complications. It was all so perfect when she didn't need him to support her. He loves her strong side. Why can't she just be strong again?

He feels an incoming text. Hey, think of the devil. It's Steph. Her text reads, *When you get a chance, please ship the stuff I left in your bathroom. I'd get it, but not supposed to go out.*

Jackson's about to text back, but doesn't want it to seem like he's just sitting with his phone in his hand. Who's he kidding? Not her. He texts, *Sure thing*. And waits. But no other texts come. Damn.

Fine. He checks his email and sees there's a message from his mother, which makes him smile. Let's open that. Jackson loves both his parents, but no one dotes on him like his mother. The women in his culture are all so strong. Maybe not in a way that's obvious to outsiders, but there's no mistake who's in charge. He thinks, I am a mama's boy and proud of it. The email reads:

Dear Jacky,

I didn't want to call and interrupt your good work. We're all so proud of the money you raised to help out people you don't even know. What a blessing you are to us and others. Your father and I find ourselves bragging about you to anyone who will listen.

How is your sister? She doesn't communicate with us and we worry about her. I can't tell you how it comforts us to know that she is living under her brother's watchful eye.

Jackson can hear Ruby humming in the kitchen. She seems much more interested in cooking since she met Benji. Cooking and sci-fi. And gaming. She also seems happier than he can remember her being since they were kids. True, happy in her way, but happy. He continues reading.

I look forward to hearing from you both. And I thank you for taking wonderful care of our family's home.

So much love,
Your mother

Jackson looks around at all of the ninja equipment that he's drilled into walls and ceilings. Does that fall under the category of "wonderful care?" Likely not. He just won't mention that right now.

Instead, he decides to share with his lovely mother the good news of how happy Ruby is. Yet, as he ponders the source of Ruby's new happiness, he's struck by the fact that Benji, this awkward guy, is so much better at being in a relationship than he is. It's a conundrum. He wonders if he should talk to his friend. So embarrassing.

GATHERINGS

BETTY'S HOUSE

The Joy is in her mother's bedroom, about to help her maneuver from a cream-colored easy chair with a floral print, to her wheelchair. Betty now prefers sitting on regular furniture whenever possible. She says it makes her feel less like a patient and although it creates more work, The Joy can't argue it. She's standing in a half squat in front of Betty, waiting for her to lean forward, placing her head on the Joy's shoulder. The cue to initiate lifting. Betty makes the move and The Joy hoists her up. Betty calls out, "Ow! Stop grabbing my bosoms!"

"Then don't keep them behind your back."

At that, mother and daughter break into shared laughter. Betty catches her breath, "It's so sad. I used to love my bosom. Now I just try to keep them where I can see them."

The Joy lowers Betty into the wheelchair, wondering if maybe their ladies' night will be fun. How nice would that be? Then Betty slips into control-freak mode. "Now, I decided that I don't want to set up in the living room. I want to move everything into the Florida room. That way, Carol is less likely to take over the piano. That woman has a voice for humming. I don't know why I let you talk me into inviting her. So, you can distribute everything between the coffee table and the end tables. And I want you to go to the Harris's. They just got back from their daughter's and Janey needs you to help her bring over a few things for tonight. She shouldn't be carrying anything with her back. You're much more...solid. I told her you'd be coming over."

At that, The Joy takes a deep breath and thinks, Pretty feet. Pretty feet. Focus on your pretty feet. Out loud, she says, "Any more commands before I go?"

"These aren't commands."

"Demands?"

"Why do you have to be so dramatic? Now, wheel me into the living room and go help Janey."

"Aye, aye." The Joy proceeds to push Betty into the living room. As they walk she adds, "First, I have to run The Fred over to the vet. His anal glands are leaking."

Betty shakes her head. "That damn cat."

STEPH'S APARTMENT

Steph's walking through her space with cell in hand. She shoots a text to Kimi, *Wanna hang tonight? Needing a girls' night.* While she waits for a response, she travels around her sofa, then her dining table/desk. She leans over to her screen to see if there are any new work emails. None. What does that mean? Anything? She continues her track around her apartment, which is feeling smaller every day. Her TV is on. She's been watching a lot of *Fleabag* lately. For the time being, she prefers to not watch people who are succeeding.

Finally, she gets a text back. *Honored.*

Carmen want to join?

I'll tell her she has no choice.

Must be great to be your girlfriend.

That's what I tell her. [*Three laughing emojis.*]

Steph wanders into her bedroom and stares at her bed, thinking about her nights with Jackson. They were good together in bed. And on the floor. And that time on the balcony. She thought they might be good in life as well. What went wrong?

Steph texts Kimi back, *Should we see if The Joy is free?*

If she's not free, she reasonable. [*five laughing emojis.*]

You love your own material.

[*Three sad emojis*] *Better?*

Should we invite Ruby?

Mistress of the dark?

Just a thought.

I can do a little crazy if you can.

6:30?

I'll check with my secretary. And...fine.

Thanks.

Steph is about to pocket her phone and realizes she doesn't have pockets. She shoves it into her sports bra and goes to the mirror above her bureau. What should she wear tonight? She wants her look to read: Not devastated. After taking a long look at herself, she thinks whatever she wears, she better start with a shower. How many days has it been? She's losing track of days of the week. She's down to shower and non-shower days. This is definitely a shower day.

JACKSON'S APARTMENT

Jackson is on his ninja hopping ball birthday present bouncing through the apartment. Absently, forgetting that he's not in a relationship any more, he wonders if he should call Steph to join him. Then he remembers that A, they're no longer dating and, B, she's mad at him. Well, she hasn't said she's mad at him, but she asked for her stuff back. You don't have to be brilliant with women to know what that means. Fine. Move on.

As he bounces, he thinks about how he likes the feeling of his hair moving up and down now that it's gotten longer. So he keeps bouncing. He makes his way down the hall towards Ruby's bedroom. He's about to bounce past but thinks, no. He should see if she wants to come out and play. Maybe make a night of it. Why not? He bounces up to her closed door and knocks.

From inside Ruby calls flatly, "What?"

"Would you like to hang out?"

"No."

"Come on. It'll be fun. We could order Chinese and watch an old kung fu movie."

"I have plans."

Jackson doesn't buy it. "Bullshit."

A moment later Ruby opens the door, holding her camera. Ever since she was a child, she's been fascinated by photography. Her favorite subject is odd people. She sees her brother, bouncing in front of her and takes his picture. "You're such a child."

"Oh, and your goth look is so mature."

"I'm not goth. I'm post-apocalyptic."

"Yes. That's way more advanced. Come on. Come for a bounce with me."

"Told you. I have plans."

"You don't."

"I do."

"Prove it."

Ruby pulls out her phone and finds the text thread to show him. "Steph invited me to hang out with the girls tonight."

Jackson's stunned. How is he on the outs and Ruby's on the ins? She closes the door in front of him.

JANEY'S HOUSE

The Joy stands at the Harris's front door. It looks just like Betty's front door. And all of the other front doors in the community. She rings the bell and waits. She can hear an argument on the other side of the door as Phil Harris opens it. He's a tall man in pastel yellow and pink golf pants, and a cream color polo shirt. Phil is still calling over his shoulder into the house as he stands with the door knob in his hand. "I'm telling you, you don't use chopsticks for Thai food." He turns back to The Joy and shrugs. "Hello, Joy. Nice to see you. My wife thinks it's OK to ask for chopsticks in a Thai restaurant."

From within the house, Janey calls to him. "I think it's OK because it is OK."

Phil stands aside and lets The Joy into the house. He calls back to his wife, "You're making a fool of yourself."

"You're the fool."

The Joy comes into the house that is much like Betty's. Rattan. Flowers. Pastels. She does feel that her mother has more interesting art. Janey is in the kitchen, which can be seen from the pass-through opening in the dining room wall. She's a sharp looking woman in blue pastel pants and a crisp white blouse. She gathers her offering for Betty's party and sees The Joy. "Oh, Joy. Sweetheart. How nice to see you."

As if she's still in high school, The Joy responds, "Nice to see you, Mrs. Harris."

"Please. It's Janey. Thanks for coming."

The Joy heads to the kitchen. "How can I be of service?"

"Well, for starters, you can tell my fool of a husband that you can use chopsticks at a Thai restaurant."

Phil calls in, "They're laughing at you."

The Joy confides in Janey, "I think you can use chopsticks with anything."

Janey calls out to her husband. "Did you hear that?"

Phil sits himself on the sofa and settles in to continue the long-distance disagreement. "I heard that, and it's crazy."

"I know I saw people using chopsticks when we were in Thailand."

"You didn't."

"Now I don't know what I saw? I'll settle this." Janey calls out to the room, "Alexa, do they use chopsticks in Thailand?"

The monotone voice of Alexa answers, "Historically, people in Thailand used their hands to eat, with some occasion for utensils like spoons and forks. While the Thai do not use chopsticks for rice dishes, as in other Asian cultures, they will use chopsticks for certain noodle dishes."

Triumphant and vindicated, Janey calls out, "There!"

Phil just throws a hand up and reaches for his golf magazine.

Janey smiles to The Joy, "He hates when Alexa tells him he's wrong." She then goes to the dry-erase board on the fridge. The board is titled, "Alexa Says I'm Right." Janey adds a new tally mark under her name. "Score another one for me. I'm now up five for the week."

The Joy quickly figures out what's going on. "You score your arguments?"

"Well, I can't beat him at golf. A gal's gotta do." With that Janey gives The Joy a friendly shoulder bump. "OK, if you can grab the platter and that canvas tote..." The Joy does as told and follows Janey to the front door. As they pass Phil, he says "Don't drink too much."

Janey looks offended. "Please. If anyone drinks too much, it's you."

"You drink more than I do."

"No, you."

Phil calls out to the room, "Alexa, which one of us drinks more, me or my wife?"

Again, Alexa answers flatly, "I'm sorry. Please rephrase the question."

Janey nudges The Joy along. "Alexa, don't bother. We're leaving."

Alexa repeats, "I'm sorry. Please rephrase the question."

THE JOY'S APARTMENT

Kimi is mixing cocktails in a large glass pitcher. Ever since The Joy went to Florida, she's been feeling like it's her duty to take up the mantle of bartender. So, after careful consideration, she decided that the choice for tonight should be white Russians. A good amount of hooch, but creamy and dessert-ish.

Carmen, looking lovely in brown leggings and an oversized white t-shirt, comes in from the fire escape carrying a fashion magazine. Kimi thinks, If I wore that, I'd look homeless. Oh, well. She can see that Carmen has quickly mastered the art of stepping over the window-sill juju. Beautiful and graceful. "There you are."

"Not many places I could be."

Kimi smiles and keeps mixing.

Carmen comes over and picks up the Kahlua bottle. She runs a finger around the rim and licks the sweet liqueur from it. "I was talking to Stella."

"Really?"

"Really."

"What did she have to say?"

"Nothing. Just girl talk."

Kimi raises an eyebrow. Should she be concerned? Is Carmen confiding in Stella in a way that she can't with Kimi?

Carmen heads to the bedroom. "I'm going to change for the call."

"Why?"

"I want to look nice. Don't you?"

"I changed already."

Carmen laughs as she disappears. "Oh."

Kimi watches Carmen disappear and calls after her. "Hurry up. The call starts in a few." Kimi finishes the drinks and puts together a plate of cheeses and crackers. She likes having someone to prepare things for. There was no reason to make life special just for herself. Or, at least she never saw the reason.

By the time Carmen emerges from the bedroom, the coffee table is set with drinks and snacks. Kimi's laptop is perched on a pile of books so they'll be framed just right. The lighting is soft and plenty of pillows are ready to be arranged as needed. Kimi plops herself on the sofa and pulls in her feet so she's sitting cross-legged. Carmen looks virtually the same as before she left to make herself over, except now? She's radiant.

Kimi shakes her head. "How do you do that?"

"You need to move."

"What?"

Carmen goes to sit on the side of the sofa that Kimi's on. "Scoot. Scoot." Kimi scoots to the other side. "I need you on my left. I'll be turning to you and my right side is better."

"It's not fucking high tea with the Queen." Kimi shakes her head and hits the appropriate computer keys to start the video call. Almost immediately, they see Steph. Her hair is freshly flipped. Kimi starts, "Look at you, right on time."

Steph: "Where else do I have to be? Hey Carmen. You're looking lovely."

With mock formality, Carmen responds "Why, thank you. So are you. Is that a Prada top?"

Steph is thrilled to talk fashion. "It is. Would you believe I got it on a promo shoot for the station? The stylist let me keep it."

Carmen coos. "You're so lucky."

Steph: "I know."

Sarcastically, Kimi jumps in. "Oh, my God! What a beautiful slice of who-gives-a-shit."

Carmen: "I give a shit."

Steph: "See?"

Kimi: "I can end this call right now."

Steph: "Fine. We can talk about something else. What are you drinking?"

Kimi: "White Russians for the Asian and the Cuban. We're going totally international tonight."

Steph: "Me, too. I popped for a Barolo." Steph holds up her wine glass. Kimi and Carmen raise their cocktails and the three cheers. "Where's everyone else?"

Kimi: "Just waiting for Ruby."

Steph: "No The Joy?"

Carmen: "Nope."

Kimi: "Carmen thought she'd rather pass on The Joy tonight."

Carmen: "The bitch slept with my girlfriend. I'm making her pay with a night of missing out."

Steph: "I guess that's fair. And it *will* make her crazy."

Carmen: "That's all I ask for."

Kimi bobs her head in Carmen's direction: "Don't fuck with a Cuban woman. She'll cut a bitch."

Steph: "I'll remember that. Where are you set up?"

Kimi: "On the sofa. Way more comfy than the counter for a hang."

Steph: "And it's a better angle. More flattering."

Kimi: "Yes. Carmen had me raise the computer."

Carmen: "I hate being shot from below."

Steph: "Who doesn't?"

Kimi: "You're five nine. I only ever see you from below." Carmen just smiles.

Steph: "If we learned nothing else from Liz Taylor, it's always be shot from above."

Carmen: "Cheers." Carmen and Steph drink to that.

Kimi: "I swear to Christ, I'll end this right now."

BETTY'S HOUSE

Ladies' night is well underway. Almost everyone's there, Kate, Janey, Franny, Denny, Mindy. The only one missing is Carol. Each woman is dressed in white and pastels. It could be Easter. And Betty's in the center of it all, right where she likes it. The Joy helped her get onto the love seat when she got back from Janey's. The way the room is laid out, the setting sun will give her a lovely sidelight without making her a dark silhouette. The Joy is playing caterer and bartender, but she doesn't mind. She's enjoying the energy in the room. She comes out of the kitchen with a tray that holds seven glasses. "Everyone want punch?"

Franny pipes up. "Punch? I thought we might get something with a bit more kick."

The Joy: "Oh it's kicky."

Franny: "What's in it?"

The Joy: "Never you mind."

Betty: "Joy, don't kill my friends."

Janey: "I'll have one."

Franny: "I'm in. Devil hates a coward."

The rest of the ladies follow suit and take a glass. Mindy, the only one in closed-toe shoes announces, "To our bartender." They all raise their glasses and drink to Joy.

Denny: "Oh my. I feel warm all over."

Franny: "You're such a lightweight."

Denny laughs. "I know."

The Joy's about to disappear back into the kitchen, but Mindy stops her. "No. Don't leave. Come. Sit."

The Joy looks to Betty for the OK. Betty raises an eyebrow. "You might as well hear your future, now."

The Joy happily takes a seat next to Franny. "OK. Tell me my future."

Franny: "It's almost exactly the same as your present. You don't learn from your mistakes. You still adore gossip...er, 'tea.' You're always going to start your diet tomorrow. On the up side, your knees hurt all the time."

Betty: "And you can't wear shorts because the veins on the back of your legs look like you have matching maps of I-95 drawn by a blind drunkard with a blue marker."

The ladies all laugh.

Janey: "And now when I sit, I make a little noise."

They all agree and overlap each other as they acknowledge her.

"You do."

"I've heard that."

"It's like an, 'Ugh.'"

"No, an 'uuuugh.'"

Janey raises her glass to her own failings.

Kate: "Oh, and the second you feel too hot and take off your sweater, you'll get too cold and put it right back on."

Mindy: "Five times."

The Joy looks horrified. "Why?"

Janey: "Menopause, sweetheart."

Kate: "I was a particular fan of waking up in the middle of the night soaked and having to change the bedding."

Franny: "You got up? I just laid there in my shame." More group laughter.

Denny: "It wasn't that bad for me."

Franny: "Oh piss off, Denny."

Betty: "For some reason, our Denny is proud that she breezed through menopause. As if she had a special skill."

The Joy: "I'll pass on all of that." She shudders at the thought of what these ladies are sharing with her.

Mindy: "She's so funny, Betty."

Betty: "Joy, this is life."

Franny: "It's not like I wake up every morning to someone asking me if I want to be twenty-seven or sixty-seven. And I bravely say, 'You know, everyone is picking twenty-seven. I'm gonna zag and try the sixty-seven I've heard so much about it.' I love how young people think they get a choice. Like they're smarter because they chose to be young."

Betty: "I like how you think we all buy that you're sixty-seven, you old bat."

Lots of laughter at that.

Franny: "See? Nothing changes. Just as dumb as I always was."

THE JOY'S APARTMENT

Still on their group call, the trio is in mid-toast. Kimi: "Truer words. Truer words." Suddenly, Ruby's screen pops into the group. She's wearing her usual dark makeup and her black hair is purposefully going in different directions. It's starting to take on an anime look that's similar to Benji's. All of that, combined with sitting in a dark room with one low light angled up at her, creates a sinister effect. "S'up?"

Steph raises her wine glass. "Glad you could join."

Kimi: "Ruby, this is Carmen."

Ruby: "Hey."

Carmen: "Nice to meet you, Ruby."

Steph: "Kimi was just bitching about novels."

Kimi: "No. Not *all* novels. Just the ones that start with..." Kimi switches to an overly sweet voice for effect, "Jessica was perfect in every way. Tall, thin, everyone loved her and she used her parent's immense wealth to travel about at whim. Her only problem was—"

Steph: "She had her picture plastered across the internet, hanging from the ceiling wearing underwear and no mask, with her legs wrapped around some unidentified swarthy man?"

Kimi: "Don't interrupt. I'm on a tear. Where was I? Oh, yeah. Perfect Jessica. Fuck Jessica! You think I give a shit what Jessica's problem is? I don't. I hate her right on page one. You know who I care about? Martha. What if a book started with, 'Martha squoze into her jeans after a night of binge eating. She guzzled the only liquor in her small apartment, which was in random airplane bottles, and got herself ready to face the inevitable parade of greasy-faced dipshits that plagued her at her low-end job, asking her things like, 'How much is 50% off?' How the hell was Martha going to get through it yet again?' Now I care. I fuckin' love Martha. Martha's my peeps."

Ruby tries not to laugh, but does. "Yeah."

Kimi: "See? Ruby's on my side."

Steph: "I'm just saying that people who seem to have it all worked out have problems, too. So much is happening in the world and I'm sitting in my apartment collecting stats on how far spit travels."

Kimi: "The fact that you even think I'm talking about you is part of your problem."

Carmen shifts focus: "Ruby, what do you like to read?"

Ruby thinks for a moment. She's reluctant to say anything that might be judged as not worthy. She doesn't have many girlfriends. Well, any girlfriends. She doesn't want to fuck this up. Messed up as this group seems, she already likes it. Since any answer could be wrong, she finally opts for the truth. "Mmm, sci-fi, graphic novels and historical fiction."

Steph expected the sci-fi and graphic novels, but, "Historical fiction?"

Ruby: "Yeah. Michener. Clavell."

Steph: "I love Michener. God, I never want those books to end."

Ruby: "Yeah."

Steph: "And Clavell, the beginning of *Shogun* was so hard..."

Ruby almost smiles. "The boiling?"

Steph: "Yes!"

Kimi: "Oh, my God. Is this turning into a fucking book club now?" Sarcastically she adds, "Wait, let me get my 'Wine is my favorite meal' t-shirt."

Carmen: "You're so sarcastic, mi amore."

Kimi: "That's part of my charm."

Carmen: "Go ahead. Keep calling it charm."

Steph: "Ruby, what are you drinking?"

Looking at her glass, Ruby says, "Cranberry and soda."

Steph: "You don't drink alcohol, do you?"

Ruby suddenly feels herself becoming not one of the girls. She sticks to short answers: "Nope."

Carmen: "Is it a Muslim thing?"

Ruby: "Yep."

Steph: "So why does Jackson drink?"

Ruby: "You'd have to ask him."

Kimi announces: "New topic." Ruby is relieved for the shift in focus. "I introduced Carmen to the joy of the supermarket line."

Steph gets wistful. "Oh, you said The Joy."

Kimi: "Sorry. The *magic* of the supermarket line."

Carmen: "Dios Mio, those people. They are crazy. And I love them all. So different. But all the same. Yes? Yesterday I saw a man with his mask below his nose trying to explain to the woman in front of him that it was still effective to wear it like that. And she told him that she hoped he doesn't explain to his son how to use a condom. Get it. It's funny. You know, because if you put the condom on wrong it doesn't work."

Kimi kisses Carmen's head. "It was one of the Lemon Ladies. And oh, my God, you're so bad at funny."

Carmen: "What? It's funny."

Kimi: "*It* is. *You*, not so much."

Carmen: "Remind me why I love you?"

Kimi stands up and runs a hand up and down her form. "Because of all this." At that everyone laughs. Even Ruby. She's slowly starting to get in the rhythm.

Carmen: "You are all that and a bag of nori." Everyone laughs again. "See, I'm funny."

Kimi: "Yes you are. Once a week."

Steph: "Hey, did someone say condom? God, I miss sex." Steph sees Ruby look down at that comment. "Sorry, Ruby."

Ruby: "It's OK. I know you had premarital sex."

Needle scratch on the record. Kimi, Carmen and Steph all give Ruby quizzical looks. There's a long pause and Ruby realizes that she just made herself stand out again.

There's a long, awkward silence. Finally, Kimi steps to the plate. "Guess I'll have to field this one. So, no sex yet, Ruby?"

Carmen: "Kimi! That's too personal."

Steph: "Unless Ruby *wants* to share."

Ruby: "It's OK. No. I won't have sex until I'm married."

Kimi: "Sucks for Benji."

Carmen: "Kimi!"

Ruby: "He says he's cool for it. But I think he watches a lot of anime porn." Laughter follows.

SHAD & BENJI'S APARTMENT/BENJI'S LOFT

Benji's watching anime porn. He's on the bed, his tablet on his lap, and the lights down low. He figures it's allowable and not at all cheating. Not that he has anyone to cheat with. But even if he did, he wouldn't. He thinks of his parent's relationship. They're each other's best friends. They'd never cheat. No good person would ever do that. His parents' relationship is his benchmark. He looks back at the anime porn, but the moment is gone. Thinking about his parents killed it.

His phone is lying on the rumpled bedspread. It lights up with a text. Benji sees that it's Jackson. *S'up? You guys doing anything?*

Benji looks at his tablet with the porn still running and texts back. *No.*

Care to hang out?

Sure. I'll grab Shad and shoot you a video link.

Brilliant.

I'm gonna make us a pizza. You should order in.

Shad doesn't know how good he has it. I'll wait for the link.

Benji selects the black t-shirt from the pile at the foot of his bed. The black one is the clear choice because he likes how it looks when he gets flour on it. Like he's been cheffing.

SHAD & BENJI'S APARTMENT

Benji heads down the ladder and finds Shad and Douglas on the sofa. The Bloomberg business news is on the TV. Shad's not watching. Douglas seems to be. Shad's asleep in a work shirt and boxer briefs.

As Benji passes him he says, "Up. Jackson wants to hang."

Shad slowly starts to stir. "What?"

"Jackson called. He wants to hang. I'm making a pizza."

"Another one? Not that I mind."

Benji calls from the kitchen, "Set up a video call and send him the link."

"You think he's lonely?"

Benji just shrugs a shrug that Shad doesn't see. Shad shoots Jackson the link and just that quickly, the buddies are all together.

Jackson is dressed for a night on the town. Fitted shirt, crazy-expensive jeans and a tasteful necklace. His ever-growing hair is looking fabulous.

Shad is taken with the effect: "Damn, brother!"

Jackson: "Look good. Feel good."

Shad calls out to Benji: "Get over here. Check this dude out."

Benji comes in from the kitchen. "I just had to set the oven to get to temp." Standing behind the sofa, he leans in to look at the screen. "Wow. You look handsome." He climbs over the back of the sofa and takes a seat.

Jackson: "I thank you both. So. Good to see you."

Shad: "You too, man."

Benji: "Did you order a pizza?"

Jackson pulls out his cell and starts to work it. "Thanks for the reminder. I was so excited to see you that I already forgot."

Benji: "Well, if it matters, we're having shrimp, bacon and sausage. I'm calling it The Un-Kosher Pie-Pourri."

Shad turns to Benji. "You didn't ask me what I wanted on it."

Benji: "What do you want on it?"

Shad: "That. Oh, shit. Beer. Hold on." Shad scoots to the fridge and returns with two cans and two pint glasses. He pours the frothy, friendly liquid for himself and Benji and raises his glass. "To us." Benji raises his glass. Jackson raises an animal horn mug with some kind of a crest on it. Shad asks, "Dude, what's *that*?"

Jackson: "It's a drinking horn. And that's my family coat of arms. There's a date palm tree, a royal crown, and the monkeys of the mountains are for virility."

Shad: "You live in a different world, my friend."

Jackson just smiles. Benji asks, "Are you up to speed on Mandalorian?"

Jackson: "Of course."

Benji: "So, when Cara Dune fights—"

Shad: "No! I cannot do another *Star Wars* geek-out night."

Benji: "But—"

Shad: "No. Real people. If you can't touch them, they don't count."

Jackson: "Who have you touched lately?"

Shad: "Besides myself?" They all laugh.

Jackson: "I'll drink to that!"

Shad: "To Mr. Left Hand."

Jackson speaks with a Spanish accent: "There is something you should know. I am not left handed."

Benji: "*Princess Bride!*"

Jackson: "To Inigo Montoya!"

All: "You killed my father! Prepare to die!" They all drink.

Jackson: "I miss you guys."

BETTY'S HOUSE

The room now has the backbeat of a Motown soundtrack. The ladies are all a bit further in the bag. Things that wouldn't have been funny an hour ago are now hysterical. They take turns sharing gossip and making fun of people The Joy doesn't know. People who are likely their friends. The Joy sits back and watches the show thinking, Franny was right. Nothing changes. They might as well be her own friends from New York. If her friends from New York wore a shitload more pastel. And there's Betty, in the middle of it, casting her thumbs up or down on their opinions. They all seem to want her approval.

A new song comes on and Mindy jumps to her feet. "Oh, I love this one! Come on, dance with me." She starts moving to the beat. Franny gets up and Kate and Denny follow. Betty starts dancing in place, moving her arms to the beat. Now Mindy's singing and not well. Not that she cares.

Denny: "Come on Joy! Show us how it's done."

Why not? The Joy's about to join the fun, but just then Carol comes into the room with a tray of something chocolate. Loudly, she says "I was ringing the bell, but no one came, so I let myself in." The Joy gets the tray from Carol. "Allow me."

"You're sweet. Those are my white- and milk-chocolate bars. They're really just saltine crackers with butter and chocolate melted over them. So simple." The Joy smiles and takes the tray over to set on the piano with a few other dessert-like offerings.

Carol starts telling the group, "Sorry I'm late. My grandbabies surprised me with a visit and—"

Kate cuts her off. "If you're going to talk, you have to dance."

Carol looks around and awkwardly adds her dated version of dancing to the group. It involves hand rolling and side stepping followed by a 360 spin. It's almost impressive until it becomes clear after about four passes that this is her only move. "I was saying, my grandbabies were here. I got so many hugs. I just loved it."

Franny: "Carol, where did you learn to dance? The University of Sad?"

Carol, not seeing the problem: "What? My brother taught me."

The ladies all laugh. Kate sends an olive branch, "Carol, you're fine. You do you."

The dancing continues until the song ends. The next song is slower and everyone takes a seat again. Carol reaches for a sandwich from a platter on the coffee table. The Joy can see Betty's watchful eye taking it in and silently counting calories for her. As Carol eats she asks, "What have I missed?"

Mindy: "Let's see. We covered what a garbage golfer Janey is."

Janey: "Bitch."

Mindy: "We complained about men."

Kate: "Oh, I forgot to share. Listen to this. Buster comes home from his physical yesterday. I asked what his doctor said about hearing aids. You know what he said? He said the doctor told him he didn't need them. I said, 'How do you know you heard that right?'" That gets a good round of fresh laughter. "Men."

Mindy picks up where she left off. "We also talked about that time we all went to New York."

Carol: "Wasn't that fun. I love musicals. Betty, sing for us. I'll play the piano."

Betty: "No. I couldn't."

All the ladies start egging Betty on. It's an overlap of begging that lasts for some time.

Betty: "OK." A cheer goes up in the group. "But only if my Joy sings with me."

The Joy is stunned at this. She puts up her hands as if to stop oncoming traffic. And now the ladies are insisting more strongly. Kate, who's sitting next to Betty, gets up from the love seat. "Here, Joy. You sit next to Betz." The Joy feels trapped. After another round of drunken urging, she takes her place next to her mother.

Carol goes to the piano and calls out, "What will it be, ladies?"

The Joy looks to her mother for an idea, but Betty already has a plan and plows forward. "'Bosom Buddies' from *Mame*, in F major."

Carol is delighted. She looks up as if the music might be on the ceiling. "Wait. Hold on. Wait."

Franny: "Do we have a choice?"

Carol proclaims, "I got it!" She starts playing the intro. The Joy wonders if she'll remember the words. Betty always loved Broadway show tunes and played them in the house all through The Joy's childhood. That included sing-alongs. What the hell. It's not like there are theatre critics in the room. She looks at Betty. Well, just the one. The music starts.

Betty looks Joy straight in the eye so they start in unison. Together they sing, "We'll always be bosom buddies, friends, sisters and pals..."

The song is filled with backhanded compliments as each declares their devotion to the other. While The Joy's voice is only fair, there's something about the blending of mother and daughter that makes the sound appealing and the connection enviable. Both Betty and The Joy slip into a musical lane they've obviously traveled before. The women witnessing this are aglow and delighted to be part of it. When the song is over, the ladies all leap to their feet and the applause is thunderous. The Joy looks at Betty who seems to approve of the performance. And The Joy has to admit, if only to herself, she enjoyed it too.

The women all shower the duo with praise. "Encore! Encore!"

Betty holds up her hands. "No. No. Always leave them wanting more."

Kate: "Just like you did with that young man in New York?" All the ladies look at Betty.

Denny: "Who?"

Betty: "You don't know anything, Miss Kate."

Kate: "I know that you disappeared with that nice usher after the first act of *Les Miz* and didn't return until Jean Valjean took his final curtain call."

Franny: "Betz, how many curtain calls did *you* take?"

The Joy can't believe she's hearing this, but she's thrilled. "Betty, were you a tramp?" Lots of laughter at that.

Betty: "You're all disgusting."

Mindy leans in, "Throw us a bone Betz. Fess up."

The Joy can see that Betty is starting to enjoy the attention. Perhaps it's the mix of cocktails and pain pills. That's always worked for The Joy. Finally, with a sly smile Betty says, "What happens in New York stays in New York."

Franny: "I knew it!"

Betty: "You don't know anything."

Kate: "Joy, I think we need more punch."

The Joy jumps to her feet. "I live to serve."

Franny calls out to The Joy, "And I think we'll need the recipe for these."

Mindy: "Oh, we definitely need the recipe."

The Joy returns with a large pitcher and starts refilling glasses. "You like it? I just invented it for this very occasion. It's got the holy trinity of juices." They all look at her like they have no idea what she's talking about, because they don't. She further explains very matter-of-factly, "Orange, pineapple and cranberry. Then the holy trinity of rum: white rum, dark rum and spiced rum. Then I float a Hostess Snoball in the middle just for fun."

Franny: "Jesus. What do you call it?"

The Joy: "A Snowball's Chance in Hell." Much laughter.

Kate: "It's genius. Betz, can we keep her?" Betty looks at her daughter and shakes her head. But not in a disapproving way. There's acceptance there.

Mindy: "Yes, Joy. You should stay. There's a bungalow opening up on Beverly Way. Marla Horton died." No one seems upset with this news.

The Joy: "That's so sweet. But I miss my Big Apple people."

Franny: "You mean, you miss sex."

The Joy: "So much!"

Betty: "I don't want to hear this."

Mindy: "We do."

Carol: "Let's not make Betz uncomfortable."

Kate: "No, let's."

Franny: "And it's better than hearing about her sex life. Would you just sleep with Nate already? Unless of course you already did." She winks at Betty.

The Joy is suddenly uncomfortable. She says to herself, "Please change to subject. Please change the subject."

Betty: "I did not."

Franny: "I'm just saying."

Kate: "Betz, go ahead. Get your chimney swept."

Betty: "I don't need my *chimney swept.*"

Franny: "Sure sounds like you do."

The Joy tries to think of a topic away from this fishbowl of a community. "I could see if Vlad has an older brother."

Kate: "What's a Vlad?"

The Joy: "Oh he's my..." she makes air quotes "...*Package Guy.* I like to think of him as my meat delivery system."

Mindy: "Now we're getting to the good stuff."

STEPH'S APARTMENT

Steph is on her sofa with her laptop, feet up and still on the video call. There's a large bowl of popcorn at her feet. She's almost at the bottom of her bottle of wine. "Hurry up. I need more wine."

Carmen and Ruby are still on the call, but Kimi is missing. Kimi calls out from off screen, "Keep your pants on, you wino."

Steph: "Wino? Seriously?"

Kimi jumps into frame wearing an outfit from The Joy's armoire. It's the yellow one-piece with the large orange flowers.

There is no holding back Steph's laughter. "Oh, my God. That's her favorite. I can't believe she didn't take it with her."

Kimi does her best impersonation of The Joy. While she can't get the sound right, the rhythm is spot on. "I have three of these. One never knows. Am I right?"

Steph is now stomping her feet on the sofa with laughter. "Serious, she has three?"

Kimi: "I do. If it's worth doing once, it's worth doing thrice."

Carmen: "You're so bad."

Kimi comes around the sofa and sits on the sofa with Carmen. "Kiss me, baby."

Carmen recoils. "I pass."

Kimi: "What, you're not into tall Anglos?"

Carmen: "I only have eyes for Kimi. Wait. Hold on." Carmen fishes Kimi's red bucket hat out of the sofa and puts it on her own head. She launches into a bizarrely good Kimi impersonation talking to The Joy in Kimi's voice. "Your juju is whack, bitch."

Kimi's a bit stunned. "Wait. You can talk without an accent?"

Steph gets up and quickly goes to the kitchen for her next bottle of wine. She thinks, Am I a wino? She considers that Ruby is enjoying this call with no wine at all. That thought leads her to the wine she enjoyed with Jackson. Jackson. She returns to the sofa with her vice. "So, ladies, tell me, honestly, what makes you two work?"

Carmen and Kimi look at each other. At the same time they each say, "The sex."

Steph: "Seriously."

Kimi: "I seriously know that you're onto your next bottle because you're over using seriously again."

Steph raises her glass and takes a drink. "Guilty. But ser...really, why do you work and Jackson and I don't?"

Kimi: "I see where you're driving this train."

Steph: "Ruby, if this is uncomfortable for you..."

Ruby: "I'm cool. Jackson's always been spoiled. I know he can be a dick."

Steph, nearing drunk-ish: "Yes! Why?! But why is he suddenly a dick, right when I needed him?"

Carmen raises her hand. "I got this. Let me answer this one. It's because you need him. He got scared. When you don't need him it's easy. You upped the ante." She turns to Kimi, "Isn't that right?"

Kimi: "Mommy's little gambler."

Carmen: "Yes. Kimi was a big dick when I needed her. Weren't you?"

Kimi smile and happily says, "Yes, I was."

Carmen: "See? You needing him makes him shut down. He's scared. Such babies."

Steph: "So now what?"

Carmen: "You wait or you move on."

Kimi turns to Carmen. "Thank you for waiting."

Carmen: "I had nothing better. It's COVID time."

Steph: "Ruby, how are you and Benji?"

Ruby: "Fine. I don't need him, I guess. But I like him. He's real, you know. We have fun. I think it's cute how he pretends he can hear."

Steph: "What's that?"

Ruby: "He turned into a cotton swab freak and now he can't hear out of his right ear and he won't go to the doctor because of COVID." She smiles. "Idiot."

Kimi: "Another reason to not date guys. The man-it-out thing."

Ruby perks up. "You won't catch me dating a woman. I've heard you all." Ruby changes her voice to sound like an overly earnest female cartoon character. "Barbie said she didn't need to go out to dinner. What do you think she *really* means? Does she *want* to go out to dinner? Does she *not* want to go, but is she leaving the door open in case *I* want to go? Is she laying a trap?' Or... 'When you said I look "fine," what does "fine" *mean*? Does it mean fine or *fine*? Does it mean, *you'll do* fine? I need to know what you *meeeean*.'" Ruby laughs to herself.

Carmen and Kimi look at each other without saying anything for a moment. Ruby wonders if she went too far. Then, at the same time, they laugh out loud.

Kimi: "Spot on!"

Carmen: "Oh, my God. You are a funny lady."

Kimi: "So good."

Carmen: "But when you say, '*So good*,' what do you *meeeeean*?"

SHAD & BENJI'S APARTMENT

The video call is far from over, but Shad and Benji look full. On the coffee table are plates with pizza remnants, two large, round, empty pizza trays, and a pitcher of beer. Shad pours himself a pint. "Why is beer so much better out of a pitcher?"

Jackson: "It's the feeling of community, my friend."

Benji leans over just far enough to let out a fart. Shad winces at the stink and tries to wave it away from his face: "Aw, geez. Guess I'm still COVID-free!"

Jackson, raising his glass: "Cheers to the canary in the coalmine."

Benji: "How will *you* know if *you* don't have COVID? All you have is Ruby. Girls don't fart."

Jackson: "You think *I* don't fart? Here. This is a song I wrote just for you." Jackson slides from the leather sofa and drops onto the wood floor. His fart is loud and snappy. He takes a big, deep whiff. "Gentlemen, I'm happy to announce, I am disease free." All three laugh and drink to their health.

Shad: "I'm sorry you missed Benji's pizza."

Jackson: "I am, too."

Shad: "My boy's got mad skills."

Benji stands up and takes a bow. "I *am* getting good. I wanna make a pizza as good as Patsy's or Totono. But our oven only gets to 550. Theirs hit 900, easy. They can get your pizza on the table before you finish ordering it."

Jackson: "Methinks you exaggerate."

Benji: "Only by about 63 seconds."

Shad: "I really love Tony's Baltimore Grill in AC. We had that every summer when I was a kid. And the place looks exactly the same today."

Jackson: "That is a good one. Question. New Haven. Pepe's or Sally's?"

Shad: "Ooh, so hard. Depends if I'm tapping the clam pie or not."

Benji giggles. "You said clam and pie."

Shad shakes his head. "You're such an idiot. What does Ruby see in you?"

Benji: "Handsome. Talent. Great hair. Handsome."

Shad: "You said that twice."

Benji: "I'm double handsome."

Jackson knows that Benji doesn't really think he's all that. He's just a nice guy. He's glad that this is the person his sister is seeing. He's glad she's not dating someone like himself. What a player. Well, maybe not a player. Maybe just immature. Then he wonders how he got to a place where Benji is more mature than he is.

Shad snaps his fingers at the computer screen. "Hey. Jackson. Join us."

Jackson: "Sorry, man."

Shad: "Where did you go?"

Jackson: "Can I tell you guys something?"

Benji: "Sure."

Shad: "You bet."

Jackson: "You can't laugh."

Shad: "Then you might want to keep it to yourself." Jackson deflates a bit. "Sorry. Man. Just kidding. Go ahead."

Jackson: "I've been having these dreams."

As if he's a doctor, Shad says, "Yes, Mr. Asghar. Go on." He and Benji chuckle, but Jackson just stares at him. "I'm sorry. I'll stop. But I'm drunk, you know."

Jackson: "That's why I can tell you. Anyway, I'm having these dreams. All different. I'm at an audition or I'm at law school or I'm being interviewed for Ninja Warrior. But every dream ends with people telling me I'm a dick. Or that I'm being a dick. Or yelling, 'Dick!'"

Shad: "And the problem is...?"

Jackson: "That's just it. If I thought these people were calling me a dick, I could live with it. But these are my dreams, so I'm calling myself a dick. Right?"

The three sit for a moment just nodding. Benji thinks about this new puzzle. "Yeah. I think you think you're a dick."

Jackson: "That's what I think."

Shad: "Are you? A dick?"

Jackson: "I might be. I kind of ghosted Steph."

Benji: "Why?"

Jackson: "Great question. I'm not even sure."

Shad: "I don't think you want girlfriend advice from me. Not that I'm not a jackhammer in bed."

Jackson: "Eew."

Shad: "Benji, any advice for our pathetically dicky friend?"

Benji: "Don't be a dick."

Jackson: "Thanks, man. That was sage."

Benji: "I'm being serious. Just be a nice guy. That's the whole trick. And if that doesn't work, it wasn't right in the first place."

Shad looks at Benji. "Jesus, can I date you?" With no warning, he kisses his roommate. Benji's not quite sure what to do with that.

Jackson: "Can it be that easy?"

Benji: "If you want it to be." He looks at Shad and warns, "Stay back."

BETTY'S HOUSE

It's late and things have wound down. Most of the gals have gone home, or at least left Betty's. Franny and The Joy are moving empty plates and glasses into the kitchen. Betty calls out, "I wish I could help."

Franny answers, "You just sit there looking pretty."

The Joy: "She is pretty, isn't she?"

Franny: "And I hate her for it."

As The Joy puts her load of dishes into the sink, something catches her eye outside the window. It's a blinking light followed by a dark figure moving quickly in the dark and disappearing into an open back door. In just above a whisper she says, "There it is again."

Franny: "What?"

The Joy: "The blinking lights."

Franny: "That's the booty blink. A very low-tech system for getting one's end wet, as it were."

The Joy: "I love that!"

Franny: "Yeah. We do some really silly shit when we get older. But it's better than what's on TV."

The Joy smiles and tries to picture herself at seventy, running through the dark for sex. Yeah, that's gonna be fun.

Franny turns to leave the kitchen. "I'm going to do one last lap of the living room before I go." The Joy turns and joins her. They look around but all the evidence of party seems pretty well gone. Franny goes over to Betz and sits on the edge of a chair. "Okay, kiddo. Thanks for a fun night."

Betty: "Thank Joy. She did most of the work."

Over her shoulder, Franny says, "Thank you, Joy." Back to Betty she says, "Now, is there anything you want to tell me before I go?" The Joy gets where Franny is going and starts to panic. Maybe she should throw a plate. Fuck, they're all gone!

Betty: "Don't step in a gopher hole in the dark?"

Franny: "I mean about Nate. You can tell me. Are you sure you two didn't..."

Betty: "No. Why do you keep asking?"

Franny: "Well, I saw..." Franny stops right there. The Joy wonders if Franny just did the math and knows it was her. Franny looks over to The Joy and changes her tone. "Oh, no reason." She looks back at Betty. "You know me. Ever hopeful."

Betty: "Well, I'd appreciate it if you'd focus on your own chimney."

Franny gets up. "Roger that. Thanks again for a great night." She passes The Joy on the way to the front door and gives her arm a good hard pinch. The Joy mutes the pain.

"Goodnight, Franny."

"Goodnight, Joy."

ZOOM FORWARD–OCTOBER ALREADY?

BETTY'S HOUSE/THE JOY'S BEDROOM

The Joy has her eclectic New York clothing folded in a towering pile on the bed next to her new pile of Florida-wear. Her bags are out and open. It's hard to imagine her piles all fitting into the available luggage space, but she assumes that because she wants it to work, it will. The alarm on her Hello Kitty bedside clock sounds and The Joy nearly jumps out of her skin. Zoom call, any minute. She catches her breath and abandons her packing.

Moving as quietly as possible, The Joy heads to the kitchen to fix a drink. She doesn't want Betty to notice her. As she makes her way, she considers how challenging it is to be this big and to try to make yourself small. She's about to fix her libation, but decides to grab a few bottles, a glass and prep her cocktail in her bedroom. Less noise. Less chance of a confrontation.

Back in her small sanctuary, The Joy realizes she forgot the ice. Damn it. No going back. She'll have to slum it. She pours a little of this and a bit of that into her glass. Once she's satisfied, she gets on the bed, pulls the laptop onto her lap and logs onto the video call.

Kimi and Carmen are already there, as are Jackson and Benji and Shad. Kimi immediately gives The Joy some of her own medicine. "Unacceptable. You're seven minutes late."

The Joy: "Ugh. I know. I had to mix my drink in the bedroom and it slowed down the works. No ice. I feel like an animal."

Kimi: "The horror."

Shad: "Well, glad you could tough it out."

The Joy: "Go ahead. Laugh it up. You try equal parts vodka, gin and tequila with no ice."

Jackson, who's wearing a skintight, NYU t-shirt asks, "What do you call that?"

The Joy: "Clear and Present Danger. And without swag. All my cocktail animals are packed."

Benji: "Are you coming home?"

The Joy: "Surprise!"

Kimi: "Wow. Warning would be nice."

The Joy: "Betty's kicking me out. Meant with love."

Shad: "Did she find out about that old man?"

Benji: "Nate."

The Joy looks around in a panic while she shushes them. "Shh! Loose lips! Loose lips! She hasn't said anything. That's how my people roll. Ignore it, pretend you don't care, and it will go away. She's ignored me for weeks and now I'm going away." The Joy considers this. "It's actually a very effective system."

Jackson: "Well, I for one look forward to your return."

The Joy: "Thank you, Jackson. I also think she wants me out of the way before the President comes."

Shad: "President of what?"

The Joy: "The President of the US! The *President* President. He's coming here to golf and Betty is hellbent on meeting him. She's so excited, she's willing herself to walk again. It's like the movie, *The Miracle Worker*."

Kimi: "Wasn't that Helen Keller who was blind and deaf?"

The Joy: "Potato, patahto. It's a fucking miracle. So I'm out."

Kimi: "Well, I was going to save my good news, but I guess I'll share it."

Just then, Steph's screen joins the others. She's looking very business-like in her readers. Without asking anything about anyone else, she flies into her rant. "I know. I'm late. Sorry. I've been researching a political piece. I'm not sharing any details because I know we don't talk politics, but holy shit! You would not believe who said what to whom, and then pretended that they didn't say it, but there's video of them saying it, but they're saying that the video has been altered to make them look like they said it and now, now..."

Shad: "Steph! Steph! Sunshine! Take a breath!"

Benji: "I thought *I* was Sunshine."

Shad: "You're OG Sunshine. Steph is Li'l Sunshine. Kimi was about to share great news."

Steph: "I'm sorry Kimi. I got carried away. It's just that you won't believe...no. Sorry. Kimi, you go. What's your great news?"

Kimi: "Stick Of Butter died."

Shad: "I'm sorry, Steph. Continue."

Kimi: "Fuck you. This is big."

Steph: "Is anyone else lost?"

Benji raises his hand. The Joy raises hers as well adding, "Lost. Yes."

Carmen turns to Kimi: "Oh, my God. Stick Of Butter died? I didn't know he was sick."

Shad: "Who the hell is Stick Of Butter?"

Kimi: "Our neighbor across the hall. Older guy, short. Always in that ratty bathrobe."

The Joy: "Oh no. Ratty Bathrobe Guy died?"

Kimi: "Don't be so sad. Dig this. He was the one who got your hairstylist license revoked."

The Joy: "That bastard!" She thinks for a moment. "See, I knew Karma liked me. She slapped the shit out of Ratty Bathrobe Guy."

Carmen: "I don't think we should be celebrating someone dying,"

Kimi: "No? Well, as they were rolling him out, I got in touch with the landlady and guess who's moving in to Stick Of Butter's apartment?

Jackson: "I'll field this one. You?"

Kimi turns to Carmen. "And Carmen, I hope. Carmen, would you like to move in with me?"

Carmen takes this all in: "Leave Miami? Permanently?"

Kimi: "I was going to ask you in private, but..."

Steph: "Oh, my God, you guys. Seriously. This is so sweet."

Carmen: "It's not that sweet. We *are* engaged."

The Joy makes an angry cat hiss and mimes claws scratching.

Kimi: "Thanks for the help. I got this." She turns to Carmen and then gets down on one knee. She reaches into her bra, pulls out a door key, and holds it up as an offering. "What do you say?"

The gang all leans in, waiting anxiously for Carmen's answer. Carmen is clearly in deep thought. "I have a condition."

Kimi: "Shit."

Carmen: "Not shit. But I want you to tell your parents. If you tell your parents that we're a couple, I'll leave my life in Miami and move in."

The Joy sings: "Whoomp, there it is!"

Kimi throws her head back. Ugh. She knew the time would come when Carmen put her foot down. She just hadn't planned on it being a public event. It's her own fault. She made it public. Damn it!

Benji starts chanting: "Do it. Do it." The others begin joining in. "Do it. Do it. Do it. Do it. Do it."

Kimi: "Argh! Fine! Yes. I will tell my parents." The gang cheers. Carmen kisses her. "You'll all hear the explosion. And then I will be written out of the family bible. Oh, and my picture will go up in the Chinese market with the caption, 'Shīlwàng Del' which, of course means, 'Disappointment.'"

The Joy: "Are you sure it doesn't mean 'drama queen'?"

Carmen: "*Mi amor*. And you're in luck. Sunday is National Coming Out Day."

Kimi: "I *am* a lucky girl!"

Steph: "You'll be great." They all sit for a moment, thinking how not great she's going to be.

Benji: "You know what? I think I'll introduce Ruby to my parents on Sunday."

Shad: "Wow, man. One up top." Shad high fives Benji. Benji looks pleased with himself.

Jackson: "I'm impressed. I don't believe Ruby has ever met anyone's parents before."

Benji: "You always remember your first. Wait. That sounded wrong."

Jackson: "Yes, it did."

Shad: "That's OK, Wingman. You're doing better than the rest of us."

At that, Jackson looks away. Changing the topic, he interjects: "Hey, more good news. Marathon In Place Dot org has three new races scheduled. Two 5ks and a half marathon. People are starting to use the platform to initiate their own races. And better news, we get a cut."

Shad: "Right on." Shad high fives Benji again. "I feel really good about this. We created something of value. Hey, Steph…"

Steph: "Don't even. I have no power at the station. I'm just a research grunt."

Jackson looks at Steph's screen, "I'm still so sorry."

Steph: "You should be. But not for that. That was on me. The rest is on you."

Jackson takes his medicine quietly. After his advice from Benji, he was going to go to Steph and explain himself. But the longer he waited, the more he felt like he'd let too much time go by. And now, so much time has passed, he feels it's too late. He's added regret to his daily to-do list.

The Joy: "This is so Hallmark channel. God, I wish I had popcorn!"

Benji: "Excuse me." Benji gets up and scoots out of frame.

Kimi: "See what you did? You upset the boy."

Benji calls from off screen. "I have to go to the can! I can leave the door open!"

They all yell.

"No."

"Don't!"

"We're good."

"Agh!"

"No!"

Benji, still calling from the can, adds: "I don't want to miss anything!"

Shad: "But we do!"

Benji: "Wait. Almost done!"

Everyone is shaking their heads. Carmen starts snickering.

Benji: "Wait for it. Wait for it!" That's it. Now everyone is laughing. "Just the dismount left!" With that, tears start flowing. Then, they hear a toilet flush. But something's wrong. The flushing sound doesn't finish. "Shit! Shit! Water! Shit!"

Shad flies up and runs out of the picture. The group all lean in and strains to hear the argument happening away from their curious eyes.

Shad: "Dude, what did I tell you? Way too much paper, man. Way too much."

Benji: "I have to wrap my hand."

Shad: "You don't."

Benji: "Well, I can't take it out now."

Shad: "You call the gal this time."

Benji: "She hates me."

Shad: "Damn man, did you eat my burrito? I was saving that."

Benji: "Sorry."

Shad: "Just dial."

The gang is rolling in their seats. Steph can hardly catch her breath. "Oh, my God. I can't breathe."

Shad leans back into frame: "Sorry, guys. We're gonna have to deal with an issue."

Between deep, laughing breaths, Steph gets out: "Want us to order you a new burrito?" She falls to the side, crying.

Shad: "Oh, you heard that?"

Steph sits up again: "I'm so sorry for laughing."

Kimi: "I challenge. I think you're not sorry."

Steph: "Not at all. That's my first big laugh in months. God, I had no idea how much I needed that. Thank you."

Shad: "Glad my toilet could brighten your shitty day."

Still in the bathroom, Benji calls out: "I'm glad too!"

Shad looks over his shoulder and back to the gang. "I gotta go."

The Joy: "Wait. She holds up her glass and they all raise their drinkables. "To my homecoming. Oh, and to our Kimi scoring an apartment. Nice job, neighbor."

Kimi: "Oh, FYI, you'll be cutting our landlady's hair for a year." Right after the words are out of Kimi's mouth, she and Carmen salute and their screen goes black.

The Joy laughs. "Shows her. I'm too drunk to care."

THE BATHROOM CHRONICLES

SHAD & BENJI'S APARTMENT

Shad and Benji are in the bathroom, watching the water. It's at the brim of the bowl, and slowly spinning clockwise. Douglas gets his paws up on the rim, and becomes equally mesmerized by the swirling. Right before the trio gets completely hypnotized, the doorbell rings.

Benji says, "You get it."

"It's your mess."

"Please."

Shad throws his hands up. "You're pathetic." He heads for the front door and calls out. "Yeah?"

A woman's voice responds. "Super."

Shad looks through the peephole and sees the superintendent, distorted by the lens. She's wearing a doo rag, coveralls and tool belt, and is holding a red tool box. Shad opens the door. In she walks like she owns the joint. She's average height and weight and of mixed ethnic origin. She looks to be about thirty. Barely acknowledging

Shad with a nod, she heads right for the bathroom. Shad follows her. Dryly, he says "Welcome back."

"Mmm."

When they get to the bathroom they find Douglas still watching the water swirl. Benji is gone. The super assesses the situation. "You use too much paper."

"It's not me."

"OK."

"No. It's not me."

"It never is." She reaches down, gives Douglas a strong pat and scratches his ears. As she moves him aside she says, "OK, buddy. My turn." She puts down her tool box and starts getting to it. After a moment, she turns back to Shad. "You don't have to watch. I'm not gonna steal anything."

"No, I... I'm just... Watching."

She goes back to work. "Live it up."

Shad shoves his hands in his pockets and tries to make small talk. "How'd you learn about plumbing?"

She doesn't look at him. "Because I'm a woman? How did a woman learn about plumbing?"

"No, I—"

"It's cool. I get it all the time from guys like you."

"Like me?"

"Yeah. Corporate types."

"I'm not a 'type.' "

"No? You don't work for a big company? You don't measure your worth by your salary? You don't look at yourself in the mirror while you workout? You don't do beer and football with the guys and talk about which celebrity you'd sleep with?"

"As a matter of fact, not that last one." He got her with that and she laughs just a bit. "I'm Shad."

"I remember from the last three times."

"Well, I don't know your name."

"You never asked."

"I'm asking."

"So, it's get to know your super day. OK, *Shad*. I'm Esther."

"Nice to meet you."

"Nice to snake your toilet."

"Seriously, how did you get into this?"

"How did I become a super? Easy. I like the free apartment that comes with the gig. My family has a heating and air company. I learned a lot of DIY shit growing up in the shop, so..."

Benji calls in from the other room. "You gonna be a while? I gotta go."

Shad calls back, "Again?" No answer. Shad asks Esther, "How long do you think?"

"One never knows, but about 17 minutes."

Shad calls back, "17 minutes."

Benji comes in, looks at them both, grabs Douglas' litter box and leaves the room without saying a word. Shad and Esther look at each other with eyebrows raised. They're now sharing an inside joke.

THE JOY'S APARTMENT/BATHROOM

Kimi is sitting on the toilet, reading one of Carmen's bridal magazines. She flips past pictures of women in flowing gowns who are holding precisely arranged flowers. One after the other. Perfect. Perfect. Perfect. She thinks, They're selling an impossible dream. No real woman looks like these women. Is this what Carmen expects? So many women talk about their *dream* wedding. Dreams aren't real. And when Kimi dreams, it's never about her wedding. She's still shocked to find herself in a committed relationship. So many unknowns. Then she wonders if Carmen ever thinks about her dream wedding while sitting on the toilet.

JACKSON'S APARTMENT/BATHROOM

Jackson steps out of the massive, white marble shower, drying off his torso with a small hand towel. He was never one to feel the need to immediately wrap a big towel around himself. He never felt vulnerable in that way. In the mirror, Jackson looks at himself. Everything is right where he left it. Pecs, abs, quads. He's in good ninja shape. Is he fooling himself with his ninja quest? No. He's always found a way to get what he wants. He should be on the show. Between being a law student and launching a successful charity for restaurant workers, he now has a good story. One people will want to cheer for. Then he thinks about who would be on the sidelines rooting for him. Lots of Middle Eastern fans. His sisters. His parents. But no wife. No girlfriend. No kids. He thinks about Steph. What is it about her? Answer? Everything. And he blew it when things got hard. Speaking of hard. He drops his towel, which lands on Li'l Jackson. Thinking about Steph does that to him.

STEPH'S APARTMENT/BATHROOM

Steph has assumed the position. Her magazine rack is all travel and expat porn. She's thumbing back through a magazine that contains her favorite article about Croatia. After a lot of research, something she's getting quite good at, Croatia is calling her name. She's even contacted a local news station there about a possible internship until she learns the language. Sun, beach and city. She also likes the proximity to Italy. And who knows? Once Europe opens up again to Americans, she could look into making that move. Italy has always seemed romantic to her, ever since she was a kid. She'd watch Sophia Loren in *Houseboat* with Ida and think about how lovely and sophisticated the olive-skinned beauty seemed. As if on cue, Steph's phone vibrates. It's Ida. She decides to show her mother the small respect of waiting until she leaves the bathroom to call her back.

How in the world will she tell her mother she's leaving the country? Is there a strategy for that much disappointment? Maybe lead with a diversion. But what? "Mom, I just want to tell you: I don't have cancer."

AIRPLANE LAVATORY

The Joy is sitting on the seat with the lid down. On her lap is her cargo-sized, tangerine-colored handbag. She's rifling through it. It's in there somewhere. She keeps rooting through the clutter. Finally, she gets her hands around the small glass vessel and pulls out an airplane-size bottle of Baileys. Treasure. It's her last bottle for the rest of the flight. She'd done her due diligence and learned that the airline was still not selling liquor. Her math told her that three bottles would do it. One bottle every hour on the hour seemed responsible.

As she struggles with the tight cap, she thinks about her last moments with Betty. So cold. At the time she thought if she handed her mother an olive and poured gin over the woman, she'd have a fine martini. And this time, it had been all The Joy's fault. They were doing so well. But Betty sitting there with a copy of *The Scarlet Letter* in her lap made it all clear. The Joy had fallen even further from grace.

Crack! The cap gives way. As The Joy savors her first swallow of the sweet, creamy treat, she thinks, Maybe Franny is equally to blame. There was no need to rat me out. Who does that? Hadn't we become friends? Or maybe she should be happy that Franny is loyal to her mother? After all, they'd been friends for years. The Joy is just an interloper. A gatecrasher. A carpetbagger. Well, she'd been invited. Just, not to have sex with her mother's boyfriend. When will she learn? Maybe never. Look at all those Florida people down there. They don't seem to have learned much. Maybe this is just how humans are. Maybe we never get any better. And if that is the case, why beat yourself up for something inevitable? Isn't it her game? So, it's her rules. And her ruling is she's just being human. Either her logic or the Baileys is making her feel better.

She takes another swig and drains the tiny bottle. Just then, there's a banging on the door. From the other side, she hears a man's voice say, "You've been in there forever."

"I'm taking care of important business."

The strained voice says, "This is important, too."

As The Joy collects her stuff to exit, she finds one more bottle of Baileys. Surprise. She'd forgotten that she'd packed a bonus bottle just in case. She thinks to herself, "See, I can learn." As she exits the bathroom, a massive guy with a stressed look on his wide face squeezes past her. As he closes the door behind him she says, "Keep my seat warm." And waits by the door.

NOW WHAT?

THE JOY'S APARTMENT

Carmen and Kimi are putting things back in The Joy-acceptable order. Which actually means making things look less in order. Carmen is laying scarves over lamps and Kimi is pushing a stack of boxes out of The Joy's bedroom. "Where the hell are we going to hide these?" Carmen just shrugs. "Come on. It was your idea to keep them here."

Kimi lets her mind travel back a month or so. She'd finally stopped squashing Carmen's ideas. But it took a huge blow up. Carmen had unleashed on her. Who knew she was a thrower? But it got Kimi's attention. They'd been eating dinner on the sofa. Kimi was once again complaining about her small profit margins. When Carmen tried to share her thoughts on changing Kimi's business model, she was met with resistance in the form of being scoffed at. Carmen said—or more accurately, yelled—for a solid ten minutes then ended with, "And guess what, I'm smarter than you!" Then she threw her plate. Wow. Talk about right between the eyes. Kimi was OK with Carmen being the pretty one, but if she got to be the smart one, too? But it was clear that Carmen was far from OK with that setup. And rightly so. But it was a huge adjustment for Kimi. She still has to remind herself to respect Carmen's ideas and give them a chance. In fairness, that's not special for Carmen. Kimi doesn't give anyone's ideas a chance. But Carmen is special. So special. And, apparently, smart.

But the truly crazy part was letting Carmen be as smart as she is was a game changer. Kimi was so used to doing things on her own for so long. But now she's not on her own. Carmen had suggested that Kimi stop selling her masks print-on-demand. Instead, she now orders them in bulk. Then, as customers order masks, Kimi ships them herself. It's a classic, old-school business model. The change means that she now clears an extra $4.75 per mask. And the fact that she doesn't have to tough everything out all alone is so huge that it almost made her cry. Almost.

But now, they have boxes of masks and no place to put them. They won't be able to move anything across the hall for at least another week. Something about fumigation. Carmen throws her hands in the air in a but-of-course move. "Got it. We put them behind the sofa, lay scarves over them and top it and add some juju. Like an occasional table."

Kimi thinks for a moment. "Genius." Together, they turn the boxes into temporary furniture. As they continue redecorating, Carmen says, "I was thinking about the wedding."

"Were you now? Beguile me."

"I've been going back and forth on waiting until the pandemic dies down, so we can do something beautiful, and have our friends and family there."

"My family?"

"I'm ignoring that. Or, we could just do it. Just have an officiant and us and do it. What do you think?"

"I thought you wanted the whole fairytale dress and flowers and shit."

"I do, but, I don't know. What do you want?"

Kimi shrugs. "I'm ambivalent."

That's clearly not what Carmen wanted to hear. Without looking at Kimi, she says, "I'm taking a break." Carmen goes to sit in the front window. Since moving in, Carmen's favorite activity is New-York people watching. After a moment, Kimi calls to her. "Want me to join you?"

"I'm ambivalent."

Kimi comes and stands behind her. "Guess I deserved that." They both scan the supermarket line, looking for their regulars. It's a nice day. Sunny and still warm enough that not everyone feels the need for an outer layer. There are a good number of new faces. How can that be, after all these months? But there they are. New people. A trio of young girls just to the right catches their attention. Two Asian and one white, all about thirteen with colorful masks on. The larger Asian girl has on a t-shirt that reads, "I'm with stupid." The white girl is rail thin with a t-shirt that reads, "I'm stupid." The other Asian girl has an unfortunate case of acne and a t-shirt that reads, "Don't f * with stupid." They all speak quickly, enthusiastically and with lots of hand and facial gestures. Large Asian Teen is saying, "I need fresh basil for my savory biscuits. If I don't get fresh basil, it's so not even worth it."

Skinny White Girl: "I know. My mother said the dried basil is the exact same thing. As if."

Acne Asian Girl: "Right?"

Large Asian Girl: "One hundred percent!"

Skinny White Girl: "It's like, she doesn't even get cooking. Like, why not just live on takeout?"

Acne Asian Girl: "Right?"

Large Asian Girl: "Same."

Skinny White Girl: "Last night on Chopped, Alex Guarnaschelli said—"

At the mention of Alex Guarnaschelli, the other two girls squeal as if a hottest teen idol just drove by. Large Asian Girl exclaims, "Oh my God. I love Alex Guarnaschelli!"

Acne Asian Girl: "I totally want to be her!"

Skinny White Girl: "You so could."

Acne Asian Girl: "No!"

Large Asian Girl: "You totally could. You're like the best cook in school."

Acne Asian Girl: "Alex-Guarnaschelli good?"

Large Asian Girl: "One hundred percent!"

Acne Asian Girl: "Oh, my God. I love you guys." At that, they all make the "Ooh!" sound that signifies they believe they'll be friends forever.

Kimi rests her chin on Carmen's head. "I love them."

Still looking at the teens, Carmen says, "One hundred percent."

SHAD & BENJI'S APARTMENT/SHAD'S BEDROOM

Shad's in the team meeting. He's half listening to Max and half thinking how glad he is that these meetings no longer intimidate him. He thinks, Go ahead. Ask me a question. I dare you. I'm ready. With confidence, he feels his core tighten and his posture improve. Max is addressing Original Sandra. Ever since her outburst, Max has treated her with more respect. Quite frankly, she's been treating herself with more respect. Shad's been forced to reevaluate her worth. Perhaps he's not the best judge of character.

"Shad? Shad would you care to join us?"

Shad realizes that Max has been talking to him. "Right here, as always."

"This is your 'As always'? I wouldn't hang my hat on it. I said I'm looking for solid end-of-year charitable deductions for our higher net worth people. Does Marathon In Place have legs or not? See what I did there? Legs? Marathon?"

What Shad sees is that Sandra D. is impressed. "I see it. And yes, we are solidly up and running. See what I did there?"

"I see it. Don't get cocky."

STEPH'S APARTMENT/BEDROOM

Steph's standing nude in front of her bedroom mirror. She's holding the printout of an email from a men's magazine. It's offering her an article and photo spread. She knows that the article is just filler. The pictures are what they want. She also knows it's something she'd never do. Still, does she look good enough to pull it off? She can't imagine what that photo session would be like without thinking about what her parents would say. She grabs her phone from the bureau and calls Ida. Why not?

"Hello, New York. What's wrong?"

"Nothing's wrong. Nothing's new. I'm fine."

"Then to what do I owe the honor?"

Steph continues to look at herself in the mirror as she talks. "I just thought I'd let you know that a gentlemen's magazine—air quotes on 'gentlemen'—wants me to pose for, shall we call them, art photos."

"Nudies!"

"That's another word for it."

"I hope you told them where they can stuff their nudies."

"I haven't said anything. I figured I'd call you first."

There's a long silence. Ida finally says playfully, "You little bitch."

"I had you going."

"Did they really ask?"

"They really did. I'm holding the letter."

"Well, you have a lovely figure."

"Thank you."

"I used to have a lovely figure. Then I had you."

"Thank you, again."

"How are you?"

"Fine. Bored. I hate research. I'm weighing my options."

"What kind of options?"

"Moving."

"Where are you going to move?"

"I don't know. Honestly, I like Europe. Croatia."

"The *jungle!*?"

"Croatia is not a jungle. It's right by Italy. Very metropolitan."

"Don't do that to me."

"Do what to you? It's just a plane ride away. They have a really strong news station and I've talked to—"

"You've talked? You're going to kill your father."

"Talking is not going to kill my father."

Ida calls out to her husband, "Mur, Steph wants to move to the jungle!"

From the distance Steph hears Murry, "She's what? I'm watching a race."

Just then a call from Bill is coming through. "Listen Ma, I have to take this."

"We're not done. You're father is very upset." She calls to Mur again, "Tell your daughter how upset you are."

Flatly Murry can be heard saying, "I'm very upset. My horse got caught at the rail."

Steph rushes, "Love you. Bye." She clicks over to pick up Bill. "Hey, Bill."

Bill is all business. "Here's the deal." Steph knows that no good conversation starts with "Here's the deal," but she says nothing. Bill continues, "I wanted you to know before it hits the news." Now Steph thinks that the prospects for good news just got darker. "Miss Molly died a few hours ago." Wow. Didn't see that coming. "She was home. Her son was with her."

Steph reflexively puts her hand to her throat, "I'm so sorry."

"I'm sure. The station's going to be airing an hour-long special celebrating her life and everything she did for children over the years. Your interview with her was her last on-camera interview." As Bill talks, Steph opens her jewelry box and pulls out the Susan B. Anthony dollar Miss Molly had given her. She feels it, smooth between her fingers. "After a lot of back and forth, Mason and Jim have decided to air your full interview as part of the special. Know this is not a promise of anything in the future. But it is a hell of an opportunity for you."

Steph's head is spinning. How's she supposed to feel about this? She'll be back on the air because a lovely human being died. "Bill, I am so sorry. For all of it."

Breaking from his business tone for a moment, Bill quietly says, "I know." And hangs up.

Steph stands wondering if she could still have a career in the U.S. after all. Then she looks at herself and realizes she took the call with Bill nude. She suddenly feels vulnerable.

SHAD & BENJI'S APARTMENT

Benji pushes his way through the front door. He's wearing a new anime facemask. His arms are full of bags of flour. He heads to the kitchen where Shad is pulling a beer from the fridge. "Think you have enough there?"

Benji drops his haul on the counter. "Pizza."

"Starting your own business?"

Benji puts the flour away as he talks. "Maybe. Mac thinks I'm getting good. But I have to practice. Einstein said, 'Only one who devotes himself to a cause with his whole strength and soul can be a true master. For this reason, mastery demands all of a person.' I think I've discovered a talent. Oh and—" Benji makes air quotes, "Everybody has a talent. It's just a matter of moving around until you've discovered what it is."

"Einstein say that, too?"

"George Lucas."

"Can't fight that. Beer?"

"Sure."

They head to the sofa and put up their feet. Shad takes a long, comfortable swig of his beer. "You can take your mask off."

"Oh. Forgot." Benji drops his mask.

"Hey. I have a question for you."

"I am your faithful wingman. Ask."

"What do you think of Esther?"

"Who's Esther?"

"The super."

"The toilet lady?"

"Don't say that. She's a person."

"I think she doesn't like me."

"This isn't about you."

Benji takes a swallow of beer and looks at Shad. Then he really looks at Shad to the point where Shad looks away. "Aw. You like the toilet lady."

THE JOY'S APARTMENT

Kimi and Carmen are at opposite ends of the sofa, facing each other with their legs stretched out, their feet sole-to-sole. They're each reading a book. Kimi's trying to not look at Carmen. She's dreading this first in-person meeting. Carmen is still holding a grudge about The Joy sleeping with Kimi. And The Joy is, well, The Joy.

The doorbell buzzes. Here it comes. Kimi looks up. Cautiously, she says, "I think that's her."

"Why would she buzz? She has a key."

Kimi gets up and heads to the door. "Because it's her." She hits the buzzer and abruptly says, "What?"

The Joy's voice crackles, "It's me!"

Kimi looks back at Carmen and shrugs as if to say, "See?" She hits the buzzer and opens the door. There she is. The Joy immediately drops her bags and gives Kimi a huge hug. Kimi's arms are pinned to her sides and she struggles for air. Her muffled voice says from inside the bear hug, "Can't breathe."

The Joy just smiles. "I don't care. I missed my little friend." She finally lets go. Kimi inhales, leans forward, and grabs her knees, gasping. "Shit, woman. Now I have to Purell."

The Joy looks over at Carmen who's now on her feet. She bounds to her. "You must be Carmen." With zero warning, The Joy gives Carmen the same bear-hug greeting. "Look at you. I can see why our Kimi fell for you."

Kimi says, "You've seen her a bazillion times on our calls."

The Joy laughs, "Bazillion. As if." She finally releases Carmen, who staggers just a bit. Carmen had decided to be cold to The Joy, but is now finding it hard to execute her plan. She's just too utterly different and too big a force to be held to the same rules as everyone else. The Joy spins with her arms out. "I can't believe how happy I am to be home." She stops spinning and looks at her roommates. "Uh, oh, I brought presents." As she goes to her bright, oversized bag, she gives Kimi the first instruction of her return. "Go make drinks for us all. I'm actually surprised you didn't have cocktails ready."

"I did. We drank them."

"Scoot. Make more." Kimi looks over at Carmen, then does as she's told. The Joy sits with her bag and reaches in. "Now Kimi, I stole something from Betty that has your name all over it."

Kimi says, "I'm truly scared."

"Hurry up and come sit with me." Kimi pours three glasses of wine, puts them on a tray and brings them to the sofa for The Joy and Carmen. The Joy takes her glass, a bit disappointed. "Wine? How Steph of you. I was hoping for something with a bit more flair. Fear not." The Joy rummages, pulls out her pouch of cocktail flair and places a plastic dolphin on the rim of her glass. "Flipper is new to the collection. Now, your gift." The Joy's reaches back into the big tangerine bag of possibilities and pulls out something silver. "Ta-dah!"

Kimi looks to Carmen for help, clearly not know what this object is. Again The Joy says, "Ta-dah!"

Kimi: "I'm gonna need help here."

Carmen: "Dios mio. It's a Shake Weight!"

The Joy: "Yes!"

Kimi: "I'm gonna need more help than that."

Carmen reaches for the item, "May I?"

The Joy: "Please, be my guest."

Carmen stands, takes the weight, flips a switch and with two hands, holds out the now vibrating hand weight, moving it all around, almost in a dance. "A Shake Weight. See, it's for working out. It shakes away the pounds, tightens and tones."

Kimi is shaking her head at the sight of Carmen delighting in this ridiculous thing. "A, why do you know this?" She then turns to The Joy. "And B, why is this perfect for me? You may answer in any order."

Carmen is having way too much fun. "How do you not know about this?"

The Joy explains, "It's perfect for you because it's little and you're little, are you not? Plus, I stole it and you're so nefarious. I can't believe I have to explain this."

Kimi acquiesces, "I don't know how I missed it."

The Joy reached back in her bag. "And you, little missy."

Excited at the prospect, Carmen sits down. "Am I little missy?"

The Joy produces a plastic bag and hands it to her. Carmen takes the bag and pulls out an object wrapped in a paper towel.

Kimi: "Is this going to be illegal?"

The Joy: "Not everywhere."

From the paper towel Carmen produces a cigar. The Joy claps, "It's Cuban! Get it?"

Carmen: "It's used."

The Joy: "Only a little."

Carmen smiles politely. "I thank you for this very thoughtful gift."

The Joy is pleased. She stands abruptly with her glass. "Now, I need you to leave me alone. I have things." And with that, The Joy grabs her bags and heads to the bedroom that's been returned to her aesthetic.

Carmen looks at Kimi who shrugs and says, "And now you know."

"I think I love her."

THE JOY'S APARTMENT/BEDROOM

With her wine glass in hand, The Joy looks around at her private sanctuary. It seems that it's been completely returned to its former glory. God, she loves this room. Wait, what's that? Who would put the Miss Manners book behind *The Joy of Sex*? Manners first. With one hand, she makes the correction. Now all is right with the world.

She takes a seat in her stylist chair. After settling in, she pulls out her phone. Yes, she knows she should do this. Feeling evolved, she texts Betty, *I made it home OK*. She thinks, Look at me, being a good daughter. Well, good-ish. She continues enjoying the feeling of being back in a space she controls. No walking on eggshells. No pretending. She feels a text. It's Betty. *Good for you. I have COVID.*

SHUFFLING THE DECK

JACKSON'S APARTMENT

Jackson's in the den doing class work on his laptop. His long hair is neatly pulled back in a Viking style. No man bun for him. As he sits back for a moment, he reflects. His courses aren't all that easy, but he's enjoying the challenge and feels that this is something else he'll be good at. It's fulfilling and with Marathon In Place getting new funding from Shad's clients, he knows he'll be able to put his degree to good use. It's all falling into place. Well, not all. Not his love life. He tells himself that he's ready to move on, but lockdown makes that all but impossible. He considers his parents. Did his father ever waver? Did things ever get tough? He fears his behavior with Steph was quite unflattering. He'll be better next time.

The door buzzer sounds. Lunch. He gets up and crosses the apartment. No sign of Ruby, not that he expected it. Jackson hits the buzzer, opens the door and waits. The elevator opens. Jeffery, the day man, comes out with a large brown paper bag. The smell of Indian food fills the entry hall. "Here you go, sir."

Jackson takes the bag. "Jeffery, I like you even more." He reaches into his back pocket for a tip.

Jeffery holds up his hands, "You don't have to tip me every time, sir."

"We're friends. You don't have to call me, sir."

"Habit."

Jackson hands him the tip. "Same." Jackson thinks for a moment. "We are friends, yes?"

"Yes, sir...Jackson. We're friends."

"May I ask you a question?"

"I can't promise an answer, but you can surely ask."

"I like that. OK. Have you ever, let's say, stepped back from a relationship when things got...challenging?"

"You mean Miss Stephanie."

"I do."

"I'll tell you what my father told me." Jeffery pauses. Jackson readies himself for some strong and sage advice. The wisdom of someone's father. This will be helpful. Jeffery continues, "He told me, 'Son, nobody's perfect.'"

Jackson stares at his doorman blankly. "That's it?"

"That's it. That's all I've got."

Jackson half smiles. "Thank you, Jeffery." Jeffery shrugs and gets back in the elevator. Jackson carries his bag into the kitchen to pull out the containers and grab utensils. As he looks at his chicken tikka, he thinks about Jeffery's offering. Nobody's perfect. Does that mean that he shouldn't expect a woman to be perfect? Or does it mean that he can't expect himself to be perfect? Or both? And does not expecting perfection, and actually expecting imperfection, make everyone forgivable? Could it all be that simple? Is Jeffery's father's advice truly genius? He suddenly knows what to do.

THE JOY'S APARTMENT/BATHROOM

The Joy is in the shower, letting warm water run over her as she thinks about Betty having COVID. They had a rather curt phone call after the text. Her mother said that she's not experiencing any symptoms. Nothing. Not even a cough. Just a positive test, so no big deal. The Joy had told Betty to lay low, just in case, and not to try and meet the President. But Betty said, "Why do you need to make such a grand deal out of everything?" She'd gotten an earful about being a drama queen. The Joy thinks about how Betty and her friends all act like there's no pandemic because they just don't want there to be one. Wish and it will be so. And here she is in the shower, wishing to wash off any possibility that she got infected too. Maybe she is a little bit like her mother. She'd snuck out last night to get tested. She'll have to avoid Kimi and Carmen until she gets the results. Just then the water flashes to boiling hot and she's forced to cling onto the far wall to avoid being scalded. God, she missed New York and its quirks.

SHAD & BENJI'S APARTMENT/BATHROOM

Shad's on the can looking at his phone. Douglas is sitting in his box looking up at him as he texts with Christopher. *So good here.*

Better here. Sure you don't wanna rethink?

Got my eye on something here.

Something or someone?

Shad thinks about how much he wants to share. There's really nothing to say. Yet. *We'll see.*

Give me something.

Shad considers this. What's something to share about Esther? Got it. *Smart.*

Oh, shit!

???

You lead with smart. Danger. Means you're in deep like.

Shad can't deny that he likes Esther. There's something about her. Yes, he's physically attracted to her, but she's not classically good looking. Her eyes are a bit too close-set. But are they? And she's strong. And smart. He likes that she can both dish it out and take it. Yet, he's not prepared to tell his A-type friend that he has a thing for a janitor. Damn. He just called her a janitor. Shad thinks, I'm such a snob.

Christopher texts back. *Where'd you go? You on the can?*

Shad smiles. *Wait. Let me flush.*

SHAD & BENJI'S APARTMENT/BENJI'S LOFT

Benji's crosslegged on his bed with his computer. He's wearing a black t-shirt with a graphic of Baby Yoda. He's on a video chat with his parents, Mike and Dayna. They're on a beige sofa in a beige, suburban living room. They're both in t-shirts and jeans and look like they've been doing chores.

Mike: "I'm telling you Benj, you won't recognize the garage."

Dayna: "It really looks like a gym."

Mike: "We have a bench and weights and a plyo box."

Dayna: "And ropes."

Mike: "It's pretty great."

Dayna looks at her husband and leans on him. "It is pretty great. Nice job."

Mike: "Couldn't have done it without you."

Dayna: "I know."

Mike: "So, Benj, what did you want to tell us?"

Benji gets a smile on his face that he can barely control. "Actually, I want you to meet someone."

Mike: "When?"

Benji: "Now. Hold on." Benji adds another member to the video chat. And there's Ruby, in a graphic Mandalorian t-shirt with dark eye makeup. Even with her headscarf on, Benji and Ruby look like two halves of a whole. Ruby is clearly the darker half.

"Mom, Dad, this is Ruby."

Mike and Dayna look at each other. They're clearly surprised to have this person thrust upon them. But they do their best to be diplomats and roll with the incongruities that come with their son.

Dayna: "Ruby, lovely to meet you."

Ruby just nods.

Benji notices nothing wrong. He's not uncomfortable in any way. "Ruby's my friend Jackson's sister."

Mike: "Oh. Hey. We know Jackson. Nice young man."

Ruby: "He's OK."

Benji: "Ruby and I have been seeing each other since Jackson's birthday. I told you about his birthday."

Mike: "I don't think so, buddy."

Benji: "Anyway. That's where we met."

Dayna: "Ruby, what do you do?"

Ruby: "Photography."

Dayna: "Oh, that's fantastic. What do you shoot?"

Ruby: "People. Out on the street."

Dayna: "Like Walker Evans or Diane Arbus?"

Ruby: "Diane Arbus? I wish."

Dayna: "Wasn't she wonderful? Such humanity."

With that, Ruby and Dayna take off on a conversation about women in photography, marginalized people and acceptance. Benji smiles and looks at his father. Mike smiles back. Father and son know that this is working. Isn't it great?

THE JOY'S APARTMENT

Carmen pulls the sheets and blanket off the sofa, folds them neatly and puts them on the chair by the back window. It's sprinkling outside. She sees Kimi on the fire escape in a rain poncho and winks at her. Kimi does a tight-lipped smile and nods to her. Today's the day. Big happenings. Carmen knows that it's best to leave Kimi be now. But she's antsy, too. She decides to go to the front window and check on the supermarket line.

Taking her spot in the window, she surveys the crowd. The inclement weather hasn't stopped people from waiting too long for things they may or may not need. There's something about the smell of rain that Carmen finds calming. She wonders if the weather will cause her hair to frizz. She wants to look fabulous when Kimi tells her that she's talked to her parents. Carmen knows that she has to be prepared for any response and looking good will help either way. It always does.

There's bitching from the people in line. The entire line seems to be disgruntled. A guy is walking past carrying a huge golf umbrella and forcing everyone in line to move over. And who's most put out? It's the Lemon Ladies. Carmen readies herself for the show.

Lemon Lady #1: "Are you serious with that thing? Why don't you just swing a sword while you walk? You're imposing on the entire sidewalk."

Lemon Lady #2: "Seriously!"

Umbrella Man: "It's a free country, lady."

Lemon Lady #1: "Well you're taking up too damn much of it."

Umbrella Man: "For Crissakes. It's just a golf umbrella."

Lemon Lady #1: "Oh, I'm sorry, Tiger. I didn't realize we were standing on the 9th green. Please, play through."

Lemon Lady #2: "Yes, please. Oh and, Mr. Woods, it's breaking to the left."

In turning to leave, Umbrella Man almost hits an older man with a cane, in the eye.

The old man puts his hands up, "Hey! Hey!"

This only increases the Lemon Ladies' anger. Lemon Lady #1 yells, "Hey, dickless. You're gonna blind someone!" She turns to the older man. "Are you ok?"

Nicely, Older Man says to her, "I'll be fine." He then turns to Umbrella Man and starts beating the golf umbrella with his cane. "Putz! Putz!" The supermarket line applauds the old man's actions.

In the window, Carmen laughs and claps. Umbrella Man is beaten, literally. He grumbles as he continues down the sidewalk to even louder applause.

The Old Man looks at Carmen and gives her a thumbs up. "I was going to call him a schmuck, but with all the golf talk, I felt that putz was funnier." She smiles at him. "I agree. Much funnier." She looks at the Lemon Ladies. "Nice to see you, ladies."

Lemon Lady #2: "Hey."

Lemon Lady #1: "Where's your friend?"

Proudly Carmen says, "Oh, just telling her parents that she's an engaged lesbian."

Lemon Lady #2: "No shit! Congratulations, I hope."

Carmen: "I hope so, too."

With a smile, Lemon Lady #1 teases, "You know, it's not too late."

Lemon Lady #2 says to her friend, "You're so bad."

Carmen: "It's OK. I like the bad boys."

Lemon Lady #1: "You're way too nice for her."

Carmen: "She knows."

Lemon Lady #1 holds up a fingers-crossed sign to Carmen. Carmen smiles, taking the support from these strangers who've become an odd part of her world. Then she thinks, How's my hair?

THE JOY'S APARTMENT/FIRE ESCAPE

No one in the fire escape community is out. No real surprise, with the wet weather. But Kimi was hoping for the support of some of her courtyard buddies. Maybe it's better this way. She won't feel like she's being watched. She hits speed dial and waits. After four rings, Milli picks up. "Did you talk to them?"

"You were supposed to say, 'What?!'"

"So, you haven't talked to them."

"I called you first."

"Don't be a pussy. Rip the Band-Aid. I love you." With that, Milli hangs up. Shit. Tough-love was not the pep talk Kimi was looking for. But she has to admit, it was tough love. Rip the Band-Aid. Rip the Band-Aid. Before she can talk herself out of it, Kimi hits the speed dial for her mother's phone and holds her breath.

Mrs. Chu answers her cell the way she always does, as if caller I.D. was never invented. "Hello?"

"Hey, Mom. It's Kimi."

"Kimi. I was talking to your father about you." Mrs. Chu never lost her Chinese accent, but she speaks slowly and overenunciates to make up for it.

"Really."

"Well, I can't talk *to* you, because you never call like you should. But I can talk about you. Quick, put me on video. I forgot what you look like."

"How? Did you throw out my picture?"

"My paper children never talk back. Put me on video."

Kimi doesn't argue. Once her mother starts the sob story of how she only has pictures of her kids, a.k.a. paper children, there's no winning. She hits the video icon on the phone. There's her mother. Same as always. A little woman, bundled in lots of layers but very neat.

"There you are. Outside. Why you always outside?"

"Privacy."

"Oh, that crazy Joy roommate. You need to move out. We did not raise you to live in a corner. What am I supposed to tell Mrs. Wang? Her daughter is married and my daughter lives in a corner."

"Well, I have some news in that direction."

"What direction?"

"I'm moving out of the corner. I got an apartment."

"You have no job. You can't afford a New York apartment."

"As it turns out, I can. I'm selling more masks and I evolved my business model, so I have more profit."

Mrs. Chu pauses. Thoughtfully she says, "More profit is good. How did you find this apartment?"

"A neighbor died."

"That lucky."

"Well, not for him." Just then Mrs. Chu looks behind her. She speaks over her shoulder. "Come. Come. Our Kimi is on the phone. She's making money now." Mr. Chu walks up behind his wife, leans in and waves to Kimi. He points to his face. He's wearing one of her masks.

Excitedly, Mrs. Chu says, "Your father wears your mask to take out trash, go to post office, the market. I think maybe people see him and word gets out."

Kimi is surprised and tickled. "I think you're right. I think he made me a success. Pop, let me see which mask you got. What does it say?"

Mr. Chu takes off his mask and holds it up to the phone. It reads, "That's not a banana in my pocket." Kimi laughs.

Mrs. Chu adds, "I pick that for him. Your father loves bananas."

Kimi smiles. "It's perfect."

Mrs. Chu tells her husband, "Our Kimi is getting her own New York apartment."

"Not totally my own. I'm going to be living with someone."

Mrs. Chu's face drops. "No. No more crazy roommates."

"Carmen's not crazy."

"Carmen? What is that? Is that Mexico?"

"No. Cuba. Actually, she's American. Her parents are Cuban."

Mrs. Chu shakes her head. "You see. If you would just get married, you wouldn't have to live like a street person."

Kimi's not quite sure how she got to street person. But she feels like they're at the precipice. She either jumps now or she's the pussy Milli said she was. Rip the Band-Aid. No! She says, "Well, it was good to see you both."

Her mother looks put out. "You are done with us?"

Kimi feels like a complete failure. She thinks, Am I not a tough bitch? No. I am not. I'm scared. I'm afraid of a little woman under a pile of sweaters. How crazy is this? Why does this woman hold so much power over her?

Mrs. Chu says, "Was that the news? Milli said you have something very important and I should be patient. Not like always."

Kimi can't believe that Milli ratted her out. But she still left the hard part for her. What a traitor.

"OK. I'm patient. Tell me now."

"Tell me now is not being patient."

"Hey, I gotta do me."

Her mother's modern phrasing catches Kimi off guard. OK. Fine. I'll do me. She blurts, "I am getting married."

Mrs. Chu looks at her husband with excitement and surprise. Back to Kimi she says, "Who is he? Is he Chinese? What does he do? Do we know his parents? What is his name?"

Kimi says, "His name is Carmen. And he's a she." She wonders how long that lead balloon will hang in the air. But there's no turning back. A minute of the Chus looking quizzically at each other seems like hours. Kimi feels dizzy. Finally, Mrs. Chu says, "Your father doesn't understand."

"I think he does."

"Are you telling us that you want to marry a lady?"

"I'm telling you that I *am* marrying a lady. A very nice lady who loves me. And I love her. And I hope you will like her."

Mrs Chu starts shaking her head. She's clearly getting upset. "No, no, no. That can't be. That is not right. What will I tell…"

"Mrs. Wong? Tell her your daughter is marrying a dentist."

"I will not lie for you, Kimi."

"I'm not asking you to. Carmen *is* a dentist."

"How can that be possible?"

"They let women be dentists, you know. She's very good."

"But she is, a…lesbian?"

"Yeah. They let them be dentists, too."

"But how? She a donut banger."

Kimi wasn't expecting this to go well, but with that, she's about to lose it. Mr. Chu puts his hands on his wife's shoulders in a way that stops her from talking. He looks at Kimi, "Is she good-hearted person, Kimi?" Her father's accent is quite thick. He does nothing to make it better.

Kimi tries to calm herself. "Yeah Pop, she is."

He asks, "Does she honor her parents?"

"She does."

"Your mother and I would like very much to meet this Carmen." Mrs Chu turns to her husband about to object. But he looks deep into his wife's eyes and without losing eye contact says, "Your mother and I would like to meet the person in love with our Kimi."

At that monumental show of support from her father, Kimi can only swallow hard. After another long patch of silence, Mrs. Chu asks, "How much does she charge for a filling?"

THE JOY'S APARTMENT

The door buzzer sounds in the empty living room. Nothing. After a moment, it buzzes again. Finally, The Joy glides out of the bedroom in a black cat suit and a turquoise chiffon robe. She's in the middle of texting the gang their assignment for their next video cocktail call. Done. As she heads to the door she calls out, "No, don't bother yourselves. I'll get it." She hits the intercom. It replies, "Package guy!" Could it be? She buzzes him in, opens the door and leans on the door frame in her most come-hither pose. It's Vlad. He bounds towards her with a smile that his facemask can't contain.

She smirks, "There you are."

"Here I are. And there you are."

"Here I am." She looks at his pants. "I see you have a package for me."

He's rocking up and down on his toes. "Oh, I have a package. You'll have to sign for it."

"I keep my ballpoint in the bedroom."

"Prove it."

They disappear into the bedroom. After a short moment, things in the bedroom get loud. Then louder. Kimi leans in from the fire escape window as Carmen walks back from the front window. They look at each other with raised eyebrows. The sounds of sex in the next room cause the two of them to start snickering like they were back in high school and someone just showed dirty pictures. Carmen walks over to Kimi as they continue laughing. Kimi climbs back in from the fire escape and they embrace. They look into each other's eyes and have a strangely touching moment against the backdrop of someone else's intimacy. They're about to kiss when they hear Vlad call out, "Fred! Fred! Let the cat watch! Let him watch! Watch cat, watch!"

STEPH'S APARTMENT

Steph brings a cutting board with cheese and grapes over to the coffee table. A bottle of wine and a glass are already out and ready. She's in her best silk pajamas and has on a simple silver chain. She sits and puts her bare feet up on the coffee table. Her DIY pedicure is perfect. Where's the remote? She's about to turn on the TV, but decides to flip her hair first. She knows it's crazy, yet she wants to look her best for perhaps her last moment in the spotlight. A private moment. Steph chose to not tell her friends about the special. She didn't even give Ida and Mur a heads up. She wanted to keep this moment small. She laughs at the thought of keeping a national TV special small, but here, alone in her apartment, this is just for her.

The TV is already set on her channel and the intro for the special on Miss Molly has just started. She watches a montage of Molly over the years. Steph has to admit that Molly had been quite attractive as a young woman. She could have been a model.

Jim is now on screen introing the special. Steph hadn't realized he'd be anchoring this. He claims that he only does "real news." He'd usually consider this a feel-good piece and beneath him. But there he is. He calls Miss Molly a national treasure and talks about her beginnings in public television. There are several clips of her from the early years. After more clips from her children's show on their network, Jim talks about some of Miss Molly's lesser known charitable work. Steph had no idea how much this woman gave of herself. Most people never knew. It seems that that's how Miss Molly preferred it. Charity for charity's sake. She used her spotlight to lift up others.

Jim says, "Up next, we'll share Miss Molly's last interview. We hope you'll stick around."

And, cut to commercial. Someone is trying to sell insurance with an ad that feels like an excuse for a comedy sketch. Is it funny? Maybe it was the first time. After it ends, Steph wonders who it was for. She already can't remember. Then she wonders how she can be thinking about that and not how her segment will come off. She's never seen all of the footage from the interview. Yet, she doesn't feel nervous. She's more curious. It's as if feeling like her career is already over, the pressure is off. She did note that Jim didn't use her name when teeing up the segment. They've distanced themselves from her. Fine. She takes a sip of wine. Yes. She definitely enjoys a nice Barbera, but popping for the Barolo was the right choice.

Jim returns. "Welcome back to our special tribute to Miss Molly. Up next, we share Miss Molly's last interview, shot just a few months ago." And there she is. Steph sees herself and Miss Molly walking around the grounds of a large, lush property in North Jersey. Steph asks a few background questions, and they start by talking about what Molly wanted to be as a child. A vet. She'd always loved animals but couldn't have a pet because her older brother was allergic to everything. They talk about her career path, which surprisingly included an undergrad degree in math and a law degree. Oh, and by the way, she has her pilot's license, just because. Miss Molly was an onion with more layers than most.

The special then cuts to Steph and Molly in her library. It's a warm room with floor-to-ceiling books, a fireplace and rich leather furniture. On every table, there are framed drawings from children. Molly sees that a drawing in all black crayon catches Steph's eye. Molly picks it up. "It's interesting, isn't it? What do you think this says about the eight-year-old artist?"

"All black. Maybe the child was sad? Depressed?"

"That's what his parents thought. His drawings were always all black. But they were afraid to ask him about it. When the child offered this to me, I asked him why he chose to draw in all black. He explained to me that he sits in the back of the class. When it's time for art, by the time he gets to the front of the room to select a crayon, the black one is the only one that's left." Molly smiles at the drawing. "We can never be afraid to ask questions."

Molly explains that she got into children's television purely by accident. She and her husband were never able to have children of their own. But they had close friends whose kids were always over. One night after watching Molly explain a dodecahedron to their ten-year-old, their friend said he'd like to screen test her for a show he was working on. That was it. She was a television personality. Molly laughs at the thought of it. "No one can truly plan for this life. It's too unpredictable. We just have to roll with the surprises and savor what's sweetest. And, of course, happy is a choice. And I choose happy." Steph politely nods her head.

Molly looks at Steph quizzically. "You think I'm being too simple."

"No. No. It's sweet."

"But simple." Steph doesn't respond quickly enough. Molly says, "May I ask *you* something?"

"Of course."

"You're a career women with objectives and a plan."

Steph smiles, "That's not a question."

Molly smiles back. "True. Here's the question. What does happy look like to you?" Steph is about to answer, but Molly stops her. "Now, I want you to really think about it. Not just notches on a career belt. What does real happiness look like to you?"

After a thoughtful pause, a small smile grows on Steph's face. She shrugs. "I guess happy looks like my parents. Happy is loving and being loved."

"That sounds good to me."

A split second later, Steph gets a text message. She looks down. It's from Janis: *You suck so much!*

ZOOM POP!

THE JOY'S APARTMENT

The Joy is excited to be in the kitchen preparing cocktails for herself and her roommates. Along with a grayish brown duster coat she dug out of the back of her armoire, she's sporting her new hair extensions. They're dark blond dreadlocks that are currently half piled onto the top of her head. She would have never done this at Betty's. She thinks, Freedom is mine. Once the drinks are as ready as they can be, she adds tiny umbrellas, pockets a packet of something, and lines the glasses on the kitchen counter. The Joy calls out, "Ladies, we're ready for action."

Kimi throws open the curtain in front of her La-Z-Boy. Since The Joy got back, Kimi'd taken to getting her business done back in her corner. It's the only place that neither Carmen nor The Joy ever go, so until she can move across the hall, it's her office. She heads to the counter to retrieve her drink, then goes to the sofa, sits and puts her feet up. Carmen comes out of the bathroom and does the same.

The Joy watches, "What are you doing?"

Kimi cracks, "Feels like sitting." Kimi stands up and sits again. "Yeah. I'm going with sitting for six hundred, Alex."

The Joy throws her hands up. "You're supposed to sit over here. This is where we do our call."

"Life marches on. We do the calls over here now." She looks at Carmen, "Don't we?"

Carmen takes a drink and shakes her head. Kimi says, "Cuba is ambivalent."

The Joy objects. "Mutiny!"

Kimi pats the sofa next to her. "Come on, Bligh. Give it a go."

Reluctantly, The Joy grabs her drink and her laptop and joins them on the sofa. Carmen picks up the computer and props it on top of a stack of her magazines. "We all look better shot from above." The Joy looks at herself in the computer frame. "My God, you're right! Look how good I look. I mean, you're both fine too." After she's done admiring herself, she hits the keys to launch the call and assumes a raised-cocktail pose. Carmen is delighted. It's like The Joy is her new toy.

And there they all are. Well, most of them. All but Steph. Jackson now has a full beard to go with his long hair. There are lots of 'Hellos' and 'Welcome backs.' Even though The Joy is no more physically in the room with the rest of them than she was before, everyone is excited that she's returned to them.

Kimi lifts her glass. "Let's drink a toast to our little The Joy. New York sucked more without you." Everyone raises their glasses, but The Joy abruptly calls out, "No!"

Kimi: "New York sucked less without you?"

The Joy: "No. More, I'm sure. But I have a little cocktail jazz hands for my roomies, who I hope will leave soon." From her pocket, she pulls out a small packet, rips it open and pours a bit of pink, chunky powder into their three drinks. Immediately, the drinks start fizzing. The Joy declares, "Now! Cheers."

Carmen: "This is so fun." She's takes a drink while Kimi looks at her own fizzing glass with concern. Carmen nudges her. "Drink. Don't be a pussy."

Kimi looks at The Joy. "I blame you." She and The Joy take a drink as their friends watch.

Shad: "Inquiring minds. What was that?"

Kimi: "I wanna say, Pop Rocks?"

The Joy puts down her glass and claps. "Very good. Strawberry Pop Rocks. To make the occasion more festive. The rest is mostly a regular ol' Manhattan. I thought, you know, Bourbon sweet. Pop Rocks sweet. It's kind of a no brainer."

Kimi: "So many things I'm not saying."

Jackson: "It's delightful, as are you."

Benji: "I like your hair."

The Joy touches her head. "Oh, wait. You have to see the whole thing." She stands up and shows off her leather duster. "I'm calling the look, 'urban-western.'"

Benji lifts up Douglas. "Cool. Douglas approves."

Steph's screen pops on. She starts right in. "Sorry. Sorry. I know I'm late. I had a meeting to wrap up and—"

The Joy: "Wow, little doggy! Back of the line. We're talking about my new look.

Steph: "So very sorry."

The Joy takes a seat. "Where was I?"

Carmen: "Urban-Western."

The Joy: "Yes." Everyone waits for her to add to her thought, but she doesn't say anything else.

Shad: "And...?"

The Joy: "Oh. That was it."

Shad: "OK then. New topic. Steph, we saw your Miss Molly special. Nice work."

Steph: "Thanks."

Shad: "Why didn't you tell us?"

Steph: "I... I just thought I'd keep this one to myself."

Kimi: "Yourself and the country."

Steph: "Yes. Just us two."

Benji: "I really liked it."

Steph: "Thanks. So did a lot of people. The station's been getting a ton of positive feedback."

Jackson: "You deserve it."

They all pause, each wondering what will happen between Jackson and Steph.

Steph, politely: "Thanks, Jackson."

Kimi cuts the tension. "Christ, woman. You're like a cat with a billion lives."

Steph: "At least two. OK. OK. Enough about me. Someone else must have something worth making someone uncomfortable about."

Carmen holds up her hand. "May I go?"

Jackson: "You have the floor."

Still looking at the computer, Carmen gives Kimi a hug. "You'll never guess what this one did this week."

The Joy: "Should we?"

Carmen: "Should you what?"

The Joy: "Guess. Should we guess?"

Carmen: "No guessing. Just telling. Miss Kimi told her parents that she's an engaged lesbian."

Steph puts her hands over her heart. "No!"

Carmen: "Yes."

Jackson: "Wow."

Shad: "I think I need to hear this from the source."

Kimi: "I did."

Steph: "Holy shit. What did they say?"

Kimi: "So, so many crazy things. My pop was great. My mother is still worried that I'll end up a street person, which is apparently the fate for Asian lesbians. I don't really get how that works. But she's comforted that she might not have to pay to get her teeth cleaned."

Everyone applauds Kimi, who makes herself even smaller in Carmen's embrace.

Shad: "You're a rock star."

Jackson: "Well done, my friend."

The Joy: "You make me so proud."

Kimi: "That was my goal. Okay, someone else go."

The Joy holds up her hand. "Me next. Then, it's on to our assignments." After a bit of grumbling The Joy continues. "I'm ignoring that. First, you'll be glad to know, I don't have COVID."

Reflexively, Kimi slides away from The Joy. "What?!"

Steph: "Did you think you had it?"

The Joy: "Maybe. Not really."

Kimi: "And you didn't tell us?"

Carmen: "That was not nice."

The Joy: "I'm sorry. But it's not my fault. It's Betty's fault. Betty has COVID."

Steph: "Oh, no."

The Joy: "Oh yes. She has COVID, like all of her *tea* ladies. Which is code for booze ladies. Anyway. She has no symptoms and she hasn't changed her life one little bit. She's still having song nights and breathing on everyone, and her friends are still playing booty-blink."

Benji: "That's so wrong."

Shad: "It's crazy."

The Joy: "Wait. Here's the really crazy part. You know that the President, our President, is coming down to her neighborhood to play golf. She's still insisting that she's going to meet him."

Steph: "Seriously?"

Shad: "No?!"

The Joy: "Oh, so very yes."

Jackson: "Can't you talk her out of it?"

The Joy: "I tried."

Steph: "What did she say? How can she justify risking the health of a national leader? The national leader?"

The Joy: "She told me that I don't get to tell her what's right and wrong since I slept with her boyfriend who she wasn't even going to sleep with anyway because he's a slut and has already slept with half of her friends."

Kimi: "Crazy says what?"

The Joy: "Right?"

Steph: "Wait. What?"

Shad: "She won't. I think she's just screwing with you."

Benji: "You said screwing."

Jackson: "She'd have to be really crazy."

The Joy: "Where do you think I come from?" That shuts them up. Wow. No one knows what else to say as their minds extrapolate the nuttiness they just heard.

Benji: "Aren't we supposed to get smarter when we get older?"

The Joy: "That's the thing. Franny, you remember Betty's friend who ratted me out? Well, she told me that we don't learn a thing. Nothing. It's like we're all living in this crazy loop of repeating all our stupid petty high school mistakes forever. Oh, and our knees are gonna hurt."

Kimi: "Well, that just sucks out loud."

Carmen turns to her. "You can repeat your stupid, petty, annoying mistakes with me."

Kimi: "Great."

Shad: "On that note, I need a refresher. Anyone?"

Benji: "You bet." Shad disappears from his screen for a moment. The Joy gets up and heads for the kitchen to retrieve her cocktail pitcher. Steph pours herself another glass of wine. She feels that by not drinking right out of the bottle, she's making great strides. Jackson reaches down, out of frame, then rises up holding an elaborate red beer stein. Is that what he was drinking from before? No one had noticed. Shad returns with two new beers, steps over Douglas and hands Benji his drink. The Joy refills the three empty glasses on the coffee table. Carmen's about to drink, but The Joy stops her so she can sprinkle in more Pop Rocks. Carmen smiles. Everyone settles back in for round two.

The Joy: "Are we ready to continue?"

Kimi holds up her glass. "Pop Rock me."

The Joy: "So sorry." The Joy adds the pink dust to Kimi's drink and it starts to fizz.

Kimi: "Quite alright."

The Joy turns to the group and leans forward. "Assignment: the question, 'What was your most interesting cab ride ever?' Let's switch to best."

Shad: "I'm going last. No one's gonna wanna follow my story."

Jackson: "Way to throw down the gauntlet."

Shad: "I'm just sayin'."

Jackson: "OK. I'll go first if no one minds."

The Joy: "Please proceed."

Jackson: "My best cab ride was my first cab ride. We were moving to New York. I was...six? We landed at JFK and we all piled into this cab. It was a minivan cab. The driver let me sit up front. When we got close to the bridge, and we could see the lights of the city, I was so excited. My father told me that we were moving to a palace and that everyone in the city was thrilled that I was coming. I didn't know if I should believe him. My sisters teased me. But when we got here, the cab driver let me say, '10-4' over the intercom and the doorman knew my name. I was sure my father was right. That's my story."

Kimi: "Ripped from the pages of Aladdin."

They all snicker. The Joy tells Jackson, "That was a lovely, magical story. A whole new world." More snickering.

Carmen jumps in: "I only have one possible choice. When I got here from Miami to be with this one. That was my best."

Kimi: "I'm calling that my best cab story too."

Carmen: "Oh. That's so sweet."

Shad: "Carmen, what the hell have you done with our Kimi?"

Kimi: "Shut up, fuck face. I *am* sweet."

The Joy: "You are *fucking* sweet."

Kimi: "See? And it's a better story than the time I told my mother that some smelly cab driver gave me his number and she berated me for not calling him." Kimi proceeds to impersonate her mother. "You wasting time. This could be the last chance. It dangerous for older women like you to have babies."

They all laugh at Kimi's impersonation. Shad adds, "Wow."

Steph: "OK. My turn. It was when I got here out of school, before I had a job. I was so excited to be on my own, and there were parties everywhere and all kinds of happenings that I wanted to be part of."

Kimi: "Next up, Cinderella."

Steph: "Ignoring. I was running out of money pretty fast. I didn't want to go back to Ida and Mur for more cash—"

Kimi: "God forbid!"

Steph: "Anyway, I got an interview at the station for an entry-level news job. Not a secretary. Not an intern. A real news job. A shitty news job, but news. And no guarantee of anything. Just an interview. I was down to my last twenty dollars. I got dressed, went out and got a cab. The ride came to twelve dollars and I told the guy to keep the change. Mur always says, 'Scared money never wins.' I got the job and had to ask for an advance to get home."

Carmen: "That's a great story."

Shad: "You know, you could have walked home."

Jackson: "Not the same poetry to that."

Steph considers Jackson for a moment. She doesn't want to be mad at him. He is what he is. Limited. But they've been friends since high school. Does she need to throw out the baby with the bathwater? She looks at her fingers that are flipping over the coin from Miss Molly. It hasn't dawned on her until just now how much her cab story was like Miss Molly's cab story. She decides to choose happy, and be nice to Jackson. To him she says, "Thank you."

Jackson smiles a small smile and thinks, Maybe.

Benji: "Now me. My best cab ride was after Patrick's birthday bash last year. I took Sophie Maddox and she left with another guy."

Steph: "Seriously?"

Benji: "Oh yeah. She's awful. Anyway, I was bummed, so I left early. When I got in the cab home, I found a wallet stuffed in the seat with no identification and a little over five thousand dollars in it."

Kimi: "Get the fuck out!"

Shad: "You didn't tell me that."

The Joy: "I want to ride in cabs with you."

Benji: "So I turned it in."

The Joy: "Oh, no."

Kimi: "What the shit! You turned it in?"

Jackson: "Hey. It was the right thing to do."

Kimi: "Says the kid from the palace."

Benji: "Someone could have really needed that. It could have been for like some kid's operation."

Jackson: "That's right, my friend. Then what happened?"

Benji: "So I turned it in and waited the appropriate time. And they called me to say that no one claimed it, so it was mine."

Steph: "What a feel-good story. How did that not make the news?"

Benji: "I didn't want to be on the news."

Kimi: "Smart. I would have hit you up for cash."

Shad: "What did you do with the money?"

Benji: "Invested it with you."

At that moment, Shad believes Benji to be a magical presence. He holds up his beer to cheers with Benji. "To my investors." Benji cheers him and they both drink.

The Joy: "I didn't make any money on my best cab ride, but I could have."

Kimi: "Here it comes."

Steph: "Should I get a cigarette ready?"

The Joy: "Lady, you do what you need to do. My best cab ride was with B-R-A-D, Brad Fist."

Kimi: "No, it was not!"

Shad: "That's such a porn name."

The Joy looks thoughtful. "Maybe that's why he got into porn. The name."

Steph: "You had a cab ride with a porn guy?"

The Joy: "Don't knock it. Anyway, we were going thirty-two

blocks through midtown around lunch time, so I figured I had seventeen to nineteen minutes."

Carmen folds her legs on the sofa, holds her drink in both hands and settles in for the story. "I love smut."

The Joy: "Then scoot a little closer. OK, Bradly said he'd never received oral pleasure in a cab—"

Kimi: "Bullshit."

The Joy turns to Kimi. "Please. I didn't interrupt your crappy little story. If you stop me again, I won't tell my super-fantastic story."

Carmen: "Let the lady finish." Kimi shakes her head. Who is she marrying?

The Joy: "Where was I? Oral pleasure. Yes. So, I let Bradly know, in my own subtle way, that I could assist him with that bucket-list item. So the cab starts going down Park Ave and I start down Bradly. Which, by the way, was an extra challenge with his leather pants. Oh, also by the way, he had the best smelling Johnson ever. So I'm performing fellatio, and he's really into it. He starts moaning. Like, loud. And he gets louder as he enjoys it more. And I can see the cab driver looking in the rearview mirror. And now Bradly's really loud. And we're stopped at a light. I didn't realize that the driver's window was down and the people in the next car can hear this. But whatever, right. I'm never gonna see them again. Wrong. The people in the next car were cops. And the next thing I know, it's all siren and lights. They signal to our cab driver pull over. Which he does, and gets out of the cab and steps away. The cops open the back door and there's Brad and Brad junior, both saluting them. So, of course, I saluted them too." The Joy stops right there. Everyone is leaning forward waiting for more.

Steph finally bursts. "What? What happened?"

The Joy: "Well, that's when I started dating Officer Bob."

Silence.

Kimi: "Only you."

Carmen: "That's so wonderful." Carmen toasts with The Joy.

Kimi: "Wash that glass."

The Joy: "OK, Shad. Follow that."

Shad: "Well then. I may need a second to shake that off." Benji snickers. Shad resumes. "OK. Alright. First, I loved this assignment."

The Joy: "Yay!"

Shad: "It's been so long since I've been in a cab. And this story is awful, but just thinking about what used to be normal for New York made me nostalgic. Here it is. I was at a meeting uptown. O.G. Sandra from the office is there. And she doesn't feel well. Something about being pregnant. I don't know. Anyway, she's gonna walk home. She was more junior then. So I say, if you can wait five minutes, I'll call a car and drop you off. Oh shit. This was a hired car. Does that count?"

Asking the group, The Joy says, "We need a ruling. Does a hired car count?"

Everyone agrees. It counts. Shad continues. "Great. So, she waits the five minutes. Maybe ten. We get in the car and as we're approaching the Port Authority, she says she's gonna be sick. Like throwing-up sick."

Carmen: "Oh, no."

Shad: "Yeah. And I'm like, no, no, you're not gonna be sick. And she's like, yeah, I'm gonna be sick. So I try to get her to relax. In my most calming voice, I tell her that she needs to focus on something else. Not on herself. She needs to take a deep breath and focus on something outside of the cab. And she does. She looks around and focuses on this rather large woman with this really skinny guy carrying two huge, blue suitcases. And she's breathing and focusing and just then, skinny guy puts down the suitcases, puts his hand on a stop sign and throws the fuck up."

Jackson: "No!"

Shad: "Yes. Skinny guy is like a vomit geyser. And that's it. Sandra looks around in a panic, picks up her purse and starts pulling things out of it and shoving them in my lap." As Shad is telling this, the gang's all starting to laugh. Even Shad is laughing. "And I'm all, 'What are you doing!?' And she tells me she's gonna throw up in her bag. And I say, 'You're not.' And she says, 'I am.' And she did. She has her head down and starts throwing up into her bag. And now we're in stop-and-go traffic and every time the driver hits the brakes, Sandra hits her head on the back of the front seat." Now everyone is in a good hard, rolling laugh. "And by the time we get to her house, she's had to open the cab door twice to empty out the bag. End of story." But not end of laughter. They're all roaring and Shad has tears coming down his face.

The Joy: "Hey, I threw up in a cab once."

Benji: "Me, too."

Steph: "Guilty."

Kimi: "We've all thrown up in a cab. If you live in New York, you don't notice pee smell, you yell at strangers and you throw up in a cab."

The Joy reaches over and hugs Kimi. Hard. With Kimi buried deep in her friend's enthusiasm, The Joy says, "I missed you. You are too sweet."

Carmen joins in the hug-fest, wrapping her arms around them both. "Let's make a Kimi sandwich."

A muffled voice whispers out from beneath her friends. "I hate you both."

BACK IN PLACE?

STEPH'S APARTMENT

Steph stands at the wall of windows in her dark apartment and lets the lights of her city reflect on her face. As she thinks about the roller coaster of her career, she doesn't even realize that she's shaking her head. It's all too impossibly crazy. But there it is. One minute you're a pariah, the next everyone loves you again. She almost doesn't feel her phone vibrate in her back pocket. She's gotten so many calls to congratulate her that she's becoming numb to her cell. Who was it now? She looks. Bill. Better pick that one up. Before she answers, she tells herself that he could say anything. Roller coasters go up and they go back down. She tries to manage her own expectations.

"Yeah, Bill."

"Yeah, Bill. Same as always."

"Well, you are still Bill."

"Last I checked. Do you want the good news or the bad news first?"

"Surprise me." She wonders why she doesn't have a glass of wine for this.

"Here it is. Mason wants you out. He said, and I quote, "I'm tired of reporters getting by on good looks and bad behavior. This isn't a reality show. It's the news. Then he added a few remarks about, in his day, respecting the job and walking ten miles to school in a blizzard. But, the public has decided that they love a phoenix rising from the ashes story and this week, you're the phoenix. He can't argue with the numbers, so you not only have a job, they're going to try you out on the desk."

The word "desk" rings in Steph's ears. Is he seriously talking about the anchor desk?

After a complete lack of sound from Steph, Bill says, "You have nothing to say?"

"Sorry. I was taking it in."

"Yeah. It's a lot and honestly, I think it's wrong. You let yourself become the story and it burned you. Then you became the story again and you're being praised. The news is not supposed to be about the reporter. And I fear that you were built to be the story."

"It was never my intent."

"I believe that. Which is why I agreed with Mason. I can recognize bullshit, even though after having COVID, I can't smell it anymore."

"So, now what?"

"Now, I'll support you and try to guide you to being the best reporter you can be. And you'll keep your shirt on at all times, even in the shower. I want you to study Jim. Watch the piece he did on 9/11. Clean. factual. The right balance of gravity, pathos and objectivity. That's your high bar. Start there."

"OK. And, thanks for...whatever you did that you're not telling me."

"You're welcome. Now, earn it." Bill hangs up.

Steph wonders what it is about her that makes her "built to *be* the story." Is she? She doesn't want to be. She decides that she's not going to be. Here's her line in the sand. She's a newswoman. Period. She folds her arms and looks out on the city that she's devoting herself to and feels powerful.

When her phone rings again, she automatically answers it without looking. "Yeah."

"You picked up."

Steph realizes that she just let Jackson in. Mistake. Mistake. No, she's powerful. She can handle this. "I did."

"Great. I need to talk to you."

"Talk."

"I want to apologize."

She says nothing.

"I was, maybe I was scared. But I'm not now. I think we should try again."

"I tried the last time."

"You're right. I'm ready to try again."

"You mean, you're ready now that my life is back on track and I don't *need* you? Now that it's easy again? I don't think so, Jackson. I'm not going to hang up *on* you, but I am going to hang up now." As promised, she hangs up. Powerful.

JACKSON'S APARTMENT

Jackson is sitting on the ninja hopping ball that Steph got him for his birthday, staring at his phone. She hung up on him. Well, not technically *on* him, but it was a slap in the face, none the less. That's not how it was supposed to go. He's had his epiphany. No one's perfect. He's ready to be there for her. Now what?

He texts Benji. *Got a sec?*

Jackson bounces a bit on the ball while he waits for a response. Come on Benji.

Finally, Benji responds. *Working.*

Important.

S'up?

Relationship problem.

You're not in a relationship.

That's my problem.

Jackson keeps bouncing and waiting. Steph is all of a sudden the most important thing. More important than ninja training. More important than law school or his charity work. It's like a wave has washed over him and is pulling him under. The feeling is overwhelming. It seems impossible that everyone doesn't feel the exact same urgency as he does right now. More bouncing. More waiting. Shit. Who else can he talk to?

THE JOY'S APARTMENT

The front door of the apartment is propped open. The Joy is lounging on the sofa engrossed in the *Real Housewives of Somewhere* while Carmen and Kimi move their few things across the hall to their new digs. The corner curtain is open and most of Kimi's things are gone from the space, leaving it feeling a bit sad. She and Carmen are ready to attack the large boxes of masks. As Carmen lifts a box she lets out the smallest tuft of a fart. Kimi is stunned. "Did you just fart in front of me?"

"That's what couples who live together do."

"Yeah. Maybe. But, eww."

"Don't be a baby. It was freshly minted. It doesn't smell."

"Freshly minted?"

"You know. New."

"I literally don't know what to say."

"Say, I love you."

"I think I'll save it."

"Suit yourself." Carmen takes her box out the door and across the hall. Kimi looks over at The Joy. "Did you hear that?" The Joy doesn't respond. "I guess not."

The Joy looks up. "Oh, were you talking?"

"I was."

"Was it good?"

"It was not."

"OK then." The Joy turns her attention back to the TV.

Kimi goes back to the boxes, but before she can hoist the next load, she gets a text from Jackson. *Got a sec?*

She responds, *Moving*

Need relationship advice.

And you're asking me? You're pathetic.

I know.

SHAD & BENJI'S APARTMENT

Shad's pacing the living room. With Benji at work, he decides that now's the time to test the waters. He has Esther's cell in his phone and shoots her a text. *Mets or Yankees?*

After a couple of minutes, he gets back a text. *Yankees*

He smiles. That was easy. Let's try again. He sends his next question. *Jets or Giants?*

Saints

He likes that she went her own way with that one. She's too strong to let him frame the debate. OK. Keep the momentum. Next one. *Best athlete of all time?*

Impossible

Shad's immediately annoyed with himself. He asked her too broad a question. But he gets another text. He's excited until he sees that it's from Jackson. Crap. It reads, *Got a sec?*

Busy at the moment.

K.

Shad feels a little shitty about blowing off his friend, but this is too important. What should he say next? He wants to seem fun and casual, yet intriguing. Should he switch to movies or restaurants? But then Esther fires back: *Babe Didrikson, Michael Jordon, Martina Navratilova, Carl Lewis, Muhammad Ali, Paula Newby-Fraser*

Shad can't believe his fortune.

JACKSON'S APARTMENT

Jackson puts his cell in his pocket. He thinks. He feels like he's having a hard time breathing, then he gets an idea. He bounces down the hall to Ruby's bedroom. Who knows? He knocks. Through the door, Ruby says, "Yeah?"

Jackson doesn't say anything. He just knocks again. Ruby responds, "What?" He still says nothing. More knocking. Finally, Ruby comes to the door. "Oh, my God. What?"

"I need your advice."

"You don't."

"Come on. Take pity on me."

"I do, every day."

"Cute." At that, she's about to close the door. Jackson changes his tune. "Wait. I'm sorry. I really want your help. I need your help."

Ruby looks at her brother. All of a sudden, and maybe for the first time she can think of, he seems like he's not in control of everything. Like the golden boy is maybe not so shiny. She stands back and lets him bounce into her room.

THE JOY'S APARTMENT

The Joy is enjoying watching Carmen and Kimi work. It's always so nice to see things getting done and not have to get up. They carry their last few items across the hall and close the door. The Joy feels accomplished.

Her cell rings with the tone that can mean only one person. Oh, hell. The Joy had resigned herself to the fact that her relationship with her mother is back to the cold dead thing that it was before her trip to Florida. She quickly tries to center herself. Nope. Not going to happen. She answers, "Betty. How lovely to hear from you."

Her mother's voice is devoid of emotion. "If that's sarcasm, I'm choosing to ignore it. I have something...inevitable to tell you. And I want you to hear this from me first."

"OK. I'm ready."

"I'm not. I need to work my way in. Tell me how your diet is going."

"I'm not on a diet."

"It's never too late to start. Carol has lost five pounds since you left. Granted, it's a drop in the bucket, but..."

The Joy can't take it. "Betty, spill it."

Betty stops. Then, "Can you keep a secret?"

"You know I can't."

"Hmm. Fine. I'll talk to you another time."

"No! Wait! You have to tell me now. Come on. Please."

"Well, only because you're begging."

The Joy listens to her mother relate her highly sensitive information. All The Joy can say in a whisper is, "No!!!"

All Betty can say in a whisper is, "Yes."

STEPH'S APARTMENT

Steph's in the kitchen staring into her fridge. After thirty miles on her Peloton, she's ready for a protein shake dinner, and feels she's earned two percent milk. She laughs at herself for thinking of it as an indulgence, but that doesn't squelch the enthusiasm. She takes her time prepping her liquid reward. Metal cup, ice, handheld drink mixer. From now on, she wants to do everything just right. As the cold, frothy chocolate drink hits her lips, the phone rings. Of course.

"Hello, New York."

"Hey, Mom."

"That's it?"

"Sorry. Ida! I'm so glad you called! I was just thinking about you."

"You're full of shit."

"I am."

"Fine. I'm calling to tell you that A, I've watched your special ten times already. You looked so beautiful."

"Well, that *is* the point of the news."

"And B, Mrs. Golding called and said she would be willing to let you talk to her daughter."

Steph laughs. "She'd *let me?*"

"I know. Where was she when you were a social outcast? She didn't want anything to do with us when everyone hated you."

"I don't think everyone hated me."

"Oh, baby, they did." After she lets that settle in, Ida gets back to the point. "It's just like her. You know what Mrs. Golding bought us as a gift for our fortieth anniversary party?"

Steph takes a drink of her shake. "A picture frame."

"That's right. And the—"

Steph finishes Ida's sentence with her. "—price tag was still on it."

"That's right. Who does that? I'll tell you who. Someone who wants you to know what they paid."

"What did she pay?"

"I don't remember."

"You know you do."

"So..."

"So what?"

"Are you gonna call Mrs. Golding's daughter?"

Steph's doorbell rings. Is it a neighbor? Anyone else would have to be buzzed in. "Listen Mom, I gotta..."

"I know. I know. You have more important things than your old mother. That's fine. But call Mrs. Golding's daughter. It's the right thing to do."

"Love you, Mom."

"Love you, too."

Steph hangs up and walks what's left of her shake to the front door. She looks out the peephole but sees nothing. Should she open the door? Sure. There, bouncing on his ninja ball is Jackson. He's clean shaven and his hair is cut. He's wearing a gray t-shirt which has been written on in black marker. It says. "I'm sorry."

Steph's not quite sure what to say. She'd been strong with him. It felt like the right thing. But here he is. She says, "You let me down."

Jackson grabs the bottom of his t-shirt and pulls it up over his head revealing another t-shirt that reads, "I was scared."

"Life is scary."

Jackson grabs the bottom of that t-shirt and pulls it up over his head revealing another t-shirt that says, "I'll never let you down again."

"How can I know that? And why am I having a conversation with a t-shirt?"

There he goes again. He lifts his shirt off and reveals a shirt that reads, "I heart you."

Steph stands and looks at this man bouncing on a ball with discarded t-shirts littering the floor by his side. She thinks, Was that enough of a gesture? Can she trust him? Does she love him? She knows that she does.

As she's about to tell him so, her phone buzzes. She glances at the device and sees that The Joy has texted the words, *Urgent News*

She quietly says to Jackson, "Urgent news."

Jackson asks, "You love me, too?"

"That's probably not The Joy's message."

"Is it yours?"

Steph wonders if she's going to say the words. She wants to, but she also doesn't want to let him off the hook. Yet, a beautiful life flashes through her mind.

Her phone buzzes again. She can't help herself. She looks. Her eyes go wide.

Jackson wonders if he should be concerned, "What?"

"The President got COVID!"

"So?"

"He got it from The Joy's mom!"

THANK YOU

Thank you for reading *Daughter Of Careful-Ish*. If you enjoyed it, please take a moment to leave a review on Amazon, Goodreads, or your preferred online retailer.

Reviews are the best way to show your support for an author and to help new readers discover their books.

To link directly to the *Daughter Of Careful-ish* page on Amazon, visit www.DaughterOfCarefulish.com

ACKNOWLEDGMENTS

Bill, the guy who cared enough to plus it. Downtown Johnny D., the dude with bottomless financial intel. Olivia, the gal with a genius party plan. Jackie & Jeff, the folks with a goldmine of parent crazy. Brooke & Kristina, the ladies who shared clappers, marchers and pandemic wedding hurdles. Jer, the man with the business advice and horse stories. Janet, the friend who threw down the acknowledgement gauntlet. Blaine, the man who sent me to Florida... and continues to send me.

ABOUT THE AUTHOR

Honey Parker's *Careful-ish*, the best-selling first book in the series, was written during the early days of the COVID-19 pandemic. She figured we could all use a laugh. *Daughter of Careful-ish* is follow up. Honey has also co-written and sold several screenplays which, as per Hollywood tradition, are circling various levels of that place known as Development Hell. A former standup comic and advertising copywriter (the two jobs are more alike than you might imagine), Honey was once crowned The Funniest Person In Advertising.

Honey is married to her best friend and business partner, Blaine Parker. Her other accomplishments include performing standup at various Club Med locations around the world, racing aboard a sailboat in the North American Fireball Championships despite the fact she cannot sail, and sparring with the world female boxing champ, a feat for which Honey is most proud that she neither bled nor cried.

You can find Honey online at www.HoneyParkerBooks.com